Rayflin: the return home

Rayflin: the return home

Kathy G. Widener

Deeds Publishing | Atlanta

Published by Deeds Publishing in Athens, GA
www.deedspublishing.com

Printed in The United States of America

Cover design by Mark Babcock
Text layout by Ashley Clarke

Library of Congress Cataloging-in-Publications data is available upon request.

ISBN 978-1-947309-48-7

Books are available in quantity for promotional or premium use. For information, email info@deedspublishing.com.

First Edition, 2018

10 9 8 7 6 5 4 3 2 1

For
My husband, Jimmy
Children: Melanie, Jason and
Tristen
Grandchildren: Emily and Jacob
And
In Memory of the daughter we lost
Lori Paige
1978 - 2017

Also by Kathy Widener

RAYFLIN: WHERE MEMORIES LIVE

Introduction

LEON, LOUISE, AND ELSIE COULD BARELY CONTAIN THEIR EX-
citement knowing they would soon be returning to the home they
had shared with their mother. She was no longer there, but they
knew everything that meant home was, including their beds and the
rooms they had occupied. They only had to pack their clothes and
what few other personal items they had to return.

Kelly had been to visit almost every day since he and Mrs.
Florence had announced their marriage so abruptly. He was still
working at the chalk mine and at their Uncle Roston's store in the
evenings.

"Florence is getting the house cleaned and in order for y'all to
return. She wants everything to be nice and perfect. She has been
sweeping, dusting, and putting clean linens on all of your beds,"
Kelly had told the children. "She is just as excited as the three of you
to have you back home. She is a good person and she will treat y'all
with love and kindness, please show her the same."

"We will, Daddy, don't worry," they all replied in unison.

Kelly had been truthful with his children, Leon, Louise, and
Elsie; Florence was excited at the prospect of having the children
come home. She had always loved children and was a kind person

by nature. She would try her best to welcome them and let them know their happiness and well-being was important to her.

Kelly had been good to Florence and had given her two wedding gifts. No one had ever given her gifts before. Her parents were so poor, they couldn't afford extras. Kelly gave Florence a gold wristwatch in an olive green hinged box. It was absolutely beautiful and she had never had anything so nice.

Years before, when her father, Thomas, had been plowing a field, his plow had turned over something shiny, a flat bar brooch evidently stepped on by his mule. The fastener on the underside was bent over and the top had a dent, but he had given it to Florence and she had treasured it ever since. She immediately stored this treasure in the box that contained her watch.

Florence had also received a new set of dishes from Kelly. They were white with a ridged rim and a blue and red flower paired on the four compass points. He told he wanted her to have something new, something that was just for her to begin housekeeping with.

"I know we have everything we need in the realm of housekeeping goods, furniture, linens, and such, but I wanted you to have something new to use, something that was originally yours," Kelly had told her.

She had few things of her own to start a life with her husband. All she brought was her meager clothing, two pair of shoes, and the quilts her mother, Ella, had given her. There just wasn't that much that Ella could spare. There was no dowry. Kelly had no concern for that; all he wanted was Florence and his children.

Now they could return home.

One

MEMORIES ARE THOUGHTS BURIED IN THE RECESSES OF THE mind, only to flood forth with a tug of the familiar. That tug was all too evident two weeks later, when Leon, Louise and Elsie packed their belongings and moved back to their father's house, a place they had only seen in passing for the last three years.

When they were in this place, their mother, Mary, had dominated every aspect of their daily lives. Seeing Miss Florence standing at the wood cook stove, sweeping the floors, washing clothes in that old black wash pot or making the beds was all too familiar. Familiar, because every piece of furniture, every dish, except for the new ones Kelly had presented to Florence, every item they used, was the same. Only Miss Florence was different.

Florence had stored her new dishes from Kelly in the top of the Hoosier dish cabinet. She was a product of her raising, poor all her life, and thought the new dishes were too nice to use for every day. She would always save things, even though Kelly had suggested they were for her to enjoy. She had never had nice things and refused to use them.

The children all agreed among themselves, *Miss Florence just makes us miss our mother more.*

"She's a nice lady and takes care of us, and everything around us in this house is the same, except she's here and not Mamma," Leon added. "That's an awfully big thing to be deal with, but I respect her. She is now in charge of this house, we'll just have to accept her. She is awfully kind, I must admit."

From the start, Florence was good to the children. She cared for them as if they were her own. She was a shy person not given to shows of affection, to them she became Miss Florence, not Mamma. In their minds she would always be Miss Florence.

Every morning when Florence woke the children for school, she would have their breakfast waiting in the kitchen. They appreciated her taking care of them and secretly thought their daddy had made a good choice, if a choice had to be made.

Now they lived in their house, not at Rayflin; the walk to school was not as far. *It's a mile closer than Rayflin, which in itself is a good thing*, the children concluded. *We don't have to get up as early and walk as far.*

When planting time came around the end of March, Leon would stop at home after school long enough to change into some work clothes, and then head out the door to his daddy's fields or down to Rayflin to help his Grandpa Kel.

Kelly had taken over the management of his fields once again and with the help of his son Leon, Arthur Moore, Joe Hardy, and young Willie Burkett, planting was right on schedule. Kelly still had his job at the chalk mine, but every evening, he walked his fields and gave instructions to Joe or Arthur.

By the first of March, Florence was beginning to feel real queasy in the mornings. She had witnessed the same malady afflicting her mother, Ella, as soon as she was expecting. *I guess I'm pregnant,* she thought excitedly to herself. *I hope Kelly will be pleased.*

That evening after supper, when the children had gone to bed, Florence told Kelly of her suspicion that a baby was on the way. Kelly's face lit up at the news.

"I hope you're all right with the idea of another child, Kelly. I know you already have three to provide for."

"Of course, I am, Kelly replied. I'm not just all right with it, Florence, I'm thrilled. I hope it's a boy. I sure could use another son."

"I hope the children will be happy about the baby when they find out. In a couple of months, it will be apparent even to the children: my condition, I mean. We don't discuss such things with children, I know, but they'll figure it out on their own pretty soon."

By the end of July, it was quite apparent to the children. Elsie said to Leon and Louise, "Don't y'all think Miss Florence is getting fat around the middle?"

"Of course, she is, you big dummy," replied Louise. "Women get that way when they're going to have a baby."

"You mean we're going to have a little sister or brother? But why hasn't Daddy or Miss Florence told us about the baby?" Elsie asked.

"Because, Elsie," Leon answered, this time speaking very slowly, implying she was dense. "Grown-ups-don't-discuss-having-babies-with-children. They figure it's really none of our business."

"But Leon, you're not really a child anymore, you're almost thirteen," said Elsie. "They could have told you."

"I may be almost thirteen, but they still consider me as a child. Besides, what do I care about babies?" Truth be known, Leon was just as excited about the new baby, but no way would he let his two little sisters know his feelings; it wouldn't be manly to take on about a baby.

* * * * *

School started again for Leon, Louise, and Elsie in September 1923. Leon had always had somewhat of a behavior problem in school. Miss Opie Barr had been so nice to him when he got in trouble bringing critters to school; he kept his behavior in check when he was with the younger group that she taught. He felt so kindly towards her and didn't want to be a nuisance under her teaching.

School started back in 1923 at a new two story wooden building across from Mr. Abe Hall's pond, not as close to the church and the train depot. Leon was moved up to a higher level with the older students and there were now three teachers and more students. His teacher was Miss Gladys Hallman. Miss Gladys was not nearly as endearing to Leon and wasn't as easy to befriend as Miss Barr had been. Leon had always liked to entertain in class; anything for a good laugh. He began to do little irritating things to Miss Hallman. Nothing malicious of course, but something that the other students would appreciate. He was always looking out the window, mind miles away, not paying attention to the lesson, slumping in his desk or hitting Greco or Nina Lee in the back of the head with small objects. Nothing that would hurt, of course, just to make them turn around in surprise and say, "Leon, quit that!"

Sometimes Greco would threaten, "Leon, I'm going to give you a knuckle-sandwich at recess if you do that again!"

All the commotion and infractions would demand Miss Hallman intervene. She was constantly saying, "Leon, sit up in your desk, stop staring out the window, pay attention, and stop irritating the other students."

Finally, the day came. Leon overstepped the line with Miss Hallman. It was in the fall; he had developed a cold and runny nose. He was constantly wiping his nose on the sleeve of his flannel shirt.

Miss Hallman was getting pretty disgusted with this behavior. "Leon, I know you have a cold, but please stop wiping mucous on the sleeve of your shirt. For goodness sake, use a handkerchief."

That's when Leon saw fit to make a smart remark that the other children would laugh at. "Miss Hallman, I know you're a smart lady, but you should know I'm not wiping mucous on my sleeve, that's *snot,* plain and simple." Of course, that started the whole class giggling and embarrassed Miss Hallman.

"One more remark out of you, Leon, and you will receive a severe spanking in front of this class, understand?"

"Yes ma'am, I do and I apologize, I just thought everybody knows what snot is," more giggles followed.

Things quieted down momentarily and Leon decided to overplay his hand. He crammed a large sheet from his paper tablet in his mouth and began to chew until it was good and wet, then when Miss Hallman turned back to the blackboard, he threw it.

Splat! it didn't come anywhere near Miss Hallman, he never intended that, but it did slide down the board leaving a wet trail behind as it made it slimy way to the bottom.

"That's it Leon, you have tried my patience long enough!" Miss Hallman couldn't help but yell. "Go outside, cut me a good-sized switch, you have fifteen minutes and you better not return with a little, bitty one. I want something that I can use on your bottom that will make a lasting impression, understand?"

"Yes Mam, I understand," Leon said as he departed amid smirks and shocking expressions on the faces of his classmates, head drooped if really contrite about his behavior. They understood this to be serious.

Leon was never serious when it came to entertaining his classmates. It was kinda fun being considered the class clown. He was intelligent and made good grades, even though he appeared to be occupied elsewhere. He didn't really dislike Miss Hallman, but he found he could try her patience without too much trouble, so he did. He followed her instructions and cut a stout switch growing at the base of a sycamore tree behind the school. He trimmed off all the sycamore leaves, which left a good size switch about four feet long, definitely not a little bitty one. He paused to wipe his runny nose with a handkerchief he had in his pocket the whole time. That's when the idea came to him. He took out the pocketknife he carried and began to ring the large switch about twelve inches from its base and every three inches above, cutting deep enough to go through the top layer of bark without cutting the whole switch apart. The cuts were not noticeable and he was sure Miss Hallman would not notice since the bottom was completely intact. Then he headed back to the school to receive his punishment.

When he opened the door, everyone was suddenly quiet. You could have heard a pin drop. Leon walked slowly to the front, his head bowed, as if feeling deeply contrite for all the trouble he had caused in Miss Hallman's class. He handed her the switch with a whispered, "Will this do, Miss Hallman?"

"Yes, Leon, you picked just what I had in mind. Now please bend over my desk to receive your punishment."

He did as he was instructed and Miss Hallman held the base of the large switch for maximum impact with Leon's backside and swung, like Babe Ruth swinging a bat. When the switch connected with Leon, at least a dozen pieces flew across the front of the room. The children burst out in laugher and Miss Hallman turned deep red. She was so angry that Leon had outfoxed her again with another ploy for the class's entertainment.

"Pick up these small sticks, dump them in the trash can, and *sit down immediately.* You have tried my patience for the last time. I will be driving you home this afternoon to speak to your parents. I'm sure Mr. Gantt will be able to impress upon you the error of your ways. This class can't learn anything; they're too busy laughing at your antics."

"Uh oh!" Leon realized the gravity of his situation. Kelly would tear his behind up. He decided then and there that his days of being the class entertainer would have to come to an end.

* * * * *

Leon was too busy after school working down at Rayflin and on his daddy's land to be concerned about when a baby would arrive. It was harvest time for the cotton and stalk cutting time in the cornfields. Time to get the ground prepared for winter and butchering time to restock their meat supply.

November 6, 1923 was just another day. It was a Tuesday and when Leon, Louise and Elsie headed out the door that morning to school, everything was as usual. Miss Florence appeared fine to them except for the fact that she had a huge belly and had trouble squeezing between the kitchen table and the dish cabinet, but that had been a problem for the last several weeks. She was in good spirits and didn't complain of any aches or pains. But then, Miss Florence was not a complainer. You couldn't always tell what she was thinking or feeling.

It was a beautiful fall day. The temperature had dipped down to freezing the night before but the day was clear and sunny with a nip in the air. The trees on either side of the road were stripped bare and underneath their limbs, the ground was carpeted with brown, orange, and red leaves. The color green had totally disappeared from the landscape. It was the beginning of that dormant time of the year when nature prepares for the sleep of winter. The smell of burning leaves reached their nostrils as the children passed Mr. John Gunter's house on the way home from school that afternoon. He was raking mounds of leaves from around his front porch, adding them to the pile already ablaze in his front yard. He waved to the children as they passed.

That afternoon, the first thing Louise and Elsie noticed as their house came into view was a strange Model T parked underneath the cedar tree near the front porch.

Leon didn't even notice. Running ahead of them, he was too intent on what chores were expected of him before dark. He just dashed into the house and changed clothes and took off down to Rayflin. He knew his Grandpa Kel wanted him to finish cutting the cornstalks in that bottom field down near the river.

Louise and Elsie quickened their steps as they drew near the front porch. Strange automobiles were an unexpected occurrence and could only mean one thing; the baby was coming.

"Do you suppose that could be the doctor's car?" Louise asked. "It is time for Miss Florence to have her baby, let's hurry."

The strange automobile belonged to Miss Willow, the midwife, and she had been there attending Florence since about nine a.m., when the labor pains had started in earnest. Louise and Elsie were concerned when they heard moans coming from their daddy and Miss Florence's room. All they could do was sit down in the hall and wait.

The door opened and Miss Ella, Florence's momma, appeared. "Don't be frightened, children, Florence is about to have us a baby, that's all."

"Miss Ella, where is our daddy?" Elsie asked.

"He'll be here soon, child; I just called him over at the chalk mine. It makes no sense having him leave work when there is nothing he can do. He'll be along directly. Florence is fine and the baby will be here soon."

She had no more than gotten the explanation from her lips when they heard the cry of a newborn baby. Ella turned and went back into the bedroom, leaving the children standing in the hall.

"The baby's here, Elsie!" Louise whispered breathlessly. They hugged each other excitedly.

"Now I'm not the baby anymore," said eight-year-old Elsie. "We have a baby brother or sister."

Immediately, they heard their father's automobile chugging down the road and both headed out the door to greet him with the news. As soon as he had stopped the car, he leaped out and in long strides headed towards them, bounded up on the porch, and kneeled before them.

"Is he here yet?" their father asked, a bit out of breath.

"The baby's here alright," Elsie said with a grin. "We just heard it yell, but we don't know what it is yet, Miss Ella hasn't come back to tell us."

"Well, let's go find out," Kelly said.

Shortly, Kelly and the two children were ushered into the room by a smiling Ella. It was a beautiful baby boy with a wisp of blonde hair on top of his head and deep blue eyes.

"He sure is beautiful, Miss Florence," Elsie said. "What are we going to name him?"

Kelly answered the little girl's question for Florence. "His name is Robert Kelly Gantt, and we expect both you and Louise to help take care of him. Is that a deal?"

"Sure, Daddy," they both answered in unison.

"It's nice to be a big sister for a change," replied Elsie.

* * * * *

Leon came in dirty and tired from working in the fields; the sun had already dropped below the tall junipers of the river swamp on this dark, chilly November day. Elsie and Louise met him as he hesitantly drug his body up the front steps.

"I'm in no mood for your joyful teasing," he warned.

"But we have happy news, Leon, we promise, and you'll be pleased," his sisters replied.

"Really? It better be good, or you two will regret pestering me, I promise too."

His mood changed abruptly when they explained that he indeed had a happy surprise waiting for him: a new baby brother.

Two

LEON PLOPPED DOWN ON THE SANDY BANK BESIDE THE
road, bent over, and rolled his britches legs up a turn. It was a pleasant spring morning, the last day of April 1924, warm enough that Leon and all the other boys at school had been going barefoot for the past two weeks.

"Come on, Leon, those girls are going to beat us to school if you keep messing around," Greco said with a hint of agitation in his voice. "They're already way ahead."

Leon wiggled his bare toes in the sand before standing. "Shaw, we can catch them pokey girls running backwards. Let's go!"

Leon, Greco and J Hugh sprinted down the road, passed the girls—Elsie, Louise, Marvellene, Clara, Nina Lee and Sis—and slowed down to walk a good hundred feet out in front. The girls completely ignored their passing; they were too absorbed in their chatter to pay the runners any attention. They were at the train depot at the edge of Steadman when Leon began to survey the sky to the northwest.

"Looks like a bad cloud coming up over yonder—we might have a storm," he observed. He turned, walking backwards several paces, and yelled to Elsie and Louise, "If it's raining when school lets out, you two hightail it to the depot and we'll catch the train to Rayflin!" Hearing no response from his sisters, he yelled, "Do you hear me?"

"You don't have to yell at us," Louise yelled back. "We hear you!"

The new school at Steadman was a two-story wooden structure, forty by sixty feet. It was constructed in the summer of '22 on the west side of Mr. Abe Hall's pond, some two hundred yards away. There were two large classrooms downstairs and an auditorium covering the entire upper floor. Three teachers taught close to one hundred and five children from ages six to seventeen reading, writing, arithmetic, history, and geography. There were few students in the older category; most were between six and twelve. Older students tended to drop out, especially the boys; they figured book learning was not as important as working on the family farm.

At 10:45, all the children were marched up the stairs to practice for commencement exercises less than a month away. Mrs. Hallman played the piano while different groups of students practiced their assigned songs, followed by recitations on each grade level to convey their accomplishments for the year.

By 11:15, the wind began to pick up, rattling the windowpanes. No rain had fallen yet, but the sky to the northwest was as black as coal. The three teachers felt anxious about the approaching storm.

Not wanting to upset the children, Miss Hallman rose from the piano bench and announced, "Children, we're going to conclude our commencement practice early today, y'all are doing so well. Please line up in an orderly fashion and don't push going down the stairs." She made her announcement with a big smile, hoping the children would not notice the apprehension in her voice.

Leon was the last student in the line as they began their descent down the stairs. Standing on the landing, gazing to the northwest through the window, stood Miss Mae Burgess. Mae was twenty-two-years old, a first-year teacher at Steadman School and liked by all the students. She was young and inexperienced. When it came to discipline, she could be swayed to be more lenient when the students committed some minor infraction. She was no beauty, her hair pulled in a bun at the nape of her neck and those wire-rimmed glasses perched on the end of her nose, but when she smiled, her face fairly glowed.

Leon glanced at Miss Mae and immediately saw the look on her face. She was as pale as if she had seen a ghost. Leon paused beside Miss Mae.

"Are you alright, Miss Mae?" he asked." Following the direction of her gaze through the window, he understood the fright he had seen so plainly on her face. To the northwest, from the river swamp, a monster approached. Leon had never seen anything so frightening. It looked like a great gray barrel rolling on the ground attached to the blackness of the sky. The black storm cloud had dropped this monster from its depths and it was devouring and destroying everything in its path. Leon could see the tops of huge gum trees whirling in the mass of gray, as if they were mere feathers. He watched in horror as the monster hit the Willard Hall house less than one-half mile away, leaving only rubble in its wake.

"Miss Mae, what is that?" he yelled above the din that now seemed to surround them.

"It's a tornado, Leon!" she yelled back as she turned and grabbed his arm. "We have to get downstairs before it hits."

All the other children had been herded into the wide center

hall by Miss Hallman and Miss Hartley. They now huddled on the floor below, the younger ones crying and clinging to the older. Leon saw their ashen faces glance upward as he and Miss Mae reached the midway point in their descent. The wind outside engulfing the school sounded like an approaching runaway locomotive. As Leon reached the base of the stairs, the tornado struck. The roof disappeared above their heads and the walls literally exploded around them. The occupants were at the mercy of the storm and flying debris that now spun in every direction. Flying lumber, desks, books, and bodies were swept clean before the onslaught, as so many leaves in the wind. Leon landed in the yard in front of the school steps. He tried to stand against the downpour of rain and wind but was blown flat in the stinging sand. The vortex of the tornado lifted him for just an instant before dropping him some 200 yards away on the bank of Abe Hall's pond.

Leon lay among broken limbs and debris dropped there as the funnel cloud released him, returning skyward. He was knocked unconscious from the fall and perhaps fifteen minutes passed before he became aware of his surroundings.

Coming to his senses, his first thought was, *I have to find Louise and Elsie, make sure they are alright.*

He gingerly stood, immediately hearing cries and moans from the direction of the school. It was still raining a slow drizzle, but the wind had died down. He made his way towards where the school had stood. It was rough going; there were broken tree trunks and limbs everywhere, and automobiles overturned. Lumber, tin from the roof, desks, everything imaginable from the school, or other buildings in the path of the storm, littered the ground. By the time he reached the school, there were people everywhere. He saw Miss

Hallman and Miss Hartley, in a somewhat disheveled state, tending to crying children and trying to account for their students. He found Elsie in their mist.

He grabbed her arm, spinning her around to face him. "Are you hurt, Elise?"

"No, I don't think so," she managed to whisper between sobs. He looked her over from head to foot, determining she was. not injured.

"Where is Louise?" At first, Elsie did not answer. "Where is Louise?" he asked again, hands clasped on her shoulders. He gave her a little shake.

"She's over there," Elsie replied, pointing towards Mr. Boyd Hall's Model T. "Her leg is all bloody. It looks awful."

"Elsie, you stay right here, I have to see about Louise," Leon said as he turned to make his way across the debris-strewn yard, heading towards Mr. Boyd's Model T.

* * * * *

Jack Evans, a black man from Sugar Bottom, had borrowed Mr. Kel's old black mule, Sue, early that morning. He had some business to attend to in Steadman, and Mr. Kel was kind enough to lend him a mule for the trip. Being in no big hurry, anticipating a whole day of visiting kinfolks and stopping a spell at Mr. Woodard's store, Jack slowly made his way passed the train depot at the edge of town. He noticed the 'Swamp Rabbit' stopped in front of the depot, engine idling, and waved to the engineer, Smoke Thompson.

Thompson was leaning out the engine window, surveying the sky to the northwest.

"Better get inside," Thompson yelled, "that cloud looks mighty bad."

"Yes sir, that's where I'm heading right away."

One glance at the sky told Jack Mr. Thompson was right; it was time to seek shelter until the storm passed. Reining old Sue in behind Woodard's store, he tied her securely to a cedar limb and walked around to the front of the building. Mr. Woodard was standing there along with two other white fellows Jack did not recognize.

"Howdy, Mr. Woodard, how you doing this morning?"

"I'm fine, Jack, me and the boys here were just looking at that bad cloud over yonder; looks like we're in for some rain, and might have some wind and hail in it too."

At that moment, a gust of wind and a sprinkling of rain hit the men gathered in the yard, and they retreated inside the store, closing the door against the storm. Within minutes it seemed, the wind picked up to a roar, rattling the windowpanes. Rain began pounding on the tin roof above their heads. The combination of the two-made conversation almost impossible; the noise from outside became deafening. The volume level increased exponentially, like the pumping quiver of an approaching locomotive, and glass from the windows burst into the building, falling on the backs of the men now squatting heads down on the store-building floor.

Woodard looked up just as a section of the roof blew away. All the men inside could do was hover there in hopes the building would hold together. It was over as quick as it came; the wind and the rain began to die down. The men stood shaking the broken glass from their bodies.

"I believe that had to be a tornado!" Woodard exclaimed anxiously as they all headed outside.

What met their gaze was indescribable destruction. Woodard's store had faired pretty well considering the other buildings across the road in the direct path of the tornado were completely demolished.

"My God, the tornado hit the school!" Woodard yelled, already hurrying in that direction. "Jack, please get down to Rayflin and let the family know. Our young'uns were in the school, and now the whole building has disappeared."

Jack didn't waste time; surprisingly, he found old Sue where he had left her, still tied to the cedar. Hopping on her back, he headed for Rayflin like Mr. Woodard had asked. This time, it wasn't a leisurely lope; he kept kicking old Sue in the sides, urging her to step up the pace. He was on a mission to alert the folks about the tornado. He first passed the 'Swamp Rabbit' at the water tank a quarter of a mile south of town. "How bad is the damage?" Smoke Thompson asked Jack as he trotted past.

"It's bad, sir. Mr. Woodard says that tornado hit the school with all them 'chillin' in it. I'm on my way to let the folks at Rayflin know about it."

"I will ease the train on back to the depot and see if we can help," Thompson said. "I saw the thing coming and backed the train down here to the water tank to save her if I could."

Jack didn't waste any more time. He stopped at Corrie and Jule's briefly to let them know; being as how Miss Corrie and Mr. Woodard were brother and sister, he knew her children were probably at the school. When he got to Florence and Kelly's, he stopped and told her, and then headed on down to Rayflin to alert Mr. Kel.

* * * * *

When Leon reached Mr. Boyd's Model T, Mr. Boyd was opening the front door to climb in and start the automobile. "Wait, Mr. Boyd," Leon called. "I've got to see Louise. Is she okay?"

"See for yourself, son, but we've got to get going. We have to get these youngsters to Leesville to the hospital right away."

Leon peered into the back window and saw Louise, ashen-faced in the corner, her head back against the seat and her left leg propped up on the edge. Her face and arms were bruised almost black from the stinging sand of the schoolyard, but the serious injury was her leg. Leon could see that the left leg from above the knee down was wrapped in blood-soaked rags. He had no idea what kind of shape her leg was in, but he knew it was bad.

As soon as the tornado disappeared, people from the community had immediately headed towards the school, hoping to help the survivors. In the back seat with Louise sat Clara and Miss Agnes Rowe. Clara appeared to be in a daze, and Miss Agnes was holding a bloody rag to the side of Clara's head. From where Leon stood, it looked like part of her scalp had been peeled back. Marvellene was in the front with another lady Leon did not recognize. Marvellene was bleeding from wounds on her face and neck.

"We've got to go, son. Tell your daddy I took your sister to the hospital," Mr. Boyd said as he started the engine and began to slowly maneuver around the obstacles in the schoolyard.

Walking beside the automobile, Leon said, "You're going to be okay, Louise, you hear." With a fleeting wave to her brother, Louise was gone.

* * * * *

By the time Woodard, Cal Adams, and Tom Boyd reached the school, everything was in chaos. Bruised and battered children were emerging everywhere from the rubble that had once been Steadman School. Most were crying, but some were just milling around in a daze. The tornado had ripped roofs and siding off surrounding houses, but the school had suffered a direct hit. There was nothing left of the school except the foundation and front steps.

"I'll get back to the store and unload the crates from my Coca Cola truck!" Adams exclaimed. "We need to get these injured children to the hospital at Leesville. Come on, Tom, and give me a hand."

As the two men headed back to the store for the truck, Woodard began to search the faces of the children for his nieces and nephew Leon. He saw Leon watching Boyd Hall's automobile drive away and headed in that direction.

"Are you okay, son?" Woodard asked as he reached Leon's side.

"I think so, Uncle Woodard, but Louise's leg is hurt real bad. Mr. Boyd's taking her to Leesville Hospital, along with the Gunter girls, Marvellene and Clara; they're worse off than Louise. Elsie is okay though, just skinned up a bit."

"Have you seen your cousins, Nina Lee and Sis?"

"No, I haven't, but we'll find them."

Just as they turned to cross the schoolyard, two men were lifting a battered and bruised body from beneath a section of the roof. They carried it gently and laid it on the ground in front of the front steps. Leon and Woodard rushed over to see who it was that they had found.

"It's Miss Mae," Leon said with a quiver in his voice. "It's hard to tell, she's so battered and bruised, but her wire-rimmed glasses are still on her face. I was with her on the stairs when the tornado hit."

Woodard put a hand on Leon's shoulder. "Come on, son, there are others who need our help. Let's find your cousins."

Nina Lee and Sis were with the other children gathered in the schoolyard and had only minor injuries. There were broken bones, cuts and scrapes, but it was miraculous that so many had survived. After forty-five minutes, all the children had been accounted for except for seventeen-year-old Jack Hall. Jack was finally found when Miss Hartley's Model T was flipped back up on its wheels. He lay crushed beneath the overturned automobile. Jack was gently laid on the ground beside Miss Mae and covered with a sheet, both awaiting the hearse from Parrish Funeral Home at Batesburg.

Leon wasn't going to any hospital—he was fine, or at least, he thought so. His ears did hurt a bit. They were swollen from the stinging sand. He had a few bumps and bruises, but otherwise, he was unscathed.

"I'm really O.K., Uncle Woodard," Leon said. "Just swollen ears and some bruises and cuts from where I landed on limbs beside Mr. Abe's pond. I'm going to walk around and survey the damage. Just wanted you to know not to worry if I'm missing. I'll be nearby."

Woodard just nodded to Leon in the affirmative; he was too busy helping load the other children on Cal's truck. "Just don't go in any damaged buildings. They could be unstable, understand?"

"Yes, sir, I'll be careful," Leon replied.

While the adults were seeing to children's injuries, Leon decided to explore the damage this monster had caused. He wandered between the buildings still standing near the school. Roofs had been blown clean away from houses, lumber peeled from their sides, leaving the inside studs visible. Huge oaks, pines, and chinaberry trees splintered off waist-high, as if they were match sticks. Pine needles stuck straight into trees three inches by the force of the wind, and there was even a two-by-four stud driven through the base of a pine tree. What amazed him so besides the force of wind needed to do these things was the fickleness of the creature.

He wandered through the house of Mr. Ed Gunter—at least, what was left of it. All the windows were blown out, the roof was gone, and yet the furniture in the front room appeared virtually untouched except for the broken glass, the lampshade was still perched on the base. Miss Eula, Ed's wife, sat meekly on the sofa, as if it was a Sunday afternoon.

"Are you all right, Miss Eula?" Leon asked. She just looked up at him, smiled and babbled incoherently. *She's addled in the head for sure*, Leon thought and turned away.

A small house standing not 200 yards behind the school looked as if it was untouched, even though everything around it was totally demolished. A cow stood in Willard Hall's pasture chomping grass and nursing a calf, oblivious to the two dead animals nearby.

Leon fleetingly thought of his Bible teachings. *Somewhere in Revelations, 'One shall be taken and the other left.'*

When he stepped into a puddle of water, his left foot felt as if he had stepped on a fire coal. On closer examination, he found a puncture wound on both sides of his big toe. A stick must have gone clean through, but there was very little blood.

He saw folks congregating at Mr. Willie Hall's house and headed over that way. Mr. Willie stood on his front porch and motioned for Leon to come on over. "Leon, what are you doing wandering around? Get in here and let Dr. Mosley and his nurse examine you. You look like a drowned rat; we'll find you some dry clothes."

* * * * *

Kelly was at the chalk mine working when he received his Pa's phone call about the tornado in Steadman. He jumped in his Model T, along with Cutter Gleaton, Buck Green, and Jack Colton, and headed across the river to Rayflin. Kel was standing on the porch when they drove up.

"Jack says it will be hard going getting into Steadman from the south," Kel said. Most of the railroad cars on the sidetrack are turned over—better go back across the river, follow the river road, and try to get in from the north. Olin says he's going with you."

"O.K. Pa, we will," Kelly said. "Come on, Olin. If you're going, get in here."

Three

Kelly found Elsie and Leon at Willie Hall's house. The nurse had bandaged Leon's foot and both had been examined for other injuries. Leon was wearing a pair of Mr. Willie's overalls, the legs rolled up so he could walk without tripping. They had also found some dry clothes for Elsie.

"I'd better get you two children home right away so Florence can fuss over you. I have to go to Leesville and see about Louise," Kelly said.

* * * * *

The hospital at Leesville was a long brick building on Elm Street. The parking area in front was crowded with automobiles and Adams's Coca Cola truck when Kelly drove in. Through the front doors was a waiting area with chairs and a nurse's desk. It was packed with children from Steadman waiting to be examined by Dr. Timmerman and Dr. Brodie. To the rear of the building were six patient rooms where the more serious overnight patients stayed.

Kelly found Louise in one of these patient rooms, tucked into bed, her leg wounds cleaned and bandaged below the knee.

A wisp of a smile touched her lips when she saw Kelly standing in the doorway.

"Are you okay, Louise?" Kelly whispered as he entered the room to stand beside her bed. She looked so pale and helpless, it was hard for him to keep his composure. He knew he had to be strong for her sake. He bent and kissed her forehead.

"I'm okay, Daddy," Louise replied, "but my leg hurts something awful. Dr. Brodie says it will heal in no time."

Dr. Brodie appeared behind them and said, "Louise, you try to rest. I just need to have a word with your daddy. Follow me to my office, will you, Kelly?"

"How bad is it, doc?" Kelly asked as soon as the office door closed behind them. "Louise said you told her it would heal in no time."

"I couldn't tell a twelve-year-old what I really thought. The left leg below the knee is mangled and mashed pretty bad. It's possible it will heal okay and she will only be crippled, but the biggest threat is gangrene. I think the leg should be amputated right away; I hate to take the chance of gangrene developing. I'm being honest with you, Kelly; it's up to you and Louise."

"I'll talk to her doc and explain the danger. I trust your judgment, but this will be a hard pill for Louise to swallow."

Kelly sat beside Louise's bed and tried to gently explain to her what Dr. Brodie had said. "It's too dangerous not to amputate the leg, Louise. You could develop gangrene."

"Please, Daddy, don't let them cut off my leg!" Louise exclaimed, big tears rolling down her swollen and bruised face. "It will heal, I just know it will. Please, please, don't let them take it off! Being a cripple is bad enough. I wouldn't want to live with just one leg. Promise me you won't let them do it!"

"Okay, Louise, I'll promise, but we'll have to give it a couple of weeks and see how the healing goes."

Kelly sat beside her bed the rest of the afternoon. Dr. Brodie gave her some laudanum for the pain and she slept intermittently. Finally, at sundown, he rose from his chair at her bedside. "I'm going home now, Louise," he said as he bent to kiss her cheek. "I'll be back tomorrow. You try to rest now."

Dr. Brodie was standing in the waiting area as Kelly departed. "What did you decide about her leg?" he asked.

"I promised her we'd wait. She said she didn't want to live with one leg. I just couldn't force her; I don't have the heart to do it now."

* * * * *

Clara Gunter died at the Leesville hospital that night; Marvellene lingered until the next day. They had serious head injuries that a small-town hospital was ill-equipped to deal with. That brought the death toll to four. But that wouldn't be all. Louise's leg appeared to be healing well for several weeks. Then inflammation rekindled with a vengeance and gangrene set in. By the time Kelly gave the go ahead to amputate against her will, it was too late. She died on the 30th of June, two months after the tornado, another victim of the 'Tornado of 24'. Kelly had to live with the torment of his decision the rest of his life.

"Twelve-year-olds have no business making decisions when it comes to life and death," he would often say. "I could have saved her if only I had been stronger and hadn't let a promise bind me."

That summer, the school was rebuilt, and in October 1924, the section of the pine tree with the two by four impaled through it was displayed at the South Carolina state fair in Columbia. That storm changed Leon's life forever. He lost good friends that day and it ultimately claimed a sister he dearly loved.

Four

LEON AND ELSIE WENT BACK TO THE NEW STEADMAN SCHOOL in the fall of 1924. Life is not fair; few young people realize that at fourteen, but Leon certainly did. In the space of four years, he and Elsie had lost a mother, a baby brother, and a sister. They were uprooted from their home for almost three years and now had a new stepmother and baby brother, Robert.

The loss of Louise was the hardest for Leon to cope with. He came home from school in the afternoons and immediately threw himself into work in the fields at home and in his Grandpa Kel's fields at Rayflin. Work was his only outlet for the despair he felt when he permitted himself to dwell on the loss of his sister. He and Louise were so close in age; it was as if a part of him was gone.

Leon's daddy, Kelly, found his comfort in the bottle. When he was drunk, his mind was numbed to feelings of loss he felt when sober. He still worked during the week at the chalk mine, but on weekends, he was drunk from Friday evening to Sunday. Often, he stayed out all night, sometimes the whole weekend, at Rayflin or down in the swamp at the still. Kelly and his brothers drank excessively: they also were producing their own moonshine.

If Kelly had not appeared by Sunday afternoon, Florence would ask, "Leon, please go down to Rayflin and try to locate your daddy? He's probably laid up drunk at Buck's with Rion and Sam. I'll have to get some food into him so he can sober up for the work week. I'm almost at wit's end with his drinking; it just makes him more depressed and remorseful. You know he feels so guilty about Louise's death."

"I will go find him, Miss Florence, and maybe I'll try to talk to him about Louise if he's sober enough to understand what I'm saying. You know that may not be the case."

Leon frequently had to go down in the swamp and bring his daddy home on Sunday afternoons to help get him sobered up; this had almost become a Sunday chore. He understood Miss Florence was having a hard time dealing with Kelly, but he appreciated her tolerance. *She must love that man,* he thought to himself. *Daddy has just turned into an old drunk and she puts up with it and tries to help and not nag him about his behavior.*

Leon was fascinated with the workings of moonshine stills and became familiar with the construction and operation of them. By the time he turned sixteen in 1926, he was spending a good portion of time in the North Edisto river swamps with his uncles helping run their still and began to drink moonshine himself. He still went to school during the week, and helped his Grandpa Kel on the farm, but on the weekends, he was running the still for his uncles and became quite efficient at it.

"I tell you, Kelly," Rion said, "that Leon is just a natural when it becomes to producing moonshine. I do believe that boy has found his calling."

Kelly was so drunk, he barely could mumble a "Yep I believe he has," before reverting back into his drunken stupor.

"He sure nuth has," Sam added in a slurred voice.

Sam was sitting on the ground, propped against the base of a big pine tree about twenty feet from the still. The sun was just going down in the west and the last rays of sun reflected off the bright copper still. It was almost blinding to the three men already blinded from the booze; Rion, Kelly, and Sam. The creek run was on the other side of the still from where Sam was propped against the tree.

"I guess sitting on the pine straw, I'll have a mess of redbugs eating my sorry behind up tonight."

"You want me to help you up, Uncle Sammy?" Leon asked. "I can at least get you up away from all the pine straw and redbugs. You could lean against those two fifty-pound sugar sacks in the little cart we hauled our makings here in."

"I sure would appreciate it, 'Cap,' a name he tended to use for everyone whenever he was drunk, but I'm awfully wobbly, having a mite trouble talking. Since you're about the only one of us anywhere close to sober, give me a hand and I'll try to get my sorry tail up.

Sam continued talking as Leon wrapped an arm around him and half drug him over to the cart, "Rion's right Leon, can't nobody in this country make high grade moonshine no better then you. Remember son, if you develop your expertise in the producing of high grade liquor, you will always have a way to survive, that's one commodity folks in this neck of the woods will pay for. Shaw, when you reach a state of dependence on liquor, you would walk ten miles on frozen ground to buy some, it's a powerful addiction and a hard one to get shed of."

The 18th amendment to the Constitution had passed in 1919. The amendment prohibited by law the manufacture and sale of alcoholic beverages. Of course, it turned out to be an absolute failure.

Criminalizing the production of alcohol only led to civil delinquency and organized crime, especially in big cities, like Chicago and New York. Hidden clubs called speakeasies still served alcohol to people illegally, Prohibition was more or less ignored when money was involved, law or no law, people were going to have their liquor. With Prohibition crime just increased.

The federal law imposing Prohibition on liquor made no difference to the Gantt boys, they just made their own.

The Gantt boys all agreed, "The fact that it was against the law only added a degree of adventure to their enterprise. Matching wits with Sheriff Cromer Oswald and government Revenuers kept them on their toes."

Their stills were always hidden down in the swamp near the river on land they knew like the back of their hand. Their base of operations was almost impossible to locate in the North Edisto river swamp.

Sometimes Sheriff Oswald compared them to ghosts; "they find it so easy to disappear in the thick 'underbrush, Juniper trees and black water that they know so well. Nobody can find them, if they don't want to be found."

The only chance to catch them Oswald had, came from informants and there were very few of them willing to snitch on the Gantts, legal or not. They wouldn't help the law because the men folk in that part of the state purchased liquor from the Gantts. Their whole group of friends and acquaintances were 'thick as thieves' when it came to secrecy about the Gantts' stills. If their stills were found it was hard for the law to sneak in and surprise them. They had their lookouts and signals they used if the law was around.

* * * * *

Florence did the best she could under the circumstances. She cooked and cleaned for Kelly and the children and babied Robert. He was such a sweet child and sometimes seemed like the only bright light in all of their lives. Florence knew Kelly tortured himself about Louise's death, blaming himself for not listening to Dr. Brodie in the beginning.

"You just can't dwell on what's over and done, you just have to forgive yourself and go on," Florence told Kelly, but he didn't seem to listen, just kept on trying to find comfort in the booze, a way to release him from the feeling of guilt he carried around inside him. He just could not see that Florence was right; he would never be able to forgive himself by drowning his sorrows in a bottle.

Florence thought that maybe if they had another child, Kelly would snap out of his despair over Louise's death. In the early spring of 1927, Florence again found herself in the 'family way.' She was pleased to announce her condition to Kelly and he appeared pleased too. But the prospect of another child didn't ease his tortured mind. His drinking didn't diminish in the least. Florence's condition had not improved the outlook for their marriage. It just added another burden for her.

Prohibition would eventually be repealed by the 21st amendment, ratified in 1933. In the meantime, production of moonshine was rampant all over the country, especially in the woods and swamps of Lexington County, South Carolina.

Five

1927 BROUGHT A DEVASTATING BLOW TO THE GANTTS AT Rayflin. Peninnah got up that April morning before daybreak, as usual, and started a fire in the wood cook stove.

"I have to have breakfast finished before daylight so that Kel and the hands can get to the fields early," Peninnah reminded herself. "It's already getting pretty hot in the middle of the day."

She was in the mist of her daily routine when she realized she had not heard Kel get up. She went to the bedroom to check and he lay frozen on their bed with a look of terror and pain on his face.

As she came near to the bedside, she asked, "Kel, what's the matter? Are you okay?" He couldn't answer; he only babbled incoherently.

She flew across the hall and banged on Rion and Ruth's door. "Rion, get up quick!" You need to call Dr. Gibson in Batesburg. Something is wrong with your pa."

Rion rushed into the room, still in his long johns. One look at Kel and he knew she was right. "I'll call right away, Ma, and tell Dr. Gibson we need him. You just sit beside the bed and hold his hand. Everything will be okay when the doc gets here."

* * * * *

Dr. Gibson drove up in his automobile an hour later, but it seemed like an eternity to Peninnah. She had sat beside Kel's bed while Ruth finished cooking breakfast for her and Rion. Rion called Sam and Buck to tell them their pa was bad off; they came in just before the doctor arrived.

Rion met Dr. Gibson as he came up on the front porch, carrying his black bag. "Direct me to your pa, Rion," he said, nodding to the others. "Y'all just wait in the kitchen while I examine my patient."

Peninnah, Rion, Ruth, Sam, and Buck waited quietly in the kitchen, sipping strong coffee and straining their ears in hopes of hearing some indication as to how the examination was going. From what they could tell, it was a one-sided conversation. Dr. Gibson kept asking Kel questions but only got incoherent answers.

"Miss Peninnah, you need to come in here," the doctor called from the doorway of the bedroom. "I can't understand anything Kel is trying to tell me. Maybe you can help."

Closing the door behind Peninnah, he started asking her questions about Kel's health and any problems he might have been having. "Has he had any numbness on either side of his body in the last few days? Did he complain about feeling bad last night before he went to bed? How did he appear when you found him?"

It seemed like the questions went on and on, with Peninnah answering the best she knew how. Finally, Dr. Gibson closed his bag. "You just get some rest now, Kel, you'll be up and about in no time. Do you have a cup of coffee, Miss Penninah? I could sure use one." They left the bedroom, closing the door behind them.

"Kel has had a serious stroke on the right side," Dr. Gibson said as they entered the kitchen. "We won't know how bad the damage is for a couple of weeks. He may just be partially paralyzed on the right side; we'll just have to wait and see. As far as his speech, I'm afraid it's bad. He tried to talk with me but could only babble. That might improve, but I'm afraid he'll have a hard time communicating. Just try to keep him quiet and don't let him get agitated or excited. I'll come by tomorrow and see how he's doing. There's nothing we can do except make him comfortable and for heaven's sake, don't let anyone come down here and upset him."

Dr. Gibson came and checked on Kel every couple of days for the next three weeks. Peninnah nursed him the best she could, but she just couldn't make that man rest. He was determined to get out of that bed and see about the planting. She was still cooking for the farmhands every day and with trying to see to Kel's needs, days were mighty hectic.

In less than two weeks' time, Kel insisted on getting out of bed and sitting on the front porch; one of his sons had to be nearby to help him get there. Peninnah was too small and Kel too portly for her to assist him. He was content to sit there in the shade of the porch roof, babbling to himself and watching his field hands as they went about the business of planting the fields near the house. It was so frustrating to him. He just couldn't make anyone understand what was on his mind. It was a great agitation that he had to sit and not direct what they were doing in his fields. Pretty soon, his right leg improved enough that he could get around with a cane and oversee the work. Of course, none of the farmhands could understand a word he was trying to say. His speech had not improved except for one word: "Damn." They could all understand that.

Willie told Leon one afternoon while they worked side by side in the field, "Mr. Kel shore can't talk much, not as so anybody can understand, but I can tell when he's cussing me out. He says 'damn' a lot and I can shore understand dat word plain as day."

Leon and Willie were in the field together every day now. After Kel's stroke, Leon quit school so he could devote all his time to the farming. He knew how much his Grandpa Kel depended on him, and he knew Kel didn't trust the field hands to oversee themselves, so Leon felt obligated.

Six

It was Sunday morning April 29, 1928; Elsie jumped from bed and ran across the porch into the kitchen. Miss Florence was busy cooking breakfast standing at the stove.

"Where's Daddy, Miss Florence?"

"Kelly got dressed up and left. Said he was walking down to Rayflin and to Buck's house; he'll be home after a while."

I just bet he's gone down to Uncle Buck's house, Elsie thought to herself. Even Elsie, at twelve years old, was smart enough to know where her daddy had gone; the same place he went every Sunday morning. Everybody in the community knew Kelly was meeting that Dorothy Gunter. They had a long-standing relationship, according to the gossip. Grown-ups didn't talk about such things to children Elsie's age, but they overheard enough to know what went on. Besides, Leon had told her, and he was a grown man of seventeen.

Miss Florence had to know it too, and she put up with it. *Surely she must be a good person, or she would kick my daddy's behind.*

Dorothy Gunter, her husband Ralph, and their three children— two older girls and a young boy of ten, Clint—lived in the old John Gantt house on a two-rut road that ran from Sugar Bottom across a ridge above sheep spring out to Pine Grove Church. On this particular Sunday morning, April 29, Kelly did walk down the road towards Rayflin and Buck's but left the road at the fork and headed up the foot path to Sheep Spring to meet Dorothy.

"Well, Dorothy, my sweet thing, you're already here waiting on me," Kelly remarked. "You must be wanting sex as much as I do."

"Of course, I do, Kelly," she replied. "Ralph, bless his heart, tries to please me, but he just can't, not the way you do. I look forward to our Sunday morning rendezvous all week long. I'm just crazy about you, Kelly, I can't help myself."

She was there waiting on him in their favorite spot, a deep shaded gully, where they spread an old quilt Dorothy brought, quickly disrobed, and had feverish sex. Afterwards, they spent a little time in conversation, then dressed and parted.

Kelly turned, smiled, and gave Dorothy a quick wave. "See you next Sunday, same place, same time, you sexy woman. You always could put a smile on a man's face." He left her with that comment.

Whether they cared for each other or just enjoyed the sex, it was hard to say. It certainly wasn't that Kelly didn't love Florence or he hadn't loved Mary, but both Florence and Mary were women of the Victorian era. Good women both, and the kind a man would want to marry, not the sexually, promiscuous type like Dorothy that men were drawn to purely for enjoyment.

Kelly was reputed to be the father of one of Dorothy's girls; the other supposedly belonged to his brother Roston. As far as the boy, Clint, it was questionable, but Ralph Gunter, Dorothy's husband, was said to be his father.

Suffice to say, Dorothy had her share of men, including Thurmond Rogers, a man who reportedly had a mean disposition and was jealous of Dorothy's other male friends. Dorothy refused to have anything to do with him after a short affair.

She had told Thurmond after he had treated her roughly, "Leave me alone. I don't want to have anything else to do with you, understand?"

Thurmond was not the type to give up; he stalked Dorothy and tormented her when he could, running his mouth to others about her. He tried to put his hands on her a time or two when she accidentally bumped into him down at Roston's store. Roston had even warned Thurmond to stay away from Dorothy; it was plain she wasn't interested in his advances.

Thurmond didn't care for the Gantt brothers, especially Roston and Kelly; he had heard the rumors of their relationship with Dorothy. He was determined she would be his or no other man's. Ralph was her husband, but Thurmond knew Dorothy had no real attraction to Ralph. He even felt sorry for Ralph, sort of. Ralph didn't see what was going on right under his nose. Dorothy's blatant rejection of Thurmond pushed him to his limit, and he began to plot his revenge.

She knew he could be a dangerous man but underestimated how violent he could be. She just figured he was trying to scare her and that he would eventually lose interest and leave her be.

Dorothy was not afraid of Thurmond. However, she was no fool and didn't trust him, and she kept Ralph's shotgun close by just in case. After her romp with Kelly that morning, they parted ways and she returned to her house and Kelly to his, but not before he made a brief detour to their still for drink with one of the brothers. One of them was always there when the still was in operation.

That Sunday afternoon, between sundown and dark, Thurmond

Rogers walked up the footpath from Rayflin with Ralph, Dorothy's husband. Ralph evidently had no idea the kind of sneaking around with men Dorothy was accustomed to. Thurmond knew this and had no quarrel with Ralph. They talked on the way up to the road on the ridge.

Thurmond asked Ralph, "How's your crops fairing? Your corn is probably up pretty good by now."

"It's doing right well, Thurmond, but we could sure use some more rain to help it along."

When they reached the ridge road, Ralph turned to Thurmond. "I'm just going to stop at the barn and check on my stock. See you later."

* * * * *

Dorothy was in her kitchen mixing up bread, the kitchen door closed and the windows shuttered. A fireplace adorned one wall; the rest of the room was meagerly furnished with just a table, chairs, an oil lamp, and a dish cabinet. The door from the kitchen opened onto an unenclosed platform about six feet wide; the rest of the house was attached on the other side of that platform.

The kitchen where Dorothy was preparing their supper was a separate room. The girls and Clint were in the other part of the house attached to that platform. Thurmond peeped through the wooden shutter that covered the window and saw Dorothy busy at the table. He threw open the shudder and stuck in his head.

"There you are, you God damn ass," Thurmond said. "I've come to settle our little disagreement."

"Get away from here, Thurmond, now," Dorothy remarked through gritted teeth. "I won't have you scaring the children, and Ralph will be home soon. I don't want anything to do with you. Can't you get that through your thick skull? Leave me alone—I mean it."

Thurmond just stood leaning in the window with a menacing look on his face.

Dorothy wiped the dough quickly from her hands with the dish towel and went for Ralph's gun leaned in the corner of the kitchen next to the fireplace. She discharged the first barrel accidentally—it went off in the fireplace; the kick knocked Dorothy backwards to the floor.

The lamp was lit, so from the window, Thurmond could see his advantage. Dorothy quickly pulled the trigger to fire the other barrel, knowing that was her only chance; Thurmond would be through the door in seconds. This time when it discharged, the load went under the door. She discharged the second barrel too early. Thurmond stepped onto the platform and threw open the kitchen door. With both barrels discharged, Dorothy had no time to reload; it was too late.

Thurmond shot Dorothy in the face at close range with a double barrel sawed-off shotgun; some of the shot was embedded in the doorframe.

The children came running when the shots were fired.

Thurmond stood over Dorothy, looking down at her, yelling at the kids. He screamed, "Go to Rayflin and get the damn Gantts bring them up here and see what they can do!" Then he turned and discharged the other barrel into his temple.

* * * * *

Dorothy's children arrived breathless and crying at Rayflin to report the awful crime they had just witnessed. Roston called Sheriff Cromer Oswald and he and his deputies came out to investigate. Roston went on up to Dorothy's but insisted her children stay at Rayflin with his Ma. He figured they had seen enough horror to last the rest of their lives.

Leon had heard the news and was up there at the scene the next morning kinda early. The sun was barely above the horizon. Cromer Oswald, the Lexington County Sheriff, was present.

Sheriff Oswald told Leon, "When we got here, Thurmond was slumped over on his knees. I turned him over, laid him out, and spread a sheet over him and a sheet over Dorothy."

Arriving early that morning, Leon observed that Thurmond had two or three shells in the pocket of his nasty overalls and two empty shells in the gun. They were the same as the smokeless, powderless shells that were in Thurmond's pocket. He reported his observation to the Sheriff. Thurmond was dressed in black, nasty, greasy, overalls, and a cap in the same condition.

Dr. Hutto from Wagener impaneled a jury that afternoon. The bodies were laid out on tables in the kitchen. Kelly, Victor Gantt, Gene Rawl, and Mel Rawl were on the panel. Doctor Hutto took the sheet off Thurmond.

Using scissors, he cut Thurmond from ear to ear across the top of his head, reached in, and got a few shots out. He asked the jury, "What size shot?" They all agreed it was #7 small tool shot. Then the doctor uncovered Dorothy's body, got some shot out of Dorothy, and asked the same question of the panel: "What size shot is in the victim?" They all agreed it was the same size shot. The side of Dorothy's face had been completely blown off by the blast, making it easy for Dr. Hutto to retrieve the sample shot.

"I declare this a murder suicide," Doctor Hutto said. "Sheriff Oswald, enter that conclusion in the official record please."

It had been a hard thing emotionally for Kelly to serve on the panel. He could feel tears welling up in his eyes when the doctor threw back the sheet that covered Dorothy's body, but he held his emotions inside. He knew he couldn't make a spectacle of himself in front of the others. He especially didn't want Ralph to see the feelings that would be so plain on his face. Even poor, dumb Ralph would know something was amiss if Kelly broke down when he saw Dorothy's body.

All Kelly could think was, *Dorothy was alive and happy this morning. I held her in my arms, kissed her lips, and caressed her body. Now she is lying on a table dead, her body disfigured by that crazy bastard, Thurmond Rogers. I'm glad he took his own life, or I would be obligated to do it for him.*

The examination by Doctor Hutto and those men he impaneled ended the matter. Evidently Thurmond figured if he couldn't have Dorothy, no other man would. Her children were raised by Ralph Gunter, the only father they knew.

Kelly, being a somewhat gifted carpenter, told Ralph, "I'll be glad to make Dorothy's coffin if you want me to."

Ralph gratefully accepted Kelly's offer, never knowing of Kelly and Dorothy's relationship. Dorothy was buried in the Convent Baptist Church Cemetery. Later, her husband Ralph would be buried beside her. Thurmond's family had him buried in the Rogers' plot at Mr. Ebal Church near Batesburg.

Seven

ON SEPTEMBER 14, 1927, ANOTHER SON WAS BORN TO FLOR-
ence and Kelly. This son was named Nathan Byron and from the
very beginning, he and Robert were different. Although almost
identical in appearance, both tow-headed with blue eyes, their tem-
peraments were not. Robert was a quiet, shy boy always wanting
to be good and please his mother. Nathan was boisterous and into
everything. Florence had a hard time keeping him out of trouble.

By age two, he liked to climb, and frequently Florence had to
coax him down from the top of a tree or their two-storied barn.

"That Nathan was a captain alright," Leon remarked. "He
would climb up the side of our barn, using the cracks between the
1x8 lumber on the outside just like a ladder until his head touched
the barn roof. Then he would swing around to get in the hayloft.

"We would lay around here half drunk, me, Daddy, Uncle
Sammy and Uncle Rion, and Nathan would pick it up, that 'old
black guard talk' as Miss Florence called it. We should have had our
behinds kicked, stomped in this dry dirt around here," continued
Leon. "Nathan could hardly talk; he had a temper and he could
cuss."

* * * * *

The moonshining business on Kel Gantt's place really picked up after their father's stroke. No longer did the boys worry about their pa busting up their stills. He just wasn't able. All of Kel's boys drank: Roston, Kelly, Woodard, Sam, Rion and Buck. Cyrus wasn't around, but he had been known to join in with his brothers whenever he made it home for a visit.

* * * * *

A problem presented itself at the chalk mine in the fall of that same year. Fine grit appeared in the chalk that was being mined. For six months or better, the operators sifted the grit out and continued their mining and shipping of the kaolin, but the cost of the extra time and manpower to remove the grit was not feasible to the Edisto Kaolin Company. In 1928, the Company closed operations at their Chalk Hill mine.

Kelly went back to his farming to make a living and Roston went back to running the store at Rayflin full time. More and more, the brothers turned to making liquor as their main source of income. Moonshining was a profitable business during Prohibition as long as you didn't get caught. Working an honest job just wouldn't give a man enough income to make a living.

Pretty soon, Leon was running liquor stills. The profit was so much better; he felt he had to run moonshine. As it turned out, he was especially good making liquor and grew a fondness for his product.

* * * * *

Things really got worse in October 1929 when the stock market crashed. The Gantt family didn't understand the significance at first, but they soon saw the results. Farming would no longer be profitable; you just couldn't get any money for your produce. The Great Depression would soon follow. No jobs could be found and if a man were lucky enough to get work, he couldn't make enough to hardly get by. In the towns and cities, people were standing in soup lines, wondering where they would get their next meal. At least in the country, folks could raise most of their food. They might be broke but they could at least survive.

Kel Gantt was physically able to wander his fields but still could not communicate his thoughts to anyone. Penninah couldn't understand what he wanted to say any better than his children. One summer day in 1929, Kel came into the kitchen while Peninnah was preparing their dinner. Kel grunted and babbled, pointing his finger toward the front door.

"What do you want, Kel?" More grunts and finger pointing were his only reply.

"I guess you want to show me something, right, Kel?" He smiled and nodded his head up and down for a yes. "O.K., as soon as we finish with dinner and I get the dishes done, I'll go with you and see what you want."

That seemed to please Kel, and he was content to wait. As soon as the meal was over and the dishes were washed and put away, Peninnah said, "Alright, Kel, let's go see what's troubling you."

Kel hobbled out the front door, down the steps, across the road and the pasture and up the railroad track towards Steadman. Peninnah was having a hard time keeping up with him; he was so intent on his objective. He could get around fine with the help of his cane; wandering to the boundaries of his land had become almost a passion.

"Kel, how much further?" Peninnah yelled. "We're almost a mile from the house!"

He just paused, looked over his shoulder and grunted. Finally, he left the tracks and turned west towards the river. The going was getting rough, with briars and brambles in the edge of the swamp, but Peninnah was determined to satisfy Kel and see what he was trying so hard to tell her. About a hundred feet from the tracks, she finally emerged on the bank of the North Edisto. There stood Kel, pointing into a deep dark pool of black water and trying so hard to say what was on his mind. On the bank lay a long rectangular wire fish trap that one of the boys had pulled from the river. The fish trap was now full of birds, evidently lured there by remnants of fish scales and flesh clinging to the inside of the trap.

"Is this what you wanted me to see, Kel?" A nod came from the man standing on the bank. "One of our boys took the fish trap out of the river, threw it on the bank and the birds flew in and were trapped?" Another nod. "Well, I say let's kill these birds and I'll make us a fine bird pie." By the wide smile that lit up her husband's face, Peninnah could tell that was exactly what Kel was thinking.

After the trip to the river that day, Peninnah tried to pay more attention to Kel's ramblings. She knew he got so frustrated trying to communicate when no one could understand. It wasn't as if he had enough schooling that he could write what he was thinking or feeling. She couldn't guess what was on his mind. She just had to say, "I'll go with you, Kel, and you can show me what you want."

* * * * *

The economy was steadily getting worse. Farming was the only thing Kel Gantt knew, and with his disabling stroke of 1927, he was reduced to depending on his sons and Leon to manage things. The fields at Rayflin were planted that spring of 1930, but it was evident that with the condition of the economy, the crops would not bring in enough money to cover the cost of producing them. The newspaper was full of 'gloom and doom,' stories of despair from all over the country. There had even been talk of discontinuing the 'Swamp Rabbit,' but that was still only talk. Kelly and Leon made what little they could with the farming, but the liquor business kept bread on the table.

Florence was alone most of the time with her two boys while Kelly and Leon were down in the swamp. On the weekends, she had to contend with Kelly and Leon's drinking when they were there, but that was seldom. They usually came in at night for supper, then went to meet up with the boys. Florence cooked their breakfast in the mornings during the week. Breakfast and at supper were the only times the boys got to see their daddy.

On the 28th of May in 1930, Florence's sister-in-law, Fannie,

Will's wife, asked Florence, "Will it be O.K. if I take Robert and Nathan to their grandmother Ella's for a visit? That will give you some free time while I tend to the boys."

Florence readily agreed. Both boys could be a handful, especially Nathan, and she realized Fannie was still grieving for her and Will's only son, C.W., who had died only six months before.

"Maybe it will help Fannie to have the boys to tend to, and they both love their Aunt Fannie," Florence told Kelly at breakfast that morning.

Miss Ella had a patch of ripe strawberries, and Fannie let the boys eat all they could hold. Nathan had eaten strawberries until he literally made himself sick. When Fannie brought the boys home, Nathan's stomach was upset and he developed a severe case of diarrhea.

Carrying a sleeping Nathan across the front porch to his bedroom that moonless night, Florence saw a startling apparition at the edge of the yard. It was about three feet tall, a white fog apparition that moved along slowly. She paused and followed its path with her eyes until it disappeared behind the house. She wasn't really frightened; she just shook her head, thinking her mind was playing tricks on her. Two days later, on the 30th of May, Nathan died. According to Dr. Brodie, it was colitis, an irritation of the large intestine. His little body had dehydrated so quickly, nothing could be done to save him. Florence would always blame it on the strawberries. The apparition she believed to be an omen of his death.

Kelly made his son Nathan's coffin. He loved the boy, but hardly got to know him before he was taken from him and Florence.

The day of the funeral, Mr. Reedy Gunter drove Florence and Robert to the service at Pine Grove Church in his car.

Florence sat on the front seat with Reedy. Miss Fannie, Reedy's wife, sat in the back seat with Miss Vyra Hall and Robert. Six-year-old Robert sat between the ladies, and they held Nathan's coffin on their laps. It was a small service, with only Florence and Kelly's family and a few friends attending.

Kelly had been drinking to ease his pain; liquor was his constant companion and his solace in times of sadness. Roston and some of the brothers thought it best if Kelly rode to the church with them. They could be there to support him and keep him from making a spectacle of himself. A death in the family was a good excuse for them to get tight to settle their nerves.

Leon, at the age of twenty, was a grown man, but he didn't hold with being in church drunk. He and Elsie rode to the church with their Uncle Woodard and Aunt Mamie and cousins, Chalmus and Cleola. Most of the other Gantt family was present too. Jennie and Olin took Peninnah; they decided it would be best for Kel to remain at home with some of the older grandchildren. No need for Kel to witness the interment of his little grandson or the spectacle of his son Kelly's drunken state; it would only cause him to become agitated and upset.

Truth be known, Kel didn't even realize he had lost a little grandson. Since his stroke, he was more or less trapped, mind and body, in a world of his own that no amount of explaining could shed light on. He couldn't communicate with his family, and they saw no reason to tell him the circumstances of Nathan's passing; it would be too complicated and only cause him to withdraw further behind his wall of silent despair.

Eight

ON SEPTEMBER 5, 1930, KEL GANTT HAD ANOTHER SEVERE stroke. This time, there was no partial recovery. He passed away, leaving a widow, Peninnah, nine grown children and numerous grandchildren to mourn his passing. He was a strong, independent man, always a farmer; before his death, he saw even his livelihood begin to crumble with the Depression that was just beginning to take over the country.

In his last three years, he had been reduced to expressing himself with grunts and hand signals. Kel's mind worked fine, but he could only keep his thoughts to himself.

Kel's mind was his only companion. He couldn't communicate his thoughts or feelings to any other person. Peninnah knew Kel was ready to go when the second stroke hit. Farming had been his life. She remembered before the first stroke, how important the land was to Kel. Many times she had observed him with the farmhands plowing. He would often squat in the newly plowed field, dig his hands in the rich soil and lift a fistful to his nose. Breathing in the aroma of the rich, dark soil, he would let it sift through his fingers, a wide smile would appear and a countenance of contentment lite up his face.

Jacob Kelly Gantt was buried at Pine Grove Church, the church he and Peninnah attended and that he had supported with his tithes and work for forty-five years.

* * * * *

When Kel Gantt died, his estate was left in limbo. All property both real and personal fell to Peninnah. He had made no will, trusting her to be fair and give to every child their right. Besides, he was always too busy working his fields, tending his land. Managing a large farm was sunup to sundown required labor and dedication. Taking the time to visit a lawyer and make legal arrangements never crossed his mind. When the stroke impaired him in 1927, he could not have communicated his wishes even if he had wanted to. You can't seek counsel of a lawyer in legal matters if you can't communicate with him.

There were 464 acres left of their home place. Five years before, Kel had cut off 40 acres for Woodard at his request.

"My family and I don't intend to live on the farm, Pa," Woodard had said. "Can you just go ahead and deed forty acres to me now? We have a home in Steadman, a house and a store; we are satisfied where we are." When Woodard approached his father with that argument, Kel had agreed. None of the other children had legal papers on any of the land.

Kel had been buried only two weeks when Jennie approached her mother with the idea of her and her family moving into the home place down at Rayflin.

"Jennie," Olin said, "Talk to your ma about us moving in with her; she has plenty of room and with you and the children for company, so she won't be lonely."

Jennie agreed, but of course it was mostly Olin's idea; he was a shrewd fellow and saw it could be advantageous for them if Miss Peninnah became dependent on her daughter, Jennie. He could always manipulate Jennie; he wasn't really concerned particularly about his mother-in-law's loneliness. Always the schemer, that was Rish, as Kel called him.

Peninnah thought it a good idea too and thought having Jennie and her family in the same house would be nice. There was plenty of room; Rion and Ruth had already moved, with their four little girls, into a small house up near Kelly across from Coon Branch. Peninnah knew she would be lonely without Kel and Rion's family, so she readily agreed. Jennie and Olin moved to the home place at Rayflin and Buck and Binnie moved to the Pelt Branch house that Jennie and Olin had built.

* * * * *

Delmas Delphin "Buck" Gantt was a businessman at thirty years old. He knew there was money to be made in the liquor business, even with the economy in decline. Buck made liquor for the money; his brothers, Kelly, Sam, and Rion, along with Kelly's son, Leon, made it to drink. Buck drank his share, but he saw it more as a business enterprise and he had the connections to turn a profit. Moving into the Pelt Branch house, Buck saw as an opportune move to promote his business. The house was off the main road some two hundred yards down near the creek run, away from the prying eyes of the law and any busybodies that would report the comings and goings of his customers. He and Binnie moved there in the early months of 1931, soon after his pa's death. Buck could get $30.00 a keg for the whiskey, which made running liquor stills, although highly illegal, extremely profitable.

* * * * *

Ted Gunter, who lived across the river from Rayflin, always made the copper stills for the Gantt brothers. Ted was a quiet man, walking everywhere he went, always accompanied by his dog. When someone passed him on the road in a wagon or automobile, he would turn and watch them until they disappeared out of his sight, never once waving in greeting. He didn't appear very intelligent, not in book learning, but he was wonderful working with his hands. Ted not only crafted the copper stills, he was also brilliant when it came to fixing a time piece.

Ted and his cousin Asia Gunter had similar personalities; both were artistic in different ways, Ted making copper stills and fixing broken watches with tiny wheels and cogs, Asia able to produce realistic drawings in charcoal. They were both 'odd birds,' but were well-liked by the Gantts and their neighbors.

"That Ted is a master when it comes to making copper whiskey stills," Kelly remarked to his brothers. "He is a perfectionist and his stills look as if they were produced in a factory. They are what I would call a work of art." All the brothers agreed with Kelly's observation, giving Ted a steady job making their stills.

Ted started with sheets of copper, which he cut out and seamed with salter to form a large copper pot, usually holding about 150 gallons, depending on the requested size. The top looked like a huge upside-down copper funnel, the flared edges soldered to the top of the pot. At the top was an opening with a removal cap where the raw alcohol from the mash could be poured in.

The still itself would be set up on rocks so that a fire could be built underneath. From the cap, a copper line ran to a 20-gallon oak barrel known as the doubler. The copper line ran down inside the doubler barrel to within 5 inches of the bottom. Three or four gallons of moonshine whiskey would be added to the doubler barrel, and it would be sealed up once the still was running. Another copper line ran out of the top of the doubler barrel several inches above the whiskey level. This copper line then ran 25 feet along the bottom of the creek bed. The copper line running through the creek served as the condenser unit and ended in an empty oak barrel that sat down in the creek. Ted Gunter handled the construction of the still itself, but the most important aspect of the process was left to the operator who prepared the mash.

Leon could explain in detail the workings of liquor stills and derived great pleasure from the explaining that six 55-gallon oak barrels were needed for this size of operation. The ingredients were 300 pounds of sugar, 3 bushels of corn meal, yeast cakes, and sometime barley malt syrup. A bushel of cornmeal was mixed with water until soupy in each of three barrels. The next morning, the cornmeal mixture was soured, and you could smell the raw alcohol. The cornmeal mixture was divided between all six barrels and 50 lbs.

of sugar was added to each barrel and dissolved. Each barrel was then filled with water to within about five inches from the top and capped with wheat bran, then covered. When fermentation started, it would bubble around the inside edge of the barrel and eventually the wheat bran and cornmeal would sink to the bottom. When fermentation was complete, what remained on the top was clear raw alcohol. The raw alcohol was then carefully dipped out and poured through a cloth strainer into the top of the still. Any cornmeal that inadvertently entered the still would scorch and ruin the taste of the liquor. A good fire was then built underneath the still. Once the raw alcohol got hot and began to boil, steam traveled through the copper line from the still into the whiskey in the doubler barrel and caused it to boil. This doubled the strength of the whiskey. The steam was carried through the condensing line in the creek and the condensation poured into the empty creek barrel as high proof moonshine whiskey. A still of this size could produce 35 or 36 gallons of liquor, or 3 and ½ ten-gallon kegs. Leon became so good at the process because he could explain to anyone exactly how it was done.

In the hot summertime of 1931, Leon and Rion were running a moonshine still for Marvin Miller on Juniper Island in the North Edisto River. It was July and sticky hot with mosquitoes assaulting their every move. Sipping the finished product made their work under the hot sun and with the nuisance of the biting insects at least tolerable.

"Damn, Rion, I do believe these mosquitoes are going to carry us off."

"One or two more swigs of this moonshine will fix you, Leon; you won't even feel these damn mosquitoes."

From the edge of the swamp, they both caught the sound of whistling. "I sure as hell hope that ain't the law," Rion said. "They sure have us dead to rights."

"Naw, can't be, Rion, they wouldn't be whistling."

Buck emerged from the edge of the swamp with a big smile, carrying a keg on his shoulder. "Thought I should forewarn y'all that someone was coming in. Just thought I would drop by and see how the operation is going," Buck said.

"We're doing just fine, brother, come on over and sample the wares," Rion replied.

"Don't mind if I do, but I brought a keg of liquor for Leon to run for me. Greco and Kingfish brought eight of these kegs to my house to sell, but each one is a little low, won't hold a bead, can't be 100 proof."

"Well, let's just check it out," Leon said as he poured some of the liquor into a quart jar, sealed the top and shook the contents. No beads appeared in the liquor Leon shook up in the jar. "You're right, Buck, this stuff ain't 100 proof. I'll run it through the still for you."

Leon poured the contents of the keg in the still, added clear water from the creek, and got the fire going. Leon ran seven gallons of moonshine for Buck using the contents of the keg. He then dipped an empty salmon can into the finished product and passed it to Buck to sample.

"Leon, this stuff must be 200 proof!" Buck exclaimed when he lowered the salmon can from his lips. "I do believe it peeled the skin from the inside of my mouth, that's some powerful liquor. How much will you work for? I can sure use your expertise. I tell you what, I'll give you $2.00 a charge. You run four charges a day, two days a week, and that will be $16.00 a week. What about that?"

Leon didn't have to study on the proposition for long. A charge was a still full of liquor, and at $2.00 a charge, that was real good pay. He would have to work a month at the sawmill for 60 cents a day to make what his Uncle Buck had just offered him.

"I'll get Greco and Kingfish to tend the fire and the still for you. All I expect you to do is grade the liquor and make sure everything is done right."

Kingfish was just a nickname for Augustus Gantt, a distant cousin from the Sugar Bottom section of the community. He and Greco helped Buck with his moonshine business; now Buck was making them Leon's helpers.

"Well, Buck, you've just found yourself somebody," Leon replied.

Leon went to work for Buck two days a week running his still. The rest of Leon's time was spent running stills with his daddy Kelly or uncles Sammy and Rion. He also made liquor for other fellows in the community.

"Jack Daniels can't make liquor any stronger than I can," Leon would say. "I can taste water out of a creek and tell you if it would be good water to make liquor or not. I'm a natural I guess when it comes to producing high-quality moonshine."

It wasn't just moonshine liquor that Leon produced. Along with Kelly, Sam, and Rion, he made gooseberry brandy, peach brandy, and London dry gin out of juniper berries. He and Kelly even made beer, or homebrew, as it was called, in the smokehouse behind their house. They somehow managed to make spirits from every edible fruit or plant available.

* * * * *

In August of 1931, Mamie, Woodard's wife stepped on a rusty nail in the cow lot behind their house. She developed tetanus, or lockjaw, two weeks later. At first, she appeared tried and depressed, and then the violent muscle spasms set in. It was hard for her to swallow or open her mouth due to the contraction of her jaw muscles. By the time her illness was diagnosed by the doctor in Batesburg, it was too late. Mamie passed away on the 21st of September.

Leon hooked the mule to the buggy the following day and headed down to Buck's to collect Kelly so they could head on up to Steadman Church for his aunt Mamie's funeral. He pulled up at Buck's just in time to see Binnie sprint out the front door and around the corner of the house. Roston was standing on the top step.

As Leon climbed down from the buggy, he could see Binnie peeping around the back corner of the house.

"Uncle Roston, what's going on with Binnie this morning?"

"Oh, she is hiding from Kelly. He told her he was going to beat her 'G D a double s.'"

"Why does he want to beat her?"

"Binnie told him he was too drunk to go up to Steadman for Mamie's funeral."

"Well, Binnie is probably right on that score. I won't have Daddy make a disrespectable show at Aunt Mamie's funeral. I guess I better collect him and get him home before he can get his hands on Binnie."

Funerals were always a good excuse for Kelly to get into the booze. He wouldn't even remember the next day about his threat to beat Binnie.

Nine

LEON AND HIS DADDY, KELLY, WERE MAKING HOMEBREW IN the smokehouse in the wintertime of that year, 1931. They had a moonshine still down on Coon Branch and Leon was running one for Buck on Pelt Branch, but at home, they didn't want to be idle when they could be producing something to drink. The smokehouse was the perfect place since it wasn't being used for hanging meat anymore. They used sugar, yeast cakes and Schultz malt syrup to make their homebrew. The beer they bottled up in Ne-hi drink bottles and they had a bottle capper to crimp the metal caps on the bottles.

Kelly was going to show Leon a quick way to wash the Ne-hi bottles, so he dumped a whole crate of empty bottles upside down in a # 3 size washtub full of water. It broke danged near every one of the bottles, just around the top, but they were no good and they had to be discarded.

Just before Christmas that winter of 1931, Leon went down to Rayflin to a turkey shoot. He was drunk of course; the whole crowd at the turkey shoot was about in the same predicament. It's a wonder somebody wasn't killed; liquor and firearms don't mix well.

Leon came home from the turkey shoot with some big firecrackers and decided to set them off in front of the smokehouse. He used the broken Ne-hi bottles. Each of those big firecrackers would barely fit in the top of one of those broken bottles. He would stoop down and light the fuse, stand up, and kinda turn around with his back to the blast. He was too drunk to run. Well, when those firecrackers blew up, all kind of broken glass was embedded in the side of the smokehouse; none of the glass even touched Leon. "The good Lord takes care of drunks and fools," Leon told his daddy the next day.

The same night Leon shot off the firecrackers, in his drunken state, he had decided it would be a good idea to paint his name in blood red paint on the smokehouse door. "Don't you like what I did on the smoke house door, Daddy?"

"Sure, Leon, looks real nice," replied Kelly. "Don't get into that red paint anymore unless you're sober, OK? You could have really done a job on the smokehouse—reminds me of a kid writing on the walls, not something a grown man would do."

Ten

IN FEBRUARY OF 1932, THERE CAME A SNOW. LEON, KELLY, Rion, Buck, Ed Corley, and Willie Burkett had mash down by the river behind Buck's house, between the swamp and the river, close to where Pelt Branch ran into the North Edisto. They were running eight big barrels of mash with a fence around it to keep the varmints out. It was freezing, ice coated the trees, and a brisk breeze was blowing from the northwest. Snow covered the ground but the storm clouds were gone and the moon was shining. They could hear ice cracking on the limbs above their heads as the breeze began to pick up. There was a kerosene lantern with a reflector that threw light all one way sitting on an empty barrel.

It was about ten p.m. when Willie said, "I hears somebody coming out da edge of da swamp."

Old Willie could hear good, but at first, they paid him no mind. They were too busy catching booze and punching up the fire.

Directly, Willie said again, "I tells y'all, I hear somebody coming in here out da edge of da swamp." Leon walked around behind the barrels and the fence, while the rest scattered in the bushes. A good breeze turned the lantern over with that reflector on it and the light shone directly on those hiding in the bushes. It was as though a spotlight had been aimed at them.

"Good gracious, that's the law sure as hell!" Rion exclaimed.

That's what they all thought. They took off running, Buck and Kelly towards the river, Rion and Willie into the swamp. In his haste to escape, Buck ran directly into the river, and Kelly had to jump in and pull him out. Leon was about thirty feet from the river, lying on the ground next to a big old gum tree. He didn't want to be too hasty until he was sure what they were up against. It sure seemed mighty cold for the law to be messing around out in that swamp.

Leon lay on the ground, just listening, for about 30 minutes. He kept hearing somebody moving around about twenty yards out in front of him. The river was at his back and the creek just this side of the swamp, perhaps 200 yards away to his left. He had no idea who was moving around between him and the creek run, but he thought to himself, *I be damned if I ain't going to find out who you are. I know where the river is and I can find my way out in the dark if I have to.*

"Who are you out there?" Leon asked.

"It's just me," Ed Corley replied. "What are we gonna do?"

Ed crawled over to where Leon was lying next to the gum tree.

"We've got to make a move," Leon said. "We can't just lay here behind this tree till morning. Hell, we'll freeze to death before then. Follow me, Ed."

They both slipped over and went into the river. As cold as it was, they were up to their necks in that icy water. They crossed the mouth of the creek where it ran into the river and came out at the edge of the swamp.

There was a big short leaf pine not far from the swamp; it looked like a huge umbrella. Leon sat down with his back propped against the pine. Ed sat down beside him and they waited. Their clothes were frozen slick as glass to their bodies and they were miserable, but they didn't want to risk running into the law.

"Ed, damned if we ain't going to have to make a move. My feet are getting awful cold," Leon said.

Buck and Binnie had an old bulldog named Dixie and Buck had told Binnie before they left home, "If you know there's somebody snooping around, go outside and call Dixie, and we'll know to lay low."

"I'm going to get out of here, Ed, I can't feel my feet anymore, they're almost frozen."

Ed and Leon came out of the swamp on the old road that went down to Buck's house. That's when they saw a light in the pine thicket between them and the house. They got out of the road, squatted down, and watched it for a little bit, then returned to the big pine and waited some more.

"Can't we follow the river down to the bridge and come out that way?"

"That's a dang mile, Ed. In this ice, we can't do that, but we've got to do something. We can't stay here in this condition much longer."

They got up and headed out. Just as they got to the edge of the swamp, they heard somebody calling Buck's old dog, Dixie.

"It's the law, sure as hell, Ed!"

"What we gonna do?"

"I tell you what we're going to do. We're gonna get out of here."

"But what if it is the law?"

"Well, if it is, we'll go out there where they're at and outrun 'em. At least we'll get warmed up. We can't stay out here any longer, we'll freeze to death."

* * * * *

This time, Leon and Ed went on to Buck's house. It wasn't the law after all. The light they saw in the pine ticket was Buck and Kelly with a lantern looking for Leon and Ed, thinking they might not be able to find their way out in the dark.

Buck had a big blazing fire in the fireplace. Leon took off his jacket; it was so frozen stiff with ice, it stood up all by itself. They got kinda warmed up and Ed went on home.

"You and your daddy might as well stay here the rest of the night. No sense in going home in this freezing cold. It's nigh on to three in the morning. You can just go across the hall and get in that bed in there and get some sleep," Buck said.

Leon finally got warm and decided to stay. Kelly was nodding off in a drunken stupor sitting in front of the fire; he wasn't interested in getting up to go to bed.

Leon went across the hall to the spare bedroom, stripped his clothes off except his long-handled drawers, and slipped down between the covers. "I felt something cold all back along my shoulder," Leon related later, "It wasn't long til the odor made its way out. Binnie's cat had gotten between those pillows and put a big pile of mess up there. It had a crust on it and when I broke that crust, I think it pushed the top of the house off. That stinking pile of cat dung had been in between the pillows a couple of days, and when I disturbed the crust on top, the smell was horrible."

Buck called out from the kitchen, "Leon, what in the name of God is going on in there. I think the roof just lifted up off the house."

Leon jumped up, pulled on his pants and headed back across the hall. "I'll tell you what's going on. Binnie's cat laid a big pile of cat dung between the pillows, and I just smeared my shoulder all in it. Man, this stuff stinks."

Buck got Binnie up out of bed; she filled a pan with hot water from a kettle hanging over the fire for Leon to wash himself. While Leon was cleaning himself with the hot water and soap, Binnie went in, stripped the bed of the offending linen, and replaced it with clean sheets. She found a bottle of her perfume and poured all of it on Leon's upper torso in an effort to get rid of the smell. That was a loud odor; the stink from the cat mess still lingered a little.

Finally, Leon became desensitized enough to the occasional whiff to go back to bed. He slept a couple of hours, got up, and returned to the kitchen where his daddy, Kelly, still occupied the chair by the fireplace. The fire had burnt down; only ashes remained. Evidently, during the night, as the fire began to die, Kelly had unconsciously moved closer to feel the warmth from the embers. He still sat in the chair with his head rolled forward dozing, but his leather shoes were now up in the gray ashes. On closer examination, Leon found the toes of Kelly's shoes were brittle from the heat of the fire, and if you mashed on them, the leather would crack apart. During the night, Kelly's hat had fallen off and landed on the coals; all that remained was a small piece of the brim in the fireplace.

"Wake up, Daddy," Leon said as he gently shook Kelly's shoulder. "Your hat has burned up in the fire and the toes of your shoes have almost disintegrated."

"Well son, why did you let me pull my chair in so close to the fire?" Kelly was sort of halfway sober by now.

"I didn't, Daddy, that was your own doing. I had enough to

contend with last night without being responsible for you getting in the fireplace."

Leon then related to Kelly the story of the cat mess between the pillows. While he was telling the story, Binnie and Buck got up and Binnie made them some coffee. Less than an hour later, Rion and Willie showed up. They had been back down to the still and brought the liquor to Buck's that they had run last night before the law scare.

Rion suggested they have a drink of liquor being as how it was so cold outside; they could use a little something to warm them up before heading home. The mere suggestion was all they needed.

After a drink or two, Leon related to Rion and Willie the story of the cat mess between the pillows. Of course, he embellished the story a little, but honestly, it didn't need any added touches; the truth was comical enough. At the time, of course, Leon didn't see the humor in it, but with an audience, coupled with the moonshine, it became one of his funniest and most memorable stories.

After a few drinks, a good story in front of a blazing fire, ice coated trees outside in a stiff breeze and the sprinkling of snow on the ground, Leon made mention of all the birds covering Buck's back yard searching for food. The ground outside was covered in little snow hoppers and jorees looking for something to eat in the snow.

"I say we fix us a bird trap and see if we can kill some of them birds," Kelly said.

They tore the door off Buck's outhouse and rigged up a trap. Propping the door up with a stout tree branch, they baited their trap with grits, tied a line to the thick branch, and pulled the line inside Buck's back door. As the little birds gathered to eat the grits,

Buck would give the line a jerk and the door would fall. They killed a mess of birds, picked off their feathers, gutted and cleaned them, and spent the rest of the day roasting birds over a spit in the fireplace to eat and drinking the liquor Rion and Willie had brought from the still. It was nearly sundown before Kelly and Leon finally made it home.

Eleven

BY THE END OF 1932, THE GREAT DEPRESSION HAD TAKEN A firm hold of the American economy. Banks invested their depositors' money in stocks and had to close their doors. Between the stock market crash of 1929 and the end of 1932, thousands of banks closed. Millions of Americans lost everything they had saved. Every month during this time, the economy slumped further. There was no money in circulation. Industries cut production because people with no cash were unable to buy their products. With the cuts in production, jobs were lost and the pay for jobs available was meager. Unemployment reached an all-time high of 25%. It was a vicious circle; depressed wages meant depressed spending, which in turn depressed production. Thousands of Americans lost their homes and had nowhere to go; they could either move in with family or take to the road. A vagabond society reigned as tens of thousands of young people and families wandered the country in search of employment, food, and shelter.

The situation all over of the country was dire. In the South, the railroad, textile and farming industries prevalent here suffered worse. People had always looked to banking and business to correct depressions in the past, but they were powerless now. There seemed no end in sight ,and people turned to the federal government to correct the situation.

Hoover as president had specific views when it came to the role of government. "I believe business will correct the situation without supervision of the federal government," President Hoover went on record as his opinion. "Local and state governments should provide assistance for their needy citizens." The problem with this approach was that state and local governments had no money to help their citizens.

The Gantts were never well off, but they all expressed their opinion: "As farmers who till our own land, plant our crops, and when the crops sell, buy the necessities that our land and livestock can't provide, we are still much better off than city folks. With farm production in such a chaotic state, we can't make enough money from our crops to cover the cost of producing them. We'll all quit farming for a living; only plant what crops our families need for our own survival."

Down at Rayflin, Olin, with the help of Arthur Moore and Willie Burkett, still planted Mr. Kel's fields, but just those closest to the house. Roston and his oldest boy, Raymond, helped, along with Kelly and Leon. This was still their pa's place and Olin was not entirely in charge like he thought. The fields to the north that Kel had planted in cotton and wheat lay fallow. Those closest to the house were planted in corn or peas, something they could eat if unable to sell for a decent price. Cotton was only bringing 2 cent a pound and a lot of labor was needed to get it to market. It was not worth the money it cost to produce.

Arthur Moore still lived in the same small house 100 yards northeast of the big house. Willie lived with his folks, Uncle Caesar and Aunt Maggie, up the road towards Kelly's. Uncle Caesar was getting too old and infirm to work in the fields, so Willie took care of them with what little money Mr. Roston paid him for the farming and what he received from all the brothers when he helped with their stills. They always had plenty to eat.

Miss Peninnah felt like Arthur and Willie were family and always fixed them a plate at dinnertime. All the Gantts felt the same way when it came to Arthur and Willie.

Frequently, at day's end, she would call Willie aside and say, "We have plenty of food left over from dinner. Please take it home for to Uncle Caesar and Aunt Maggie. I want to be sure they are being fed." She would admonish Willie, "You let me know if they are in need—it's important to me that they are not going without."

Willie replied, "Yes ma'am, Miss Peninnah, I will. We shore do thank you for whatever you does for us. Mam and Pap remembers all of you every night in their prayers. I don't know what my folks would do without y'all allowing us to stay in that house for free. I guess we would be like all the other hobos roaming the countryside hereabouts. We is all beholden for your generous kindnesses to us."

"We're glad to be able to help, Willie," Peninnah said with a smile. "Don't forget what I said."

* * * * *

Being frugal became a fact of life for everyone. Nothing was wasted or discarded. Everything had to be used up, worn out, or recycled into something else. Florence did her part to insure their survival.

With no money to spend, she learned to get by with what they had. When Robert started to school and needed a winter coat, Florence took an old coat of hers, ripped it apart, and downsized it to fit him. She patched their worn clothing and when they were too worn to patch, she cut them into scraps and sewed the scraps together to make quilts for their beds. Every fruit produced on the place, from plums and gooseberries in the summer to the last little wormy apple in the fall, were used for pies or jelly. No food was wasted; she used leftover biscuits to make bread pudding and left over rice to make rice pudding. Every morning for breakfast they had grits ground from their own corn and butter she made from their own cow's milk. Kelly hunted for wild game, rabbits and squirrels in the woods for their table or caught fish in the river. Occasionally they had fried chicken for Sunday dinner or pork from a hog Kelly and his brothers butchered. Kelly did the best he could. He was drunk most weekends, but no one could say he didn't provide for Florence, Robert, and Elsie; Leon could provide for himself.

* * * * *

The liquor business was booming at Rayflin, Sugar Bottom and in the whole rural countryside of Lexington County. The County Sheriff and his deputies had plenty to do just trying to make a dent in the illegal liquor business. There were so many men involved in the trade, they practically had to wear badges stating they were moonshiners to keep from trying to sell it to each other. Buck and his brothers were doing well in the business; at least, Buck was. It was not uncommon to see him with $500.00 in his pocket but it was a business with high overhead. There were the ingredients bought in bulk, cost of replacing busted up stills, transportation, and pay for the operators of his stills.

* * * * *

One cold Monday morning in February 1933, Leon left home, walking towards Steadman. Leon, J Hugh, and Greco were clearing the swamp for Uncle Jule behind his house so that a pond could be built. Working in the swamp had to be done in the dead of winter because of water moccasins. Leon walked most everywhere he went now; his daddy Kelly had to park his Model T under the shed beside the barn, with no money to buy gasoline. Leon shivered in his denim jacket; even with long handled underwear under his flannel shirt and flannel lined dungarees; he was still cold. He pulled his gloves from his jacket pockets and put them on.

Man, it sure is cold this morning, Leon thought, *and this frost is so heavy on the ground, it looks like a young snow. I sure do hope Greco and J Hugh are ready to go when I get to their house.*

Leon stepped up on the wooden step at Mr. John's and tapped on the door. Greco flung the door open and bounded down the steps followed by J Hugh.

"Let's get going, Leon. We'll do some clearing this morning, and this afternoon, maybe that mash we have down on Jule's creek run will be worked off. I know it takes a lot longer with the weather this cold, but maybe that sawdust we packed around the kegs will do the trick."

Because of the cold temperature, they had pounded stakes into the ground encircling the kegs of mash and packed the hollow space between with sawdust.

"It should be Greco; we'll check after dinnertime and see if it's ready."

Even though it was freezing cold, neither Greco nor J Hugh wore a coat or hat. Greco did have on his leather boots that laced clean up to his knees. They were used to the cold. The house they shared with their parents had no heat, only a fireplace, and the cracks in the floor were large enough that you could see the chickens scratching in the dirt underneath the house.

Leon figured, *Greco and J Hugh are just so used to the cold, they have become acclimated to the cold temperatures. The only time the cold doesn't bother me is if I'm drunk, I don't feel anything, just a pleasant numbness.*

When they reached Uncle Jule's house, his three bulldogs, Rufus, Mutt, and Jeff, came flying out from under the house, barking and growling. They would bite you too, them damn dogs. Greco caught Rufus behind his front legs with the toe of his boot and sent him sailing into the bushes up against Jule's house. Rufus scrambled up, yelping, and all three disappeared under the house.

"You better get your damn asses away from us," Greco said. We ain't got time to put up with your sorry selves."

The three skirted Jule's yard, stopping long enough to gather three axes from the tool shed. They disappeared into the woods, heading towards the creek run and the swamp. Leon set his dinner pail on a stump and they set to work chopping down young saplings and pulling brush to a pile on high ground above the swampy mire. After sufficient clearing had been accomplished, the brush piles would be burned. By midmorning, the winter sun had burned off the heavy frost from earlier and Leon had to come out of his jacket. Even in this cold, swinging an axe tends to warm a man in a hurry.

"You know, boys, when you think about it, wood warms you twice; once when you're chopping it down and a second time when you actually burn it in the fireplace."

Greco and J Hugh agreed with Leon's comment.

"Just never thought about it that way, Leon," Greco said. Laughing and talking as they worked, time passed quickly. It was soon noon and dinnertime.

"Leon, Greco and me are going on back to the house for a little while to see what Ma has for dinner. Do you want to come with us?" J Hugh asked. "We won't be gone long."

"No, thanks for the offer, but I'll just sit down on one of these stumps and have my pork and beans and cold biscuits. It will be nice to just rest for a few minutes. You boys go on ahead and have your dinner. When y'all get back, we'll see if we can run that mash."

Leon finished his can of beans and biscuits, wiped his mouth, and put the trash back into his pail. He set the pail back on the stump to be picked up on the way home. Gathering his jacket from the tree branch where he had left it, he started on down the creek towards the still 200 yards away.

I'll just go check on that mash and see if it's ready to run. Greco and J Hugh will be back soon, he thought to himself.

The still was all set up, waiting for the raw alcohol to be poured in and the fire built underneath. Leon lifted the covers from the two barrels of mash, and seeing that it had worked off completely and no cornmeal was visible on top, he started dipping and straining the contents into the still. Greco and J Hugh arrived about fifteen minutes later and they all got busy operating the still. They were so intent with the job at hand, they didn't hear Jule's bulldogs barking. By the time they heard the commotion up towards Jule's house, they were almost too late.

Leon paused. "Is that Uncle Jule's old bulldogs I hear?" Glancing towards the sound of the barking, Leon saw Ollie Roberts, one of the sheriff's deputies, standing on a fifty pound sack of sugar just across the creek from where they were.

"Y'all boys making a little shine this afternoon?" Roberts called.

They didn't answer; Leon, J Hugh, and Greco were gone before he could hardly get the question from his mouth. They took off running up the creek towards Steadman, picking them up and putting them down. They were no way going to go peacefully with the law. When they reached the area where they had been clearing hours before, Greco ran smack into one of the brush piles and was briefly entangled. Leon and J Hugh stopped just long enough to drag him out and they took off running again. They climbed across the pond dam Jule was building and slid down the other side, pausing to catch their breath. All they could hear were those bulldogs barking and raising hell out in the big cornfield just this side of Jule's house. Leon crawled to the top of the dam and peeped over. The corn stalks were dry in the field but still standing, and he could see five people milling around among the dried stalks, trying to get out.

"Those bulldogs have got those five bastards cornered in the field," Leon said as he slid back down. "I think we'll be able to slip through the woods and get away as long as Rufus, Jeff, and Mutt keep them busy."

"I think you're right, Leon," Greco said with a smile, pulling a pint bottle from his pocket. "I'll have to be nicer to them damn bulldogs from now on. They sure saved our asses." Greco passed around the bottle and they all had a slug.

Then they leisurely headed into the woods in the opposite direction from the noise and chaos of the cornfield.

Two days later, they returned to the still down on the creek behind Jule's. The law had busted up the copper still with an axe, poured out their liquor and destroyed all their barrels.

Twelve

ON MARCH 4, 1933, FRANKLIN DELANO ROOSEVELT BECAME the President of the United States. He promised the American people a 'New Deal' with programs supported by the federal government to end the Depression and put Americans back to work.

Politics would not normally be of interest to the Gantts, seeing as how making moonshine could still provide a living. In dire situations, folks had to have their vices to comfort and dull their senses to how bad things were. Farm folk didn't see the soup lines, they didn't lose money when the banks closed. If they had cash, it was more than likely buried in their backyard somewhere—most never trusted banks. They were aware, however, of the news from newspapers they received and gossip passed by all manner of vagabonds, traveling the back roads, hoping for a meal for a few hours of work. Peninnah believed it was her Christian duty to help these unfortunates and tried to impress that on her children. When she saw the drawn faces and withered bodies of these weary travelers that stopped in Rayflin, she offered them what she could.

Jennie frequently admonished her mother, "Momma, I know you feel sorry for these people, so do all of us, but we must think of feeding our own families first. This new President, Mr. Roosevelt, seems to have some good ideas. He intends to create government programs to give men folk's jobs. Why, even Kelly intends to apply for the WPA. They're going to build a new school at Fairview, so he'll have a steady job for a while. Might not pay a whole lot, but any job is better than nothing."

"Yes, Jennie and maybe Olin can work for the WPA, like Kelly. He's not doing much good at farming. Franklin Roosevelt may be just the President we need to bring this country back from the brink. I am surely hoping all these programs work. I just feel so bad for these homeless families, and their children are so raggedy and pale."

Roosevelt did implement a number of programs, putting the able-bodied to work, building schools, states parks, and roads. They worked hard and even though circumstances did not improve right away, gradually the economy did seem a little brighter.

The 'Swamp Rabbit' spur line was discontinued by the railroad in the winter of 1933, and the tracks would soon be torn up. Roston decided to close his store in Rayflin in the summer of '33. With the railroad gone, it seemed pointless to try and continue the business. He would no longer be able to have supplies brought in by rail, and besides, the folks around the community had no cash to spend.

* * * * *

The sun was streaming through the window when Leon opened his eyes. With no covering except a red ruffle across the top of the window Miss Florence had made, it was hard to sleep when the full sun flooded into the room. It wasn't quite there yet, but it was good daylight. Leon glanced across the room and saw the tousled blonde head of ten-year-old Robert in his bed. They shared a room, at least when Leon wasn't off drunk somewhere. It was warm weather now, mid-June of 1933, and a Sunday morning.

I guess I'll go ahead and get up, Leon thought, *and see what Daddy has planned for today.*

He took his time getting up, sat on the side of his bed, and pulled on his britches and shirt. He padded barefoot across the wood floor, stepped out on the porch, and bent to retrieve his shoes he had left beside the door last night. He was trying to be quiet when he came to bed—didn't want to wake little brother. The cedar tree beside the front porch was full of sparrows, red birds, and blue jays arguing among themselves. Leon gazed up at the birds while he tied his shoes, then stood and crossed the porch to the kitchen door. Opening the screen door, he saw Miss Florence leaning over the table, wiping crumbs off the red-checked vinyl tablecloth.

"Where is Daddy this morning, Miss Florence?"

"Kelly already had his breakfast about forty-five minutes ago and walked on down to Buck's. I have a pot of grits on the stove and some fried fatback—would you like some?"

"Sounds good," Leon replied.

Florence walked over to the cook stove, dipped grits on a plate, and added a big scoop of butter to the hot mixture. She stirred the grits, picked up four pieces of fried fatback from a plate on the stove, and added to Leon's plate.

Leon pulled out a chair at the table, sitting down, and asked, "Why did Daddy go down to Buck's so early on a Sunday morning?"

"Well, Kelly said last night that Buck and Binnie had a big fight and Binnie left, heading up to her sister Fannie's. I guess he just wanted to see if she had come home yet and if her and Buck had made up. The whole works are probably down there drinking by now."

"I guess I better mosey on down that way after breakfast myself, see if everything is O.K."

"Would you mind, Leon, hooking old Sue to the wagon before you go? I thought Robert, Elsie, and myself would go on out to Pine Grove for morning service."

"I'll do that soon as I finish my breakfast."

After Leon had eaten breakfast and hooked the mule to wagon for Miss Florence, he started out walking down to his Uncle Buck's house; it was less than a mile. It was a beautiful sunny morning with just the least bit of a chill in the air. When he walked up at Buck's, he could see the situation was worse than he thought. There was a whole damn crowd lying around on Buck's porch, and they were all glassy-eyed, each sipping from a glass full of what appeared to Leon to be homebrew. Uncle Sam, Ed Corley, Gus Gantt a.k.a. Kingfish, and Uncle Roston were all lounging on the front porch. Leon's daddy, Kelly, was also sitting propped against the porch wall, but he hadn't been there most of the night like the rest of the crowd, so he wasn't as drunk as them.

Uncle Sammy, with his bald head shining, spoke first. "Howdy, Cap. Come on in and have a glass of homebrew. It's pretty damn good."

"It's still a little early for me, Uncle Sammy," Leon replied. "After a while, I'll try a glass, but not now. I just had my breakfast."

Leon went on into the house and on the kitchen table was a

ten-gallon keg of homebrew with about six inches left in the bottom. Leon knew Binnie had put up the homebrew and intended to bottle it up and sell it, but Buck and his buddies found it first. Leon figured they had run out of liquor last night and discovered Binnie's homebrew sitting in the corner and had fallen in on that.

"Where's Binnie?" Leon asked Buck, who was sitting at the kitchen table.

"She and I had a little disagreement yesterday and she ran off. She'll be back after a while; I'm sure to raise some more hell. Pour yourself a glass of this homebrew."

Buck and Rion got up from the kitchen table and ambled out the door to the front porch with the rest of the drunks, glasses in hand.

There was a box of 'diamond crystal' salt sitting on the kitchen table beside the keg. Leon just could not help himself. He picked up the box of salt and dumped the entire contents into the remaining homebrew in the keg. Giving it a quick stir with a spoon he found lying on the dish cabinet, he left the kitchen and joined the others on the front porch. He sat outside with the rest of the crowd for a while talking and just listening to their conversation. Every one of those present, with the exception of Kelly, was having a hard time talking without slurring every word.

In a little while, John Gantt walked up.

"How are all you boys doing today?" John asked.

It was still early, not yet 8:30, and the whole damn works was drunk, but claimed they were doing just fine.

"John, would you like a drink?" Sam asked.

"By gracious, Sammy, I don't care if I do."

Sam led John into the kitchen. Leon followed and watched as Sam dipped John a glass full out of the barrel. John took a drink.

"How is it, Cap? Is it any good?" Sam asked.

"Yea, Sammy, but by gracious, I believe you've got a little too much salt in it."

Sam took John's glass, refilled it, and took a swig himself. Then started dipping and passing the glass around so that all the others could sample from the same glass.

"Try this, boys," he would say as he stumbled out onto the front porch with the glass full. "John says we got a little too much salt in it, by gracious, I didn't notice this before."

Each participant obediently drained the glass when Sam handed it to him, commenting on the salty taste. They were so drunk by this time it didn't occur to them that the homebrew had been doctored.

Pretty soon the whole works was outside in Buck's front yard, puking like a flock of buzzards. In the middle of this fiasco, Binnie came home. She stomped into the kitchen, discovered her homebrew was all but gone, turned red as a turkey, and cussed the whole lot out, but good. That's when the party broke up; Binnie's tongue-lashing, along with the aftermath of the salty homebrew, convinced those present that it was time to depart, find someplace to lay their heads and pray to God, if he let them survive, they would stop drinking for sure. Of course, the promise to God would only last until they had an opportunity to share another drink with their buddies, as long as it wasn't homebrew.

* * * * *

Kelly and Leon were making their own homebrew again in the smokehouse at home. The smokehouse wasn't being used for hanging meat because with the depression in full swing, they had been obligated to sell what livestock they had for a little cash. No need to waste their time when they could be producing something to drink and making homebrew. Beer was fairly cheap and easy to make.

Leon described it this way: "You take some sugar, a couple of yeast cakes, some Schlitz malt syrup, add a little water and let it ferment. Then you pour it in Nehi bottles and use a bottle capper to crimp the metal caps on the bottles. Presto! You have homebrew."

A few days after Kelly and Leon had the homebrew bottled, Kelly suggested Leon needed to trim the hedges around the yard. Leon discovered a big wasp nest in one of the hedge bushes. No way was he going to mess with a nest of red wasps; those things had a painful sting.

"I'll just save this wasp nest for Uncle Sammy, he ain't afraid of nothing; I'll let him handle it."

A few days later, Uncle Sammy came up to the house looking for some homebrew. Rion had told him Leon and Kelly had made a batch and it was ready to be consumed.

"Well, when Sammy showed up, he had already been drinking. I took him out to the smokehouse," Leon said. "I told him, Uncle Sammy, when I open this bottle, you'd better be ready to drink. You don't even have to turn the bottle up. This last batch Daddy made, he didn't think it had enough alcohol in it, so we added a spoonful of sugar to each bottle. We poured that stuff in the bottles using a dipper and a funnel. Well, when I took the cap off and handed the bottle to Uncle Sammy, he put it to his mouth, his jaws pooching out on either side, like a squirrel storing nuts in his cheeks. The homebrew started running out around the mouth of the bottle and down his chin. He just couldn't swallow fast enough."

Finishing the first bottle, Sammy said, "What makes that stuff do like this?"

Leon replied, "I'm not sure, but it's good stuff." Uncle Sammy drank two or three more bottles.

Afterwards, Leon told Uncle Sammy, "There's something I want to show you," and took him to see the wasp nest.

Uncle Sammy just reached into the hedge and plucked the nest from the hedge branch; he didn't get stung the first time. "Trying to hand it to me," he said. "These things won't hurt you, 'Cap.'"

All Leon could say was, "Get that thing away from me, Uncle Sammy; I don't want anything to do with a wasp nest."

* * * * *

"Idle hands are the Devil's workshop." At least that's what the pastor out at Pine Grove Church preached in one of his sermons that summer of 1933. Florence could see that was definitely true. Just about every man in the community seemed to be lying around drunk, making illegal moonshine or fighting sometimes with guns and knives. In fact, there were only two men Florence knew in the community that didn't make moonshine: Reedy Gunter and Tom Boyd. It was lawless times, and what most of these men needed was a job, earning a paycheck to make them feel respectable again. They couldn't control their own destiny without that paycheck to prove their worth. With all Roosevelt's promises, their fulfillment seemed slow in coming. In the meantime, the male population of Rayflin and environs was still having one big party, drinking, fighting, and running from the law.

On a Saturday night in July 1933, M.V. and Jimmie Lee, a couple of women of dubious character, 'old rips' Leon called them, were having a dance at their house over near the chalk mine. There was to be a couple fellows playing music, dancing, and lots of booze. There was a whole group from Rayflin and the surrounding community going across the river to the party.

Atwell Willis, Lever Gunter, John Gunter, Harvey Hall, and Thurmond Hall from Steadman stopped by Leon's to see if he wanted to walk with them across the river to the party. Everybody walked for lack of cheaper transportation. It was a pleasant evening, a little after dark, and the moon had just come up. Walking along with the fellows, laughing, and cutting the fool was enjoyable. They had already had a drink or two but not too much. Leon noticed the little sparks of the lightening bugs in the woods and the smell of honeysuckle as they passed a swampy area beside the road. The moon was not yet full, but bright enough that the white sandy road shimmered where the shadows of the bordering trees did not intervene. Leon noticed these things even though the others did not.

As the men approached the fork in the road where Pine Grove Road intersected it, they heard voices. Coming into the fork, they met up with two other groups of partygoers, some coming from towards Pine Grove Church and a group from down towards Sugar Bottom. The fellows were all just standing around cussing, laughing, and swigging from their bottles. There must have been fifteen or twenty congregated at the fork.

In the meantime, two hundred yards up Pine Grove road at

Mr. Bill Gantt's house, Mr. Bill and Asia Gunter sat on the porch, talking and enjoying the evening air.

Asia Gunter was a likeable fellow. He only had one major flaw in the eyes of the community; everyone was aware that Asia was a homosexual. But that didn't matter none to the Gantts or to the rest of the fellows. They felt no animosity towards Asia; he was their friend and they didn't feel threatened by his queer demeanor. There had been no more unwanted advances on inebriated men from Asia. He had not made the same mistake he had with Sam at Kelly's house back in the early twenties. He had not forgotten Roston's dire warning at the time. He still enjoyed the company of the Gantt brothers and enjoyed drinking with them. The only thing Asia had to fear was their teasing. They loved to tease Asia, mainly because he took their teasing so seriously.

"I wonder what all the commotion is down at the fork," Asia said to Mr. Bill, sitting there on his porch. "I think I'll walk on down there and investigate."

"Asia, you better stay away from down there. You'll just get hurt. It's just a bunch of these local hotheads drinking and acting the fool. It's no place for you."

Asia stood. "I'll see you later, Mr. Bill. I just want to go down there and see what's going on. I'll be fine."

With that, he descended the steps and headed down the road towards the voices at the fork. When Asia reached the group, he stood off to himself with his arms folded across his chest, just watching and listening to the goings on. Leon saw Asia standing there but realized too late that a joke was about to be played on Asia. Harvey Hall from Steadman sneaked around behind Asia and bent over, and then Lever Gunter walked up to Asia and gave him a shove over Harvey. Asia fell backward and cut a somersault, landing hard on the ground behind Harvey. Leon rushed over to help Asia back on his feet. Harvey and Lever were having a good laugh, but Leon and some of the others didn't think it funny. They got in a quandary about that.

Leon said, "Damn if I can straighten some of this crowd out." Leon cut a big stick and cracked the first head he saw. He later found out it was Rion, an innocent bystander. A fight ensued between the whole crowd, and John Gunter pulled out an old Barlow knife and had the five-inch blade opened. Leon dropped his stick, came up behind John, and locked his arms around him, pinning his arms to his side with the lethal weapon still in his right hand.

John started raising sand but didn't know who had him in such a grip. "You think you can hold me?" John snarled at his anonymous attacker.

"No hell, I don't think it, I know it," Leon replied.

John wiggled and twisted and lifted Leon up off the ground, but Leon was determined to hold on to that joker until he dropped the knife. Finally, plum tuckered out from the struggle, John dropped the knife.

Leon picked up the knife, closed the blade and handed back to John. "I couldn't let you use this knife on anybody, John; sorry I had to clamp down on you that way."

"That's alright, Leon, I should have known better. You should have told me it was you. I would have given it to you and now I wouldn't be so damn tired."

The fighting had died down and the crowd started wandering down the road to the party. Asia walked along with them as far as

Rayflin, then headed on home. He wasn't hurt physically and nothing was broken; he was just sore.

* * * * *

The following Monday morning, Leon went down to Rayflin to his Uncle Roston's store. He hadn't closed the business yet but the shelves were mighty bare. Rion and Sammy were there socializing with their brother Roston. One of them had evidently told Roston what was done to Asia up at the fork on Saturday night. Roston always loved to tease and could hardly wait to tease Asia about what happened.

Asia came in to the store about ten that morning, gingerly favoring his right leg; he was still suffering from the cruel joke played on him at the fork.

Leon even inquired about how he was feeling. "Are you OK, Asia?" He knew Asia wasn't a young man; he was forty seven years old and he had flipped backward and hit that red clay road pretty hard.

He solemnly replied, "Leon, I'm feeling alright. Didn't sleep too well, but I do appreciate you asking."

No mention was made by Asia or Leon as to the circumstances. Asia was hoping Roston didn't know; he was in for a ribbing if he did. Still Asia just stood with his arms crossed looking out the door up the road towards the fork. Roston, of course, had heard all about the ruckus up the road and the outcome and couldn't resist teasing him a little. Asia took teasing so seriously and his little mishap with those confounded scoundrels was an embarrassment. To Asia, it wasn't at all humorous.

"Asia, damn if I don't believe people is doing better around here. I haven't heard no tell of people being drunk and raising hell around here, have you?" Roston asked.

At first Asia didn't answer; he just stood gazing out the door up towards the fork with his arms folded. *Roston's just trying to get me riled up. Maybe if I ignore him, he'll let me be,* Asia thought.

No such luck with Roston Gantt; he was like an old hound dog on the hunt, never giving up.

Roston asked the question again. He just couldn't help himself when it came to Asia; he was such a serious fellow when it came to being teased. He just didn't take it well at all, which made teasing Asia more enticing.

Roston addressed him a second time. "Asia, damn if I don't believe people is doing better around here. I haven't heard no tell of people being drunk and raising hell around here, have you?"

A minute passed before Asia turned his head and looked directly at Roston. Serious as a heartbeat, never cracking a smile, he said, "I should say I have, Roston, I should say I have."

Everybody in the store burst out laughing and Asia just limped out with his arms still folded, not saying another word until he was on the way home. "I should have waited until I was better," he said out loud to himself. "I know Roston too well. He just can't resist pouring salt on a wound. Next time I see him, he'll apologize, I'm sure, and I'll forget all the embarrassment. Roston sure nuff likes to tease."

Thirteen

ON DECEMBER 12, 1933, ROSTON'S WIFE FAIRRIE DIED. FAIR-
rie was a frail woman, having given birth to seven children and
now raising her brother Elvin Jeffcoat's two children, Rudolph and
Louise. Her health was fragile. Elvin had been executed in Florida's
electric chair for killing his wife, so Fairrie and Roston were raising
his two children. They already had seven and two more didn't make
much difference. Rudolph and Lousie were happy living with their
aunt and uncle and seven cousins.

After Fairrie's funeral at Steadman Church, the whole family
was gathered at Roston's in Rayflin. Tillman Jeffcoat, Fairrie's older
brother, insisted on taking Louise and Rudolph home with him,
seeing as how Fairrie was gone.

"Those are my brother's children and now that sister Fairrie is
gone, they should be raised by their Jeffcoat kin, plain and simple.
Those two young'uns will be going home with us, Roston."

Louise and Rudolph didn't want to go with their Uncle Tillman;
they wanted to stay with the Gantts. They loved Uncle Roston and
all their Gantt cousins.

Buck was down at Roston's about half drunk and decided he
would intervene. "I'll put Tillman on the go for you, Roston, and

there won't be any more discussion about his taking those two children away."

"You just stay out of this, Buck. I'll handle it; those children will be staying right here with us."

Buck got up from the chair in Roston's kitchen and headed out the door. He crossed the road to his Ma's house, where Olin was sitting on the front porch.

"What's the trouble over there, Buck?" Olin asked.

"Nothing I can't fix, Olin, I need Pa's shotgun, that's all," he said as he opened the door to enter the house."

Olin knew he shouldn't let Buck have the gun, but he also knew there would be hell to pay if he tried to stop him, so he just sat in the porch chair and kept his mouth shut.

Buck came out in a few minutes carrying his Pa's shotgun, paused on the porch to breech it open and inserted two shells. Without another word to Olin, he descended the steps and headed back across the road to Roston's. As soon as he entered the house, Roston met him.

"What in the hell do you think you're doing with Pa's shotgun?"

"I'm going to kill that son of a bitch Tillman for you, that's what I'm going to do. That will end this discussion and he won't be pestering these children anymore!" Buck yelled.

"Oh, no you ain't, Buck," Roston said as he grabbed the barrel of the gun. "This is my affair and you stay out of it. You're drunk, little brother and you won't be helping these children or me by committing a murder. Now give me Pa's gun and calm down." Buck released his grip on the gun and Roston unloaded it and propped it in the corner. The shells he slipped in his pants pocket.

Tillman had seen Buck with the gun and had heard what Roston said, at least some of it. He decided he had no claim on Elvin's children after all and they could just stay here with Roston and his kids. He also knew Buck Gantt was not to be challenged. Tillman signaled to his wife to follow him and they sneaked out the back door, got into their automobile, and were gone. Tillman knew Buck could be mean when he was drunk, and he was certain Buck would have shot him no questions asked.

Roston saw Tillman drive away.

"I guess, Buck, you did put him on the go, and I don't think we'll have any more trouble from Tillman. All I have to do now is grieve for my Fairrie and raise our children the best I know how."

* * * * *

In early 1934, soon after his mother Fairrie died, Raymond joined the Civilian Conservation Corps, the CCC. It was one of Roosevelt's New Deal relief programs to help get young men from needy families back to work. There were CCC camps set up where young men were trained to help with conservation projects, such as planting trees and building damns. Raymond was the oldest of Roston and Fairrie's children; he would be sixteen years old on May 18th, 1934. He worked with the CCC during the week and came home to Rayflin on the weekends.

Raymond was eight years younger than Leon, but they were good friends and became drinking buddies. On the weekends, Raymond hung around with Leon and his uncles Sam, Rion, and Kelly. His daddy Roston was with them on occasion, but with all his children to tend to now, he had curtailed his drinking somewhat. Raymond started drinking like the rest of the men-folk.

In March of 1934, Raymond stole a good ham from his daddy, Roston, took it over to the chalk mine to Rose's store and traded it to her for a pint of liquor. It was bad liquor, just old backings. Leon said, "I'm an old drunk, Raymond, and I won't even drink that stuff."

Well, Olin found out that Raymond had stolen the ham from Roston and traded it to Rose for the liquor. He took his 'jingle butt' out to Fairview and called Cromer Oswald the sheriff to report the thievery. Nobody had phones in their houses anymore; they couldn't afford to pay the bill with the Depression. Cromer came down to Rayflin to see Roston.

"Yeah, that sorry son of mine stole my ham, but I won't press any charges."

Cromer went over to Rose's and made her give him the ham back, which he returned to Roston.

"Next time, I'll take that boy of yours to jail whether you like it or not. You better get him straightened out."

"Don't you worry, Cromer; it won't happen again, I promise you."

Raymond was a clever fellow and he somehow found out Uncle Olin had called the law and reported him. Raymond went up to his Aunt Jennie's with that old pint of sorry liquor; it was milky looking in the bottle.

He called Olin to come out on the porch.

"Uncle Olin, I want to give you a drink of liquor."

"Raymond, I don't believe I want any; you know I have quit drinking. I'm not drinking any of that liquor."

"Oh hell, yeah you are too." And he made Olin turn up that bottle and drink about half of that old backings liquor.

Olin would think twice before sticking his nose in business that wasn't his own again, especially if it concerned Raymond or Leon. He knew better than to tick either of those two off; they both could be real ornery.

* * * * *

Buck drank liquor something terrible. He'd get sobered up and do fine for a while, and then he would get drunk and stay drunk a month or two. He complained of having no feeling in his legs after each binge of drinking; his health was fast declining mostly because he drank so much. He and Binnie were also having their problems again because of the liquor. Buck and Binnie had three children, J.B., Vivian and Crum, but they didn't really know their father; most of the time, he was in a drunken stupor.

In April 1935, Buck and Gus, a.k.a.. Kingfish, were in Lexington drunk. One of them had a pistol and shot up a filling station. No one was injured but both were arrested. Buck didn't even spend the night in jail. Roston went to Lexington, paid Buck's bond, and brought him home.

"Buck, are you crazy? You and Gus are going to get into big trouble mixing liquor and firearms." He lectured his little brother all the way home, but to no avail.

Three days later, Buck was on another drinking binge when he went off the deep end. Binnie got him in the car; she knew she had to get some help and took him to the hospital in Columbia. On the way, he tried to open the car door and jump out. He was going to commit suicide.

"Buck, have you totally lost your mind? We've got to get you some help," Binnie told him. "We have children to raise. Think about what your actions do to your family."

On the 21st of April, the doctors at the hospital decided to do a spinal tap to find out why Buck lost feeling in his legs. He died during the procedure. He was only thirty-five years old. Buck was the youngest of Kel and Peninnah's children but the first to die.

The whole family was devastated by Buck's death at such an early age. He left Binnie with three children, ages fourteen, twelve, and seven, and eight brothers and sisters, all older than Buck. His mother, Peninnah, had lost her youngest child, and she blamed his death on his dependence on alcohol. But it didn't seem to slow her other boys down one bit.

* * * * *

Kelly had taken a job with the WPA, Works Progress Administration, another New Deal program of Roosevelt's founded in 1935. The WPA provided jobs building highways, parks, bridges, schools, all projects intended to have long-range value to the people. Since Kelly now had a job to bring in some pay again, he confined his drinking mostly to the weekends, but he and Leon still drank a lot of booze. They were consuming 1½ to 2 gallons of moonshine a week between the two of them. Leon was still making liquor for a living.

In the summer of 1935, Kelly was working on the new school at Fairview. He was a good carpenter and the WPA was in charge of the project. Leon was running a still down in Sugar Bottom for Bill Sawyer. Leon had finished running a charge at the still and was headed home. He came staggering into the backyard at Rayflin about half drunk, just as Peninnah descended the steps and headed for the woodpile to get some wood for the cook stove. It was getting close to suppertime and she and Jennie had to get busy. She glanced up to see Leon standing there as she bent to retrieve an armload of wood.

"Look at you with your sorry drunk self. I wish there wasn't a drop of liquor in the world. Then maybe you would straighten yourself out."

"Grandmamma, I agree with you 100% and I'm doing all I can to try to get rid of as much as I can. But every time I drink a gallon, somebody makes two more."

"You trifling thing," Peninnah said as she threw a piece of stove wood in his direction. "Just remember, what happened to your Uncle Buck can happen to you. I don't want to lose another one of my men folks to that demon liquor."

"I'm sorry, Grandmamma, about Uncle Buck. I know you're right and I'm going to get myself straightened out one of these days, I promise."

Leon staggered on off heading towards home, but he would remember his grandmamma's words.

* * * * *

In late November of 1935, Leon and his daddy, Kelly, were running a still down in the swamp within spitting distance of the black water of the North Edisto. The location was near where Rattlesnake Branch emptied into the river. The woods were deep and dark here very little sunlight seemed to filter through the tall, thick tree branches, even in mid-day. In these woods, it was easy to disappear if need be. When the dark came, it was eerie what the mind could conjure up in these surroundings.

The weather was extremely cold this night. After all light had disappeared; wherever the ground was damp, sprigs of ice spurted up. The leaves and grass close to the ground were soon coated with heavy frost. The ice popping up in the damp ground and the breeze stirring the canopy high above them only added to the loneliness of the darkness. Leon felt more comfortable venturing this deep in the swamp near the river, away from prying eyes, and safer from venomous snakes in the low temperatures of winter. The colder it got, the better. In this deep swampy darkness, they each had a kerosene lantern sitting opposite the cleared area where the still was placed. They weren't fearful of the dark, but the lanterns did help to push back the darkness and the thick mist that settled near the river. There was also the blazing fire built under the still that sent waves of heat in all directions and helped dispel the dark. Kelly always carried his pistol and a well sharpened knife for protection.

"Damn, if I wasn't drunk, I would feel as frightened in this dark swamp as I would waking up at midnight alone among the headstones of some cemetery," Kelly remarked.

"It's just plain crazy to even compare the two locations, Daddy," Leon replied, "the people in the cemetery can't hurt you." There are things in this swamp that are dangerous; you know why I prefer winter time deep in the swamp for running a still."

Water moccasins would often dangle in trees above the water in the hot humid summers of the South; not so this time of year. The thick undergrowth of the river bank, and the forest floor harbored other venomous vipers in hot weather, and they were hibernating in the winter. To Leon, the dark cold winter was preferable to the humid darkness of warmer weather.

"We both know cold weather is just the safest time deep in the swamp, especially if you're drunk. Drinking tends to make a man more careless about such things as venomous snakes, bobcats, and wild boars. Besides, sampling the moonshine helps keep us warm," Leon remarked.

"Me and Daddy," as Leon recounted, "were making some liquor down in the swamp surrounded by the extreme cold of late November. We saw a light approaching through the misty darkness." Knowing it had be someone privy to their still's location, they were not apprehensive. As it turned out it was Rion, who soon stood in the lantern's glow.

"I hope I didn't give you boys a start," Rion said. "I had to get away from Ruth for a little while and I knew you two would be here."

"Glad to have the company," Kelly remarked. "How's about a little drink to warm you after that half-mile hike from your house on Coon branch. It's mighty cold and damp down here near the river."

"Don't mind if I do," Rion replied.

He had to sneak out; Ruth would raise sand if she knew he was headed to Leon's still. She thought Leon and Kelly were bad influences on Rion. Of course, that was crazy, Rion did what he wanted as far as liquor drinking and making it were concerned.

"I was pretty boozy," Leon confessed. "Daddy was drunker than me. Rion arrived about 9:00 that night and fell right into drinking the booze too. When we finished the batch about midnight, the three of us came on to our house, built up the fire and decided to have another drink before calling it an evening."

Miss Florence, Elsie and Robert were sleeping in the newer part of the house. Kelly, Leon and Rion entered the kitchen quietly so as not to wake them from their slumber. Of course, they would have to make a lot of noise to disturb them, but they tried to at least enter quietly from the porch.

Ruth must have been out looking for Rion. Leon heard someone hit the steps, and the creaking of the screen door hinges, then the wooden door was thrown open; it was Ruth. She came in raising sand and storming at Rion. She wanted to know where he had been.

"Were you down in the swamp with those S.O.B.s?"

"She called me and daddy sons of bitches," Leon recalled. "Daddy didn't take too kindly to her addressing us in that manner. Even drunk, Kelly Gantt wasn't about to take no mouthing off no body, least of all Ruth."

"*I'll just slap the G. D. shit out of you, Ruth*! Of course, he didn't say it like that, the whole words just came spilling out. He got up and lunged at her and she took off out of the house."

Rion just sat there at the table, all glassy eyed. His only response to the ruckus was, "Aw, Ruth."

Rion didn't have the bad temperament that Kelly, Sam, and

Buck had possessed. Ruth's ravings and cursing just rolled off Rion like 'water off a duck's back.' He was the easy-going sort. Mostly he just ignored Ruth's angry tirades. His personality kept him out of a lot of trouble, but Ruth would give him more hell when he did return to their house. He seemed not a bit concerned.

Fourteen

ROBERT SAT CROSS-LEGGED ON THE FLOOR, LOOKING UP AT
the wooden case sitting on the table above his head. His daddy,
Kelly, had ordered the radio from Sears and Roebuck and to Robert, it was a marvelous invention. The radio itself was encased in a
beautiful oak box. The box was shaped like a cathedral ceiling, with
four paisley-shaped cut-outs backed with gold woven cloth, which
covered the speaker.

"This radio shore is a beauty," Robert remarked the minute he
saw it. "Just replacing the batteries is a highlight to me."

That was his job, and when the batteries started getting weak,
Kelly would order new batteries from Sears and Roebuck. Robert
looked forward to changing them; there was not much excitement
to be had in the backwoods for twelve-year-olds. Besides, without
electricity, the radio was their main contact with the outside world.

Robert was the only child at home now. At least, he might as
well be. Leon was always off drinking with his buddies and making
moonshine at some still down in the swamp. It was 1936; Leon
spent all his time drinking, almost to the point of destroying all
memories of the here and now of his life. Half the time, he couldn't
remember what day it was, it had taken over his life to such an ex-

tent. Even Kelly worried about how much booze Leon consumed and made, and Kelly was himself a pretty heavy drinker. The difference being, he confined his drinking to the weekends due to his job working for the WPA. Leon on the other hand, produced high grade liquor all week, so he was always in close proximity to the booze, which was the way he made a living.

Elsie had moved out in 1935.

The reason Elsie moved out according to Leon was, "She and Miss Florence both wanted to be boss and that just didn't work."

Elsie also had met a fellow she liked from down around Wagener, and Kelly had told her she was too young to be courting. Of course, truth be known, it wasn't her youth that concerned him. She was, after all, twenty-years-old and a grown woman quite capable of making up her own mind. Kelly just didn't approve of this fellow, so he told Elsie she was too young.

Elsie at first had moved in with her Uncle Woodard in Steadman. Woodard's daughter, Cleola, and Elsie were about the same age. That didn't last long either. Woodard didn't want to be responsible for Elsie's courting when he knew his brother Kelly was so set against it. Now Elsie was living with her Aunt Peggy in Batesburg. She had met a nice man, Fred Ridgell, five years older than her and she and Fred were planning to be married. Kelly seemed to like Fred Ridgell all right; maybe he just didn't cotton to that fellow in Wagener she was so crazy about.

Leon had no serious women friends. He was more concerned with making moonshine than with finding himself a good woman. More than anything, no woman he met could ever measure up to his mother, Mary. "When you lose your momma, you have lost your best friend on earth," he often quoted. The women he came in contact with drinking and partying were just not the sort of women you want to marry. He never thought about getting married and settling down.

* * * * *

It was 1936, Kelly was still working for the WPA, and Leon was still making moonshine. Leon had briefly worked with Julian Hall in the Heathwood section of Columbia in 1935 laying brick. He was going to learn to lay brick, but getting drunk was more important.

"Those boys could do some fancy brick work, but they liked liquor and I could supply them with it," Leon realized. He became their supplier and his brick-laying ambitions fell to the wayside. Leon confessed, "That's when money was money and supplying the brick masons with their booze turned out to be more profitable."

Almost the whole year of 1936, Leon was drunk. He drank liquor before breakfast and all day long while running a still.

"Shaw, as Uncle Sammy once said, 'You get where you would walk ten miles for a pint and the ground frozen, you had to have it.'" That was the way it became with Leon.

He knew his drinking was going to kill him, but he kept drinking anyway until one day in 1937.

* * * * *

On July 31, 1937, Leon and Hawkeye Gunter went over to New Holland in Aiken County to see a Mr. Kirkland about a coon dog Hawkeye wanted to buy. They were in Hawkeye's 1930 maroon Chevrolet Roadster with the top down.

Returning from New Holland that Sunday afternoon, they came by the old chalk mine, crossed the North Edisto to Rayflin, and got up to the old railroad bed when Hawkeye said, "Let's go down to Sugar Bottom and get some liquor."

"That's sounds fine to me," replied Leon.

They each bought a pint from Wayne Gunter in a brown bottle. The bottle was called Paul Jones when it had government liquor in it; now, that had been replaced by moonshine. They came from Sugar Bottom back through Rayflin up to the fork.

"Can you walk on home from here, Leon?"

"Sure, Hawkeye, no problem." Hawkeye stopped the car and Leon got out.

"I sure do appreciate you riding over to New Holland with me. Take care." With a wave, Hawkeye was gone.

Leon started on towards home about a half mile away, left the road just in sight of the house, crossed the field, and stopped at the spring down the slope behind the house. There was a dipper hanging on a limb beside the spring and Leon drank four dipperfuls of that good spring water before walking on to the house. He set his bottle of liquor down on the cook table in the kitchen and went to the bedroom to lie down.

It was quiet in the house. *I guess Daddy, Miss Florence, and Robert have gone down to Rayflin to visit Grandmamma and Aunt Jennie's crowd,* Leon thought to himself.

He didn't even take off his shoes; he just lay on his back on top of the covers with his feet propped on the iron pipe of the footboard. He punched the cotton stuffed pillow a few times and put it under his head. He dozed off to sleep, dreaming about his mother Mary. A noise awakened him and he opened his eyes to see a dove perched on the footboard of the bed between his shoes. He thought at first he had to be dreaming and closed his eyes, but when he opened them again, the dove was still there. The dove leaned its head to the left and then to the right, just staring at the man frozen in fright on the bed. The first thing that came to Leon's mind was the dream he had just had about Mary.

This dove must be my mamma returned to see what a sorry excuse her son has turned out to be, he thought.

As he opened his mouth to speak, the dove left the rail and flew out the window. He even distinctly heard the sound of the bird's wings flapping as it disappeared. He lay there for a few minutes, thinking surely he had been hallucinating. But how could that be? He was stone cold sober. He sat up on the side of the bed. Shaw! The window was down.

"I must be losing my mind," he said aloud.

He was shaken up a bit; he had heard old folks say that the appearance of birds where they're not supposed to be is a powerful warning.

This must have been a warning from my Mamma, he thought. He never opened the bottle of liquor he left sitting on the cook table. He stopped drinking that day, July 31, 1937.

Leon was a strong-willed man and never took another drink of liquor. It had basically robbed him of the past year of his life, time and memories that he couldn't ever replace. He didn't intend to lose anymore. What time he had left, he was determined to stay sober.

The economy was a little better; at least a man could find an honest job saw milling, cutting trees, and dragging them out of the swamp. The pay was not as good as the liquor business, but at least you didn't have all that excess emotional baggage to contend with, loss of time and memory, not to mention your self-respect. Kelly was still drinking but without his main drinking buddy, Leon, it just wasn't the same. Besides, Kelly had a job too, and he wouldn't let his drinking interfere with his work.

Fifteen

IT WAS A HOT, DRY AUGUST THE SUMMER OF 1939, AND ROBert was working for his Uncle Woodard in the pulpwood business. He drove a logging truck hauling the logs that Woodard's crew cut and drug out of the woods. Once the logs were loaded on the truck, Robert took them to the sawmill set up near the site. Here, the outside of the trees was sawed off to square up the logs. The removed portions with bark on one side and tree grain on the other were the slabs and were discarded as waste. The only thing the slabs were good for was burning for firewood, and Robert frequently brought a load of the slabs home to add to their woodpile.

Woodard and his son, Chalmus, picked up Robert as usual before good daylight on August 7th and headed to the job site about fifteen miles away down below the small community of Pelion.

"I just don't feel good this morning, boys," Woodard said. "I think I'll drop you two off and go on down to Wagener and see Dr. Williams; I'll be coming back after the doc checks me out. It's probably just a case of indigestion, but my chest feels real tight."

"Better still get the doctor to give you the once over, Uncle Woodard," Robert said.

Woodard dropped the young men off with the crew and went

to see the doctor. Returning two hours later, he assured them the doctor said he would be fine.

"Just gave me these pills to take," he said as he pulled the brown glass bottle from his breast pocket. "I think I'm just going to go on home, take a pill, and lie down for a spell."

Woodard had remarried Eva Padgett, nineteen years younger than himself, after he lost Mamie. He and Eva had two little girls. Eva always said Woodard was the sweetest man and father to the girls; she loved him dearly.

"Chalmus, you can carry Robert home this afternoon in the logging truck. Eva will take good care of me. I'm sure it's nothing too serious; see you at home later, son."

"Sure thing, Daddy, you go on home and rest. Everything will be fine here. I'll see you at supper time."

That evening about seven, word was sent to Kelly's family that Woodard had passed away, suffering a major heart attack just five days after his forty-seventh birthday. Peninnah had lost another son and Kelly a brother. Woodard left a widow, Eva, and four children—two grown children, Cleola and Chalmus, who belonged to his first wife, Mamie, and two little girls, Barbara and Mary Eva, who were Uncle Woodard and Eva's children. Aunt Eva lived seventy-one years after Woodard passed away. When she passed away at age ninety-nine, less than one month shy of her one hundredth birthday, she was laid to rest beside Uncle Woodard at Steadman Baptist Church.

* * * * *

Winter came with a vengeance to South Carolina in mid-December of 1939. It was ungodly cold to the folks used to a milder climate even during the wintertime. Most days, the thermometer barely made it above the 32-degree mark. At night cold seeped in around the windows, and doors and fires were kept going in the kitchen fireplace and the dining room stove. Wintertime promoted family togetherness, since everyone had to stay near the fires to stay warm. The bedrooms had no heat, and when it was time to retire, they huddled in their beds under piles of quilts until their bodies warmed a cocoon under the heavy covers.

Miss Florence placed hot bricks in the kitchen fireplace and before bed would fish them out with a fire poker, wrap them in a thick cloth and place one in Leon and Robert's beds and two in her and Kelly's bed.

"If you place hot bricks down near where your feet will be about thirty minutes before going to bed, it sure helps to have a warm place for your feet," Florence said. "My Mamma taught me that trick. She said she could never go to sleep if her feet were cold. Wearing a thick pair of socks also helps." Florence slept in a long flannel gown; the men folks wore their 'long handles.' Once their bodies warmed a spot, they dared not move outside of their cocoon.

The first order of business when the sun came up was to build a fire in the kitchen fireplace, cook stove—so Florence could get breakfast ready—and then in the potbellied stove in the dining room. This was Robert's job every morning. As soon as the sun began to tint the sky in the east, a grey dawn spread over a frosty landscape. As the sun rose above the horizon, the light became brighter outside the window by his bed. He placed his feet on the icy floor, jerked on his clothes over his long underwear, slipped his stocking feet into his brogans, and headed to the kitchen to start the fires. Of course, in order to get to the kitchen and get the fires going, he had to make a dash across the front porch. He kept his wool-lined denim jacket on a nail beside his bed and thrust his arms in it before crossing the icy porch to the kitchen. That was Robert's job, and he performed it without question every morning during the cold of winter. It didn't take long when there was a bed of embers below the ashes.

"All I need to do is stir the ashes until I locate some red coals, and add some fat lighter splinters and small dry wood," Robert remarked. "It flames right up. Then I can put on some green wood to get a good fire going. The worst part is crossing that dang icy porch in the mornings."

Florence got up as soon as she heard Robert open the hall door, slipped on her shoes and house robe, and followed him across the porch to start breakfast. Leon and Kelly lay in their warm beds just a few minutes longer, giving Robert and Florence time to get the kitchen warmed up.

With the bone chilling cold of that winter, Robert began to appreciate the fact he had hauled home all those pine slabs last summer from his Uncle Woodard's saw mill.

* * * * *

Robert was a senior at Fairview High School and his daddy, Kelly, was still working for the WPA. Leon was working for Lucius Jackson, running his farm about a mile from their house. Leon was also working for Mr. Pope Hall at a saw mill; there wasn't a whole lot to be done on the Jackson acreage in the wintertime, and he had to be making money at something.

On a raw January 25th in 1940, Robert and his daddy, Kelly, were out at the woodpile, cutting up slabs with a bow saw. It was a two-man job, one holding the slab in place between two saw horses, while the other cut with the saw. It was evening time, about four; Robert had been home from school for almost an hour when Kelly suggested they cut up some more slabs before it got dark.

"Our wood boxes are really getting low, son, and with this cold weather, we need to cut up all the wood we can before night settles in."

Florence remained in the house, cooking their supper. Stepping onto the front porch, a shawl draped over her shoulders against the cold, Florence addressed the two when there was a break between the sound of their saw. "Supper will be ready soon, Kelly. How long will you and Robert be cutting up those slabs? I don't want supper to get cold."

"It shouldn't take too long; we don't have a lot of daylight left," Kelly replied.

It wasn't windy that day, just very cold and still. The only noise was the back and forth grinding sound their saw made as they cut the slabs. Kelly and Robert laid the slabs across two saw horses before they began their cutting back, and forth, sliding the pine slab to the end of the first saw horse to cut the right length. From experience, they knew what length to cut to fit the fireplace, the woodstove in the dining room, or the cook stove in the kitchen. They separated the slabs according to the length they needed for each heating source. They had quite a pile sawed into lengths and dark was beginning to settle all around them. As Kelly bent to pick up another pine slab to place across the saw horses, the pipe he always held in his mouth fell to the ground. It was simple thing barely noticed by Kelly or Robert.

"Just a couple more slabs and we'd better call it quits for today, son," Kelly said as he bent to retrieve another slab to cut. This time, the slab seemed too much for him to hold in his left hand and it slid from his grasp.

"My left hand feels like it's asleep," Kelly said, flexing his fingers. "I think I just have a case of 'droppies' this afternoon."

Robert was beginning to suspect it was more than just accident. It was noticeably odd to him that both times his daddy had dropped something it had been on the left side of his body. He remembered the stories of his Granddaddy Kel's stroke and was beginning to think that could be happening to Kelly.

"I think, Daddy, we need to go inside and forget about cutting any more wood this afternoon. It almost dark and I'm sure Mamma has supper almost ready."

"O.K. son, but let's take an armload of wood inside as we go."

Kelly knelt to pick up the wood slabs, but before he had his arms full, his left knee collapsed and the wood in his arms fell to the ground.

"Here, Daddy, let me help you," Robert said as he bent and helped his daddy to his feet. "We need to get you inside and send for the doctor."

"What's happening to me?" Kelly exclaimed, his voice trembling with fright. "The left side of my body isn't working. I feel kind of numb on that side."

"You'll be fine, Daddy, I'm sure. We just need to get you inside now and send for Dr. Gibson in Batesburg. I'll go to Miss Willow's and call him. Don't worry, you'll be O.K."

Robert managed to get Kelly into the house and onto the bed. "I'm going to Miss Willow's and call the doctor, Mamma," he told her privately in the kitchen. "I think maybe Daddy has had a stroke. Just try to keep him calm until I get back."

* * * * *

Darkness had settled on the land as Robert jumped from the front porch and headed to Miss Willow's half a mile away. There was an old logging road across in front of their house, two ruts with high grass in the center. It was bordered by impassable forest encroaching on both sides, to the point of almost being simply a pathway through the trees. It led straight to Miss Willow's house. She had the nearest telephone so that was the place to go for help, Robert figured. It was dark on that narrow road, but Robert didn't even notice the blackness or the cold; he was too concerned about his daddy. In less than ten minutes, he saw the lights from Miss Willow's windows shining through the trees, a beacon of hope, and felt relief flood his body as he bounded up on her porch and knocked on the door.

"I think Daddy has had a stroke," he said between gasps as Miss Willow opened the door. "I need to use your telephone to call Dr. Gibson."

"Of course, Robert, come on in. The telephone is in the parlor."

Robert called and explained the situation to Dr. Gibson.

"From what you have told me, it sounds likes Kelly has experienced a stroke," Dr. Gibson said. "I'll be there within the hour. Just try to keep him calm."

"Thanks, Miss Willow, for the use of your telephone," Robert said as he descended the steps. "I have to get back and see about Daddy. Dr. Gibson is on the way."

"I'll say a little prayer for Kelly," Miss Willow called after the young man as he departed without a backwards glance.

It was pitch black in the narrow logging road as Robert headed home at a lope. Looking up at the sky, Robert could distinguish the gap between the trees on either side of him; otherwise, it was almost impossible to see his hand in front of his face. The canopy of stars helped direct his path. The moon had not yet come up, so there was no light to guide him. He knew the way home by instinct; with the short distance to home, it never occurred to him to be apprehensive of the blackness all around him. When he reached the intersection where the logging road entered the main road, he paused to catch his breath. Across the road directly in front of him, their house loomed black against the starlit sky. There was a kerosene lamp setting on the table in the kitchen sending shafts of soft light through the porch window and another lamp in the front room to the right, the parlor. Someone was sitting in the rocking chair on the front porch silhouetted against the light from the kitchen window. It was Leon. Robert could distinguish the orange coal of his cigarette against the black of the porch walls.

"Did you talk to Dr. Gibson?" Leon asked as Robert stepped up on the porch, a bit out of breath. "Daddy has had a stroke for sure."

"I talked to Dr. Gibson and he said that's what it sounds like to him. He'll be here within an hour, said we just need to keep him calm. I guess it's just a wait and see game. Not a whole lot we can do at this point. How is he?"

"Miss Florence is just sitting there beside their bed holding his hand. He's visibly upset, doesn't understand what has happened to him. I just had to get outside for some air and a cigarette. I knew there was nothing to be done but wait. He seems to be calmed down some—when I first came in he was cursing and giving Miss Florence a fit.

"I said, 'Daddy, you have to be calm until the doctor gets here, he'll know what to do. You're only hurting yourself by getting all excited. You have to stay calm. That's the only thing you can do right now.' He knew I was right and seemed to calm down and accept the situation a little more. At least I could understand his speech. Maybe it's not as bad as Granddaddy's. I hope not."

"I'll just go in and tell Mamma in private what Dr. Gibson said. I don't want Daddy to be any more upset then he is before the doctor arrives. I'll just tell him Dr. Gibson is on the way and I'll come back and sit with you until he gets here," Robert said as he headed for the door at the end of the porch.

* * * * *

Robert and Leon had been sitting on the porch, huddled against the cold in silence, for thirty minutes before automobile lights finally appeared up the road to the north towards Steadman.

Dr. Gibson parked under the Walnut tree in the front yard, got out, paused to retrieve his black bag from the back seat, and walked towards the house. Leon and Robert stood as the doctor ascended the front steps.

"Where is Kelly, boys? Sounds to me like he has had a stroke like his daddy, Kel, back in '27, but I can't make a determination for sure until I have examined him. Direct me to your daddy, boys."

Dr. Gibson was in the room with Kelly and Florence for thirty minutes before emerging onto the front porch where Robert and Leon had sat in silence. As he approached, both men stood to receive the verdict about their Daddy's condition.

"Well boys, Kelly has had a stroke on the left side. He still can speak coherently. I don't know how bad his affliction will be yet; stroke victims tend to improve or get worse in the first three weeks. When I attended your Grandpa Kel I knew that man was bad off. I couldn't understand a word he was trying to tell me. At least I could understand what Kelly was trying to say. That's a good sign that it may not be as severe as his pa's. Every few days, I'll drop by to check on him. Just don't let him get agitated if possible. He will be frustrated and ornery, so try to be patient. He should be able to feed himself since he is right handed; don't try to baby him. Let him do whatever he feels like he can do for himself. We'll just hope it gets better. Maybe he'll be able to get around with a cane. It's just wait and see for now. Any questions?"

Dr. Gibson delivered his verdict in a quite matter-of-fact manner, leaving no room for doubt that he was certain of his patient's condition and treatment. Neither Leon nor Robert had any questions for the doctor.

"I better be getting on home. Man, it's cold tonight," Dr. Gibson remarked as he turned up the collar of his coat. "Y'all boys be sure Kelly is as comfortable as possible. I'll see you boys later. Try not to worry about Kelly. Let the good Lord do the worrying. You can't change things."

Dr. Gibson descended the steps and headed for the car. "Thanks, doc, and we're much obliged for you coming out tonight to see about Daddy," Leon said. "How much do we owe you for your trouble?"

"We'll worry about that later, Leon," Dr. Gibson replied as he headed for his automobile. "Good night, boys."

Dr. Gibson paused before opening his automobile door. "Call me if there's any change. I'll be back in a couple of days." He started the engine and backed out of the driveway. Light beams bounced off the darkened woods across the road and he was gone.

Sixteen

KELLY SAT IN A SMALL-ARMED ROCKING CHAIR BESIDE THE fireplace in the room he and Florence shared. This had been the parlor, but after his stroke, Robert and Leon insisted this would be better place for his bed. When the weather had been so cold in January and February, one of his sons built a fire in the fireplace every morning to make the room more comfortable. This room had been his world for the past eight weeks and Kelly had finally resigned himself to the fact that it would continue so for the remainder of his life. Immediately after his stroke, he had ranted and raved about his misfortune, but gradually he had come to terms with his affliction.

Florence and his children had been so patient with his bouts of swearing and his disagreeable attitude, Kelly realized. "I wish I could just stay drunk, but I can't even do that without someone fixing a drink for me," he complained. So, by necessity, his drinking had almost stopped.

They would give him a drink if he raised enough sand or if one of his brothers stopped by with a bottle, but generally, he did without. Still insisting on smoking his pipe, he could pretty much manage that on his own with only his right hand, as long as the pipe and tobacco were kept within easy reach. For the first two weeks after the stroke, he was totally dependent on Florence, and he realized her sacrifice.

"She has carried all my food to this room, fed me, bathed and shaved me, I have been blessed with a wonderful wife," Kelly said to everyone who stopped by. He continually thanked Florence for all she had done. "Without you, I don't know what would have become of me," he told her. "I don't believe I really deserve all you have done to help me, and I know I have not been the best husband. Please forgive me for the hard times I've given you—I'll be better to you from now on. No woman could be a better wife then you, Florence and I do love you. Don't forget that, please."

"I love you too, Kelly, and I don't begrudge taking care of you," Florence replied.

Gradually, he began to do more and more for himself. His speech was not bad, occasionally he slurred a word or two, but hell, he had done his share of slurring words most of his life due to his drinking. Now he had a legitimate excuse.

He sat now in the rocker where Robert had deposited him some two hours ago, gazing out the window at the bright sunlight, his left arm lying lifeless across his lap and his left leg flung out before him. He had no control or feeling in his left arm at all. It hung like a useless weight to his side unless he took his right hand and moved the left to a less awkward position.

He reached for his pipe on the small table beside him, pulled the drawstring apart on his tobacco pouch with his teeth, stuck the pipe in, filled the bowl, and packed the tobacco down with his index finger. He then stuck the pipe firmly between his teeth, removed a match from the wooden box on the table, stuck it on the wall beside the mantle, and lit the tobacco. As he puffed, whirls of smoke drifted upward towards the ceiling.

Robert entered the room just as Kelly got his pipe going good.

"You make lighting your pipe by yourself almost look easy, Daddy."

"Well, son, I can't expect one of you to be handy every time I want to smoke my pipe, so I'm learning how to do it myself. What is that you have in your hand, son?"

"I've made you a walking stick and I thought we would see if you can get around with a little help. I know you're getting tired of looking at these four walls. Mamma has dinner almost ready; I thought you might make it to the table. Since Leon put in that door between the dining room and bedroom across the hall, you won't have to navigate across the porch to reach the kitchen. What about it? Do you think you could manage?"

"I don't know, but I'll be glad to give it a try if you help me get up out of this damn rocker." Kelly put his pipe in the ashtray on the table. "This is a mighty nice walking stick you made for me son," Kelly said as Robert placed it in his right hand. It was approximately three feet long and two inches in diameter. Robert had found exactly the right size oak limb, sawed it off, peeled the bark, and sanded the entire length smooth. At the top was a knot that made a perfect handle for support; other imperfections were smoothed out with sand paper and a glossy finish was applied. Robert had even drilled a hole at the head of the stick and threaded a short strip of leather through it; tied in a knot, the leather strip became a perfect hanger to loop over a nail beside Kelly's bed.

"I'm glad you like it, Daddy. Just use the stick to brace yourself and I'll lift you up."

His left leg was almost as uncontrollable as his left arm, but with the help of the walking stick and Robert to lean on, Kelly found he was able to fling the left leg outward and propel his body forward, dragging the left leg every other step. At least he could use the left leg enough to support his weight. It took some doing, but after a determined struggle, Kelly made it to the kitchen table. His weight fell heavily in the chair when he finally reached his destination, and he was sweating profusely from the effort, but it was a good feeling to be able to move again.

Beside herself with happiness, Florence could only exclaim, "Why, Kelly, it is wonderful having you join us at the table for a meal."

He could even feed himself with no problems since he was right-handed. His food did tend to creep out of the left side of his mouth onto his cheek, but not so bad as to be a nuisance. Before they had finished the meal, Leon came in from the field to join them. He was very surprised to see his daddy at the table away from his bedroom. Kelly and his sons sat in the kitchen long after the meal, just talking and laughing most of the afternoon.

After that day, Kelly had limited mobility with his walking stick and someone to lean on. Leon or Robert frequently assisted him to the kitchen table when they were home. Florence couldn't manage his weight against her because she was so much smaller and weaker than he. If Leon and Robert were not home, Florence carried his meals on a tray to his bedside, placed the tray on a small semi-circle shaped table, and helped him sit up to feed himself.

Two weeks after his first trip to the kitchen, he had attempted the long trip to the kitchen table by himself. Florence was in the kitchen preparing their mid-day meal when she heard the thump of

Kelly's walking stick in the dining room next door and the whisper of his left foot as he drug it beside him. She rushed to the doorway just in time to see him tumble to the floor.

"I'm O.K., Florence," he exclaimed as she kneeled at his side. "This damn left leg is so unpredictable; it just gave way completely with me."

It was hopeless for Florence to tug and try to lift Kelly from the floor. His weight was just too much for her to handle. The best she was able to do was make him more comfortable with a pillow placed under his head until help arrived. He had lain there on the dining room floor almost an hour, until Leon came in from the farm for dinner and got him back into his bed.

"Don't try that again without Robert or me here to help you," Leon chided his daddy. "Next time, you could break a hip. You just can't be trying to get around with that walking stick by yourself."

"I know you're right, son. But I feel so damn useless just sitting in that rocker or lying up on this bed all day every day the good Lord sends. I've worked hard all my life in my fields and down at Rayflin in that store of Roston's. And hell, I've made enough moonshine to float a boat in a good-sized pond. When I think about some of the things I used to do, some of which I regret I might add, it's hard to just sit still and watch the world go by, staring at these four walls. Just to be able to make it to the kitchen table is a big deal for me. I just wish I had something to occupy my time instead of just pondering the past in this stagnant condition I'm in now."

"I understand what you mean, Daddy. I really do, but don't ever feel like you're useless. You're not; all of your family needs you. You know more about farming than anybody I know and I appreciate your advice. I couldn't manage Jackson's planting without your help. Just because you're in no condition to walk the fields and push a plow don't mean you can't be useful."

"Thank you, son, for telling me that. I'm just thankful I have a family and I'll try not to cause y'all any worry by using that walking stick without help again."

"I tell you what, Daddy; I'll move the radio in here from the dining room. That little table it's on should fit right over there under the front window. You can listen to the radio whenever you want. That would at least be company for you when no one else is here. Would you like that?"

"That would be fine, son; you know how much I enjoy listening to some of those funny shows, like 'Lum and Abner.' They're always going on about some kind of foolishness. I hadn't even thought about having the radio in here, but it sure would be nice."

Leon moved the radio into Kelly's room that very afternoon. It sat upon a square oak table about 15 inches in diameter and three feet tall. The four table legs came out from underneath the top at an inward slant and midway down held a smaller shelf in place. The radio sat on that table in front of the window facing the road and gave Kelly hours of enjoyment every day from the very start. If Kelly was in his rocker beside the fireplace, he found he could maneuver his rocker by twisting it back and forth and pulling forward with his right foot the six feet across the creaking floor to reach the radio knob. In the warm spring and summer days of 1940, Robert would often hear the radio and his father's laughter drifting through the open windows of his bedroom. It was good to be working outside in the yard and to hear his father's laugh again.

In May of that year, Robert graduated from Fairview High School. There were only thirteen students in his class. Kelly and

Florence were so proud of his accomplishment; graduating from high school was no small feat for a rural Southern boy in 1940. He was the first in both their families to receive a high school diploma; education was not a high priority in the rural South. Unfortunately, Kelly could not attend Robert's graduation ceremony in his handicapped state and Florence wouldn't leave him. It had only been five months since his stroke, and Kelly was not about to be put on public display even if he had someone to assist with his movement. Elsie and Fred were there, but Leon was not. It wasn't that Leon wasn't proud of his little brother; he was never one to mingle with a large crowd. He didn't attend celebrations of any kind where numerous people were in attendance unless it was a funeral. He did make exceptions for funerals, only because he felt it was his Christian duty to honor those who had passed on.

Seventeen

Fall arrived that year and as the evenings became cooler, Florence insisted on closing the windows in Kelly's bedroom. She was so afraid he would catch a chill from the night air, and in his weakened condition, pneumonia could easily set in and he would be gone. Kelly hated to have her close his windows at night.

"My God, woman, why do you insist on depriving a man of fresh air? In the evening it actually feels pleasant in here, and after the steamy heat of August, I'm ready for some cool evening air."

"It can't be good for you to be exposed to the cool night air while you're sleeping. You might catch pneumonia. I'll open these windows for you in the morning, but they'll stay closed at night. Pretty soon there won't be any disagreement; we'll be having frost and you'll not be wanting the windows up at all."

Sometimes Florence had to put her foot down. She and Kelly had few disagreements and she tried to please him in everything. She cooked what he wanted, helped him shave and bathe every morning, and responded to his every request, but not when it compromised his health.

As for Kelly, he knew how good Florence was to him and he

told her most everyday how he appreciated her taking care of him. He tried not to be too contrary, but sometimes he couldn't help his frustration at the condition of things. Since Leon had moved the radio into the bedroom, he'd had a constant companion. Florence would turn it on for him as soon as she brought him his breakfast and it stayed on until she came in to close his windows at night and light the kerosene lamp beside his bed. With the radio in constant use, the batteries had to be changed often. Robert handled this, and as soon as they started to weaken, more was ordered from Sears and Roebuck. When Florence returned after delivering his breakfast in the mornings, she would move Kelly's tray to the kitchen, then help him shave and bathe in a wash pan of warm water placed on the little table beside his bed. They had discovered that although Florence couldn't help him walk with his walking stick, she could help him slide into the small-armed rocker if it was placed close beside his bed. It was only a matter of her handing him his walking stick and holding the rocker steady for him to lift his weight enough, with the support of the stick, to heave into the rocker. Florence, with some help from Kelly, could then slide the rocker back over to the fireplace and he would be near his pipe and tobacco. Kelly could pretty much handle the rest of the day. If he wanted to change the radio station, he could slide his rocker over to reach it.

After I get Kelly settled with his breakfast, bath and shave, Florence thought, *I can go about my normal chores, I only need to peep in on Kelly ever so often. That radio has added so much pleasure to his uneventful days; he isn't lonely as long as he has the radio to listen to. And it is so good to hear him laugh again.*

Most of the time physically checking on him wasn't even necessary; she could hear him laughing at one of those crazy shows he loved so much, Abbott and Costello or Fibber McGee and Molly. But his favorite was Lum and Abner. If he needed her for anything, he would just call or tap his walking stick on the floor and she was there. If she was working in the yard or feeding their livestock, she always checked on Kelly and told him she would be outside for a short time.

"I'll let you know when I am back inside; I promise I won't be outside for long."

"Don't worry about me," Kelly would say. "Just go about your daily chores. I'll be fine for a short time. I promise I won't try to get out of my rocker by myself. I'm satisfied as long as I have my pipe and the radio. It would be nice to have a little sip of my liquor, if you don't mind."

Sometimes Florence would get him the drink, but more often than not, she would bring him a glass of tea instead, and he seldom complained if she did. She didn't like him to drink much alcohol especially if Leon or Robert wasn't home at the time. She knew he missed it and that it was a hard thing to give up 'cold turkey,' so he was allowed the occasional drink. If his brothers stopped by to visit, they would usually bring a bottle and they would pass it to Kelly. She never told them it wasn't allowed. She knew he had few pleasures; a drink shared with one of his brothers was one of them.

Listening to the radio every day, Kelly became well aware of the sad state of world affairs and the march of Hitler's army across Europe. Hitler's German army had invaded Poland in 1939. At first Kelly paid little attention, viewing the beginning of the chaos in Europe as an outsider looking through a window. It was no business of ours what those foreigners did. He sympathized with their plight but that was, after all, the other side of the world. But day-by-day, as he listened to the radio reports of the German armies conquering one European country after another, Kelly came to realize we would most definitely not sit on the sidelines for this one.

Every evening beginning in the spring of 1940, Kelly gave Leon and Robert a report outlining Hitler's aggression. "Germany attacked Denmark and Norway in April, in May they invaded Belgium, Luxembourg, and the Netherlands," Kelly reported. "By the end of June, France surrendered to Hitler, and now in September, that bastard Hitler has started dropping bombs on Great Britain. Day and night, he is determined to pound even Great Britain into submission. The German armies have marched across Europe intent on conquering the whole world. We just can't sit idly by much longer," Kelly prophesied. "We're bound to get swept up in this bloodshed soon, like it or not."

"Listening to the radio all day, you know more about what's happening over there than anybody else in this community, probably in the whole county," both sons would tell Kelly in the evenings spent across from him at the fireplace in his bedroom.

Kelly would then give them an updated report of Hitler's army and what he believed they were planning. Listening to his radio became very educational; it was not only entertaining through his favorite shows, but he had also taken a big interest in people on the other side of the world. He shared these reports with Robert and Leon and they discussed the situation every evening.

To make matters worse across the Pacific to our west, Japan was at war with China and had occupied Indochina. The United States supporting China against the Japanese had added another potential enemy to the west.

"We can't stay here in the middle too long between the Germans and the Japanese without getting into this fight," Kelly told his sons. "It won't be long before we're in it too. Mark my words, we'll be at war with both countries, and it won't be long in coming."

The United States government had already switched their objective from one of neutrality to one of being prepared for the inevitable. The U.S. Selective Training and Service Act became law on September 16, 1940; the government had started a draft to build up the armed forces. To begin with, all men between the ages of 18-35 had to register. They only had thirty days from notification, so Leon had to register almost immediately, and Robert would turn seventeen on November 6th. With the world situation steadily deteriorating, both his sons could be called into service. Besides reenacting the draft, Roosevelt's government began building defense plants and giving the countries allied against Hitler aid, only stopping short of war. Roosevelt called upon the United States to be "the great arsenal of democracy." Listening to the news on the radio and the words of Roosevelt, Kelly felt proud knowing his country was on the side of right, but this patriotism came with a heavy heart, knowing what might lie in store for his sons.

As fall turned into the cold of winter, Kelly sat in his rocker and listened to the news with great apprehension. He sat beside the fireplace, feeling the heat of the embers and puffing his pipe. Robert and Leon were both working, Robert at Olympia Mills, a cotton mill in Columbia, and Leon for Lucius Jackson, running his farm. Robert rode to and from work each day with Lucius Jackson. Kelly only got to see Robert for any length of time on Saturday and Sunday, but Leon's job was more flexible. He was in and out at all hours of the day. Kelly and Leon had more time to talk about things. They still had no automobile; they couldn't afford the cost. Leon didn't drive and had no intention of starting now, but Robert was longing for a car of his own, and Kelly was sure he would get one just as soon as he could save enough money.

Leon would often walk down to Rayflin to visit his grandmamma Peninnah and Aunt Jennie's crowd. Kelly had not been to his childhood home since his stroke.

He told Leon one day, "It's a sad thing that I don't get to go visit my brothers and sisters and my ma anymore. I'm glad you at least get to go down to the old place. How is it looking, by the way? I sure would love to be able to walk those fields again."

"Well, Daddy, there ain't a whole lot of fields there anymore. Uncle Olin doesn't do a whole lot of planting. The terraces are beginning to go down between the fields and some are beginning to grow up in pines. It's not the place it once was. I'm afraid you would be real disappointed to see the shape it's in now."

"I'm sure I would, son, but with all this talk of war, Olin should be able to make a living farming those fields again. Maybe with a little encouragement from Jennie, he would get those fields in shape again. With those sons of theirs and Arthur's help, it could be a fine farm again. Arthur's getting old, but he knows a whole heap about farming. I'll talk to Jennie next time she comes for a visit. I hate to see Pa's fields disappear. We worked too hard from daylight to dark when I was a boy to clear that land."

Eighteen

On a clear, cold Monday, two days before Christmas 1940, Florence was in the kitchen finishing up the breakfast dishes when she heard an automobile pull into the front yard. Wiping her wet hands on her apron, she peeped out the window and saw Jennie open the automobile door, step out and head towards the house with a basket on her arm.

"Kelly will be so pleased to see Jennie," she said aloud, a smile touching her lips. "Kelly," she called as she headed through the dining room towards his bedroom, "Jennie is here to see you."

Delivering her announcement from the doorway of his bedroom, she could see the pleasure of the news light up his face. Kelly was still in his bed this morning. It was extremely cold outside and even with a good fire going in his fireplace, he had not made up his mind to leave the warmth of his quilts to sit in his rocker.

"Don't just stand there, woman, let her in from the cold, fix her a cup of coffee in the kitchen, and then come back and help me out of this bed. I'll sit in my rocker beside the fire for our visit."

"Whatever you say, Kelly, I'll be right back."

Jennie was standing on the front porch at the kitchen door when Florence returned. Opening the door, Florence greeted her sister-in-law with a warm smile. "Come in, Jennie, out of the cold," she said as they embraced. "It's such a pleasant surprise to see you this morning."

"I just wanted to stop by and check on Kelly and bring all of y'all some fruitcake for Christmas. Ma and I made it two weeks ago, and you know Ma, she's been pouring whiskey on it every couple of days since; Kelly should appreciate the added flavor. She would have come with me, but she says the cold gets in her bones and her arthritis acts up so bad in the wintertime. She sends her love to all of you. How is that brother of mine this morning? I haven't seen him in near a month now."

"He's seems to be doing pretty well, and I know a visit from you will cheer him up. I'm going to get you a cup of coffee and you just sit and warm up beside the fire while I help Kelly into his rocker."

Florence poured Jennie strong black coffee from the pot sitting on the cook stove into a tin mug.

"This should still be good and hot. There's still a bed of coals in the stove box," Florence said as she placed the mug on the table. "Would you like cream and sugar?"

"Just a teaspoonful of sugar will be fine," Jennie replied as she removed her wool coat and scarf, draping them across one of the ladder-back kitchen chairs. "Is Kelly getting around any better since I saw him last?"

"No, but he's still able to make it to the table with Leon or Robert's help sometimes. He just sits mostly in his rocker beside the fire listening to the radio and smoking his pipe. He does seem to accept his condition now, doesn't complain to me like he did at first. You enjoy your coffee and I'll go help Kelly dress and get into his rocker beside the fire. I know he's anxious to see you."

"Is there anything I can do?" asked Jennie.

"No thanks, I know Kelly wants you to see him at his best. I'll be back shortly," Florence replied as she crossed the threshold into the adjoining dining room. "You just enjoy your coffee and warm up."

When Florence entered the bedroom, Kelly had already thrown back his heavy covers and was sitting up on the side of the bed.

"Kelly Gantt, you know you could fall off that bed trying to get up by yourself!" she exclaimed as she rushed to his side, "And it would take me and Jennie both to get you up."

"I know, I know, but I was careful," he replied with an exasperated tone. "Now help me dress and get into my rocker please. I'm anxious to see that baby sister of mine."

Fifteen minutes later, Jennie paused in the doorway of his bedroom, a smile touching her lips as she met his warm gaze. Jennie Rish was twelve years younger than her brother Kelly and he considered her his baby sister. They had always had a good relationship, although growing up, Kelly had considered her more a nuisance than anything else due to the difference in age. Jennie was a short woman, just a couple inches over five feet, and at forty-five, she was beginning to add a few extra pounds around the middle. The strawberry blonde hair curling around her face was touched with gray at the temples. Looking at his sister, Kelly envisioned the skinny girl of his youth working beside their ma in the garden and bending over the cook stove in the kitchen. Now he could see she was just a much younger version of Peninnah.

"You look more like Ma every time I lay eyes on you, Jennie," he said with a smile, removing the pipe stem from his mouth. "Have a seat and tell me all the latest about the family."

Jennie crossed the room, bent over, kissed his cheek, and slipped into the small rocker at the other side of the fireplace. Extending her hands towards the fire, she replied, "I'm glad you think I look like Ma, I'll tell her you said that. This fire feels nice and cozy—it's freezing outside."

"Robert gets a good fire going in here in the evenings, so there's always a good bed of coals. Florence just stirs up the coals and adds a splinter or two of fat lighter when she gets up in the mornings and a couple of pieces of green wood and it's going again. Even when it's freezing outside, a good fire in the fireplace makes it pleasant for me sitting here in my rocker. Now, tell me how Ma and all your family are getting along."

"Ma seems to be doing pretty well. She wanted to come this morning but you know how her arthritis acts up in the wintertime. She sends her love and said she hopes she will be able to get up here to see you for a spell on Christmas day. We're expecting a big crowd at Rayflin for Christmas. Sam, Rion, and Roston will be there with their families. Ma was hoping Cyrus and his family could make it home for Christmas, but she received a card from him two days ago and they won't be able to come this year. I'm sure most all of them will be by to see you Christmas."

"And Olin and your chaps, how are they?"

"Oh, they're doing fine; Olin and the boys butchered two hogs last month, so we have plenty of meat for the winter. I'll be cooking one of our hams Christmas and I'll bring you and Florence one up here next time I come."

"We sure will appreciate that. It's been a long time since we have had a good ham. How about the farm? Is Olin planning to do much planting come spring? With all this war business, he should be able to do pretty well farming. I'm sure we'll all be caught up in that mess pretty soon."

"I don't know how much planting Olin is planning. The boys are getting old enough to help but we don't have the blacks to help on the place like we used to. Arthur and Willie are still helping Olin with the fields, but Arthur is getting old and can't help with the plowing and planting as much. I wish Olin would get back into farming for a living, but he just doesn't see it as profitable enough to support our family. He says it's hard to get good help at a decent wage, and the cost of fertilizer, seeds, and such is just not worth the work you have to put into it. And then there's the weather to consider. What if we have a dry spell just when the crops are beginning to grow? He thinks putting all your effort in planting is just too risky."

Kelly just nodded his head at Olin's reasoning concerning not farming his pa's fields. He didn't agree with leaving all the fields barren, but he of course had no right to add his two-cents to Jennie's pronouncement. Hell, he couldn't even get to the table without help. No need to complain about Olin's decisions. It might upset Jennie and he didn't intend to do that. If Olin ever came to visit him, he would be glad to voice an opinion, but he didn't expect Olin to do that, and to be honest, he didn't care for Olin or whether he visited or not. At least Jennie still came to see him.

"Of course, you're right about this war in Europe; we'll probably be in it before it's all said and done," Jennie remarked. "Thank God our boys are still too young for the army; George, the oldest, is just twelve."

"How about Raymond? Has Roston heard from him lately?"

"I think Raymond will get to come home on leave after the first of the year; that's what Roston believes. You know he joined the Army almost eighteen months ago, before all the business about a draft was started. Roston says he'll get to come home for a visit before he leaves the States. Roston says Raymond is to be sent to someplace in Hawaii called Schofield Barracks. I think the government is worried we might have some trouble from the Japanese. This place Raymond is going to is at Pearl Harbor, Roston says. Maybe he'll be safer there and won't have to get in that fight in Europe."

"Let's hope he will," Kelly replied. "Tell Roston to be sure Raymond comes up here for a visit when he's home. I sure would love to see that boy, and I know Leon and Robert would. Tell them brothers of mine when you see them to get up here for a visit. I sure do enjoy talking about the old days when we were all full of piss and vinegar. We sure were a rowdy bunch of boys in our day, Woodard and Buck included. That's all in the past now, but I do wish I was able to get around and visit all of you."

All was silent for a good five minutes, Kelly gazing into the fire, remembering the past, and Jennie trying to get up the courage to tell Kelly what she really came to see him about. Finally, Jennie broke the silence between them.

"Kelly, there's something else I wanted to talk to you about. You know Ma is not in the best of health and she just turned eighty on her last birthday. We didn't get this place settled two years ago because the whole works weren't happy about what Ma wanted. You know Olin and I have taken care of Ma since Pa died and we want things to be settled. Well, Olin and I convinced Ma that she needs something done legally in case something unexpected happens to her. You remember how it was with Pa and his stroke."

"I remember all of that, Jennie. Just get on with it and tell me what in the devil you're talking about."

"Well, Kelly, Ma has signed all her dowry in the place over to me." Jennie tried to deliver the announcement as a matter of fact. She wasn't sure how Kelly would take the news, now that she controlled their Ma's entire dowry in the place. That was, after all, well over half of the total acreage. She now controlled half of the lower section that belonged to Peninnah and Kel jointly, plus Peninnah's third of the half that belonged to Kel, and a third of the upper section that Kel bought outright from Aunt Merari. Considering she also was entitled to a child's portion of her father's part, she owned over 257 acres of the remaining 464 out right. After Jennie delivered her announcement, she sat quietly, watching Kelly's face for his reaction to the news.

Kelly puffed on his pipe a couple times, seemingly deep in thought. He had put so much work in this place and now Jennie was telling him their Ma had signed her part away. That didn't leave a whole lot of land as his part. After pondering what he had just heard and gazing into the fire, he looked up to meet Jennie's stare.

"You know, Jennie, I've put a lot of work into this place. I built this house, I cleared the land, and planted these fields. I trust you to be fair and as long as I have this house and a few acres of land, I'll be satisfied. It's not like I'll be needing a lot of land in my condition. I just wanted something to leave to my children, and land is the one thing that lasts."

"You know I would never take this place from you or your family. It's still going to be yours. Olin says we just need to be prepared with someone to take over for Ma if she's not able."

"I thought Olin was probably behind this. That Olin is a shrewd fellow, but I trust you, Jennie, and I know you will do the right thing. I appreciate you coming to see me and telling me this in person. I'm sure all the rest will not be too pleased to learn this news."

Jennie stayed and talked to Kelly another hour before taking her leave. No more was said about the place. They talked at length about the rest of the family and reminisced about the past and how things had changed for all of them. After Jennie said her goodbyes to Florence and Kelly, she departed for Rayflin.

Florence had already started cooking dinner before Jennie left, and they both encouraged her to stay, but she insisted she had to get home and cook for Ma, Olin, and the boys.

"Ma and I have a lot of Christmas cooking to get started on," she said as she put on her coat and wrapped her knitted scarf around her neck. Jennie gave Florence a goodbye hug at the kitchen door and she was gone.

As Florence set the dinner tray on Kelly's bedside table, she asked, "What is the news from all the folks down at Rayflin?"

"Everybody is doing just fine," Kelly replied. That's all he said.

Nineteen

LEON WALKED AT A FAST PACE, FOLLOWING THE OLD WAGON road that ran beside the field north of the house. This was the lower field, about ten acres in size; just ahead, there was a gentle slope to the top of a small rise. As the land begin to incline, a stand of pines marked the boundary between the lower field and the crest of the rise. As the wagon road turned toward the west, past the crest, another five-acre field lay fallow to his left.

"Both of these fields I'll plant in corn in a couple months," Leon said aloud to himself. He looked them over in the deepening of the early winter light as he passed. *Those two fields to the south near Coon Branch, I'll probably plant in soybeans. I'll ask Daddy for his opinion,* Leon thought. *It seems to give him purpose to be consulted about his fields even though he can't help in the planting. Kelly Gantt is still the best farmer I know, cripple or not.*

It was now mid-February and a cold, breezy afternoon. It was almost sundown and Leon wanted to check his rabbit boxes. He always set at least a half dozen rabbit boxes every winter in hopes of catching some fresh game for their table. He pulled his denim coat together in the front and buttoned all the buttons. It was getting pretty chilly this afternoon.

"If this wind lies, we'll have a heavy frost in the morning I bet," Leon said aloud to himself.

He passed the persimmon tree that stood beside the old road and noticed half-eaten persimmons lying all about underneath the tree. *Possums have been in this tree since yesterday evening,* he thought. The first rabbit box came into view off the road in some underbrush, still set.

"I do hope I catch a couple of rabbits today. We can sure use the meat."

As he reached the end of the old road and turned back south toward the swamp, he saw that the next box was tripped; the door was down. He lifted the box on its end and peeped inside the door, but didn't want to go sticking his hand down in the box until he was sure it was a rabbit. Other critters sometimes got inside the box and he didn't want to tangle with no polecat. He had had that misfortune before. It was a rabbit, and he reached inside, slipped his hand down underneath the furry creature, grabbed its back legs, and hauled it out. A swift chop to the back of the head and he broke the rabbit's neck. He continued on past the trash pile where all their discarded and broken items were thrown and through the woods towards Coon Branch. The woods were thick, tall pines, poplars, and junipers and dark this time of the evening. He checked four more boxes; two were undisturbed, one held another rabbit, and his last box had a possum inside.

"I bet you're the rascal that's been up in that persimmon tree," he said as he let it out and watched it amble away towards the swamp.

Retracing his steps, he headed back to the house and a warm fire. When he reached the crest of the little hill, he paused for a few minutes and gazed down towards their old clapboard house. His daddy had never painted the house, and even at this distance and in the darkening evening light, you could see the bright streaks of orange in the lumber from the fat lighter etched against the dark gray of the boards. Smoke curled skyward from the wood cook stove in the kitchen and the fireplace in his daddy's room. He turned his coat collar up against the cold breeze and headed to the house.

"Better get these rabbits skinned and cleaned for Miss Florence. Maybe she will fry them up and make some gravy for supper," he said aloud. "No better eating than that."

He reached the backyard just as the sun was disappearing behind the tall junipers to the west towards the river swamp. He laid his rabbits on the wash table that stood beside the path down to the spring.

Climbing the back steps, he opened the door to the dining room and stuck his head in. A kerosene lamp was lit on the dining table. Just as he thought, Miss Florence was busy cooking supper on the wood cook stove. Two kerosene lamps were lit inside the kitchen, one near the stove on her cook table and another on the mantel above the fireplace.

"I got two rabbits in my boxes this afternoon, Miss Florence. Hand me a dish pan and a knife—I'll skin and clean them for you."

"Oh good, Leon. We'll have them for supper," she said as she handed him the dish pan and knife through the back door.

"I was sure hoping you would say that; nothing better than fried rabbit and gravy," Leon replied.

Leon hung the rabbits by their back legs on a post in the back-yard. Just as he started to work, Robert descended the back steps.

"Mamma said you might need a little help with the rabbits."

"Sure, would make the job go faster," Leon replied. "You clean one and I'll do the other."

Robert pulled the pocketknife from his pocket. It was always kept sharp, something Kelly had taught him, and he set to work on his rabbit.

They worked quietly for ten minutes, both concentrating on the job at hand. The rabbits were ready in no time. Robert put their slick pink bodies, with heads and feet removed, into the dishpan and headed for the house. He knew as soon as he put the dishpan on the kitchen table, his momma would pour dippers full of water over them, clean them, and cut them into pieces. She always par-boiled rabbits before flouring and frying them in a skillet of lard. That way, they were always tender. Then she would make brown gravy with the drippings and put the fried pieces back in the gravy to simmer.

"I think I'll have me a cigarette before I come in, maybe walk up to the barn and check on the livestock," Leon called after him.

"Let me give these to Momma and I'll join you," Robert replied.

"Tell her to give you the bucket and I'll get the cow milked, and we'll get both her and the old mule in the barn and give them some feed and water."

"Sure thing. I'll be right back to help."

When Robert returned, Leon was standing at the edge of the yard smoking a cigarette and gazing at the orange glow of the setting sun over the river swamp. "Pretty cold this evening," Robert said as he pulled his coat closed in the front.

"We'll have a heavy frost in the morning I believe," Leon replied. "The wind has died down considerable just in the last fifteen minutes. Going to be a cold one tonight."

"I've already filled all the wood boxes for Mamma, including the one on the front porch; should last until tomorrow evening even if we get a hard freeze."

"That sure is a pretty sight," Leon said, gesturing towards the western sky. The towering junipers appeared starkly black, silhouetted against the bright orange sky.

"I don't think I've ever seen a more beautiful sunset, that's for sure," commented Robert.

They both stood in silence, eyes fixed on the orange sky as the last rays of the sun began to disappear.

"Let's walk on up towards the barn before the light is completely gone," Leon said. "Miss Florence will be calling us for supper pretty soon."

Leon dropped his cigarette, snuffed it out with a twist of his shoe, and headed up the path towards the barn, Robert following close behind. The barn stood some 100 yards northwest of the house. It loomed dark against the evening sky, and as the two brothers entered the double doors, Leon struck a match and lit two kerosene lanterns that hung just inside. The air inside was heavy with the pungent odor of animal manure and animal bodies. But there were also the unmistakable smells of leather, burlap sacks, dried corn, and the sweet scent of straw mingling in the air.

"I'll get the mule and old Bess out of the lot and you pitch some fresh straw into their stalls," Leon said as he unlatched the side door that opened into the lot.

The mule and milk cow were all that was left of their animals. They had sold their hogs and the other mule soon after Kelly had his stroke. The one mule, Sara, they needed to pull the plow in the spring and the wagon. The milk cow still provided their milk and Florence milked her every morning and evening. Florence also insisted on keeping a few chickens in a small coop in the backyard. During the day, they roamed the backyard freely but every evening, she fed them and closed them up in their small coop, fearful of the foxes in the nearby swamp.

Robert took the pitchfork from the nail beside the door and began to pitch straw from a pile near the rear door while Leon went outside to bring in the mule, Sara, and old Bessie, their milk cow. The animals did not have to be enticed to come in; all that was required was opening the side door to the lot.

"They're glad to get in out of cold," Leon said. "I think animals have more sense than people when it comes to some things."

Robert finished covering the stall floors in fresh straw; Leon turned the two animals into their stalls and poured feed into their troughs. They both then grabbed a bucket and headed to the spring for some fresh water, Robert carrying the lantern to light their way.

Once they came back with fresh water for the animals, Leon put the small three-legged stool that hung across the stall boards beside Bess and began the milking. The cow seemed docile and concentrated on her feed while Leon concentrated on the milk spurting into the clean bucket. He expertly squeezed her teats; he had been milking cows most of his life and Bess gave him no trouble. Cows can tell when their bag is in need of emptying for sure. As Leon milked, Robert leaned on the stall fence and they continued their conversation.

"You sure have caught a mess of rabbits this season. Just how many rabbits have you caught in your boxes so far this winter?" Robert asked.

Leon finished milking and, taking one lantern and extinguishing the other, they continued their conversation on the way to the house.

"Well, so far, forty-one, but you know I'll still have them set for another two weeks or so until the end of this month. I guess that's a pretty good season. My momma always had to have her rabbit boxes set in the winter. Daddy would make the boxes for her and clean and skin her rabbits, but she was the one that checked them every evening. She would cook them or pack them in the saltbox for later."

"When she cleaned out the saltbox one winter," Leon remembered, "she discovered a whole row of rabbits in the bottom covered in salt. They were from the season before but those things were danged good. I was just a young'un and I got tired of eating rabbits in the wintertime. I guess I get my rabbit-catching skill from my Mamma. She taught me a lot in those almost ten years she was here with me; I think about what a good woman she was most every day."

Interrupting Leon's melancholy, Robert changed the subject, not to a happier one but to the present.

"What news have you heard of the war in Europe?" he asked.

"You mean, besides our daily news reports from Daddy?" Leon asked.

"Yes, you do come in contact with Mr. Jackson every day, and he gets the State newspaper daily, doesn't he? That's the news I was meaning, printed, not just secondhand from Daddy. He might not always hear it straight, you know. His hearing ain't what it used to be."

Leon summed up the situation according to their father's exclamation. "Lucius told me this morning he heard two fellows from up at Steadman, John Hartley and Bo Kirkland, got their draft notices last week," replied Leon. "The news I get from Lucius is more about the local situation hereabouts. "Daddy keeps up with the news pretty well listening to the radio every day. He hears a lot more than you give him credit for, and I actually believe he writes some of it down. You know he expects us to ask him for a news brief every evening and wants to give us the correct information. He says the situation in Europe is in a sorry shape. All those countries over there are fighting each other. I don't profess to know what's going on, who is fighting who. Some of the places he hears about on the news I don't even have a clue where they are. I do know Germany and Italy are the main jacklegs that started this messed up damned affair, but now they have Hungary and Romania on their side. Just last month, Daddy says British soldiers invaded Ethiopia. I think that is somewhere in Africa. Now, you tell me, what are the British doing in Ethiopia? All I know is it is one hell of a mess over there and we'll be over there soon. There just ain't no way around it."

"Daddy sure gets the scoop listening to his radio all day, you're right about that," said Robert. "I don't know a whole lot about world history," Robert said, "but I do know the Italians invaded Ethiopia in 1935 and I think the British are trying to get the Italians out. You're right, the United States will have to get in the fight, and I do think it will be pretty soon. We're both registered, you know. We could be called at any time."

"Miss Florence and Daddy can't manage with both of us away in this war, that's what worries me," Leon replied. "I'll go and you'll have to stay and watch out for them."

By this time, they were standing at the base of the back steps, Leon smoking a cigarette in the twilight while Robert bounded up the steps and handed the milk bucket to his mother. Returning to Leon's side, he stated, "That decision may not be up to me and you. I'm the one that should go, not you. After all, you're practically an old man," Robert replied with a laugh.

"You think so? We'll just see about me being an old man. Why, me and couple of the old boys I know around here could put them Germans, Italians, and Japs on the run. But no need worrying about that now, time will tell."

Miss Florence stuck her head out the back door. "Supper's on the table boys and it's getting cold."

Twenty

AS 1941 PROGRESSED, THE WORLD SITUATION GREW STEADI-ly worse. In April of that year, Germany invaded Greece and Yugoslavia, and by the end of June, the Axis forces allied with Hitler invaded Russia.

To the backwoods farmers of South Carolina, the War in Europe was beginning to impact more and more on their lives.

"Sitting around the radio in the evenings listening to Daddy talk about this War business can really worry a fellow," Leon remarked to Robert. "If we're both drafted, Miss Florence and Daddy will be helpless alone, you realize that, don't you, Robert?"

"Of course, I do," Robert replied. "Mamma is just too small and frail to take care of Daddy, and she can't move him around. What could we do?"

"We'll cross that bridge when we come to it, but I'm thinking if the right person would plead our case to the draft board in Lexington, they would consider a hardship in this case and you could be reclassified," Leon stated. "That person would be Uncle Roston. He can be well-spoken and you know how persuasive he is. I'll ask him if necessary."

"I still say you're too old to be called. We might just have Uncle

Roston pleading to reclassify you," Robert countered. "Either way, you're right."

From the radio that they sat around after supper in the evenings to the people they came in contact with on their weekly trip to town, the War was the chief topic of every discussion. They went about their normal chores of planting and harvesting, sunup to sundown, working on their land or working in the cotton mills that were the main employers in every small town. Fred, Elsie's husband, worked for Burlington Mills in Batesburg and Robert still worked at Olympia in Columbia. Leon had tried working for a short spell at Burlington, but he longed for the outdoors, quit the mill, and devoted his time to farming and saw milling. It was hard work, but he couldn't stand being cooped up in a windowless building standing in one spot over a loom all day

In the fall, the United States' relationship with Japan became increasingly tense. The two countries argued over United States aid to China, the fact that the United States had frozen Japan's assets in the States, and Japanese troops in Indochina. Japan still had their envoys at their embassy in Washington D.C. but it was all a game of cat and mouse to them. What the Japanese embassy relayed to the Americans was only a ploy, a smoke screen, to divert attention from their real objective: catch the Americans off guard with their pants down.

In the afternoon of the seventh of December 1941, Robert was out at Fairview at Mr. Cleve Padgett's store. He sometimes went there on a Sunday afternoon to socialize with some of the local boys. He always bought a drink and a pack of nabs and just sat around shooting the breeze with the fellows. He had finally saved up enough money to buy a car, paying $90.00 cash money for a 1937

Ford. He sure was proud of his automobile, even if it was basically a three-door car; one of the backdoors was permanently wedged shut. On this Sunday, Robert, Clyde Shumpert, Billy Redfern, Clarence Rogers, Conwell Miller, and Mr. Cleve were sitting around on the front porch of the store, talking and enjoying what was a mild early December afternoon. The temperature was a pleasant fifty-five and the sun was shining from a cloudless blue sky. It was almost two o'clock in the afternoon when Miss Maybelle, Cleve's wife, stuck her head out the door and said, "Cleve, you and them boys better come in here and listen to this bulletin on the radio. The Japs have attacked Pearl Harbor!"

They all scrambled to their feet and hurried inside to listen. The radio announcer was just repeating the news. "This is a special news bulletin, at 7:55 Hawaii time this Sunday morning, December 7th, the Japanese, in an unprovoked attack, dropped bombs on the Pacific Fleet anchored at Pearl Harbor, Hawaii. Over 300 Japanese planes demolished the American ships anchored there. It is believed 18 ships have been sunk or severely damaged, close to 200 of our planes destroyed, mostly on the ground, and an unknown number of American casualties suffered, quite possibly in the thousands. Please stay tuned to this station for further updates, as more current news is available. To repeat, this is a special news bulletin ... "

No one spoke for several minutes as the news announcer repeated the horrible news. They looked at each other ashen-faced. No words could express what each man felt. The Pacific Fleet practically destroyed by a sneak attack! They drifted away quietly, taking their leave with whispered words of disbelief that such a calamity could befall their country. They hurried home to deliver the devastating news to their families.

* * * * *

Robert pulled his car to a stop in the front yard underneath the walnut tree, completely devoid of leaves this time of year. All the way home, his mind reeled with so many thoughts, what an enormous effect this turn of events would have on his country, his friends and his family. He thought of Raymond at Schofield Barracks near Pearl Harbor. Raymond had to be O.K., but how long would it be before they would know for sure? It must have been pure chaos out there in Hawaii; so many Americans killed and injured in a cowardly sneak attack by the Japanese.

He climbed from his car and headed to the house. All seemed so serene on this balmy December day. He saw a flash of red as a cardinal flew from the cedar tree by the front steps. How could everything appear so tranquil here, when the whole world was being engulfed in death and destruction? It was so quiet as he entered the kitchen; he knew the news had already been received. He headed for his daddy's room, where he found Kelly sitting in his rocker beside the fireplace puffing on his pipe and Florence sitting across from him. Both were listening to the radio. Neither spoke as he entered, only looked up as his mother motioned for him to sit on the edge of Kelly's bed. Soon the initial report was over, with the promise of updates delivered as soon as more were available.

The music returned and his father turned to Robert and said, "This means war for sure. President Roosevelt has already asked the Congress for a Declaration of War. All we can do now is pray to the good Lord that our family will stay safe."

They sat glued to the radio the rest of the afternoon and into the night. Leon came home about five and joined them in their vigil beside the radio. He had already heard the news. He had been at Rayflin when the first news bulletin was broadcast over the radio. The next day, December 8th, the United States declared war on Japan.

War, with all its horrors of blood, death, and destruction, was visited on American soil. The Japanese had brought the fight to the American people and they stood steadfastly behind Mr. Roosevelt and their armed services. There was no dissention on the part of any. As Roosevelt said, "December 7, 1941 is a day that will live in infamy. No matter what sacrifices we have to make or how long it takes. we will avenge our countrymen, we will take the fight to the enemy and we will be victorious. The course of our history depends on it."

Three days later, on December 11, Germany and Italy declared war on the United States and the United States declared war on them.

Two weeks later, the American people celebrated Christmas, filled with uncertainty about their future at a time that spoke only of peace and goodwill. President Roosevelt met with Prime Minister Churchill in Washington D.C. before the end of the year. They decided Germany was the prime enemy, the dominant member of the Axis, and Germany's defeat was the key to victory. Even with Japan's attack on Pearl Harbor, Germany had to be defeated first. Only those forces necessary to safeguard our vital interests in the Pacific would be diverted from the European theater of operations. The strategy would be to land in North Africa, invade Italy from there, and knock Italy out of the War, then sweep the German Armies before us from Italy, like leaves before a strong wind. Concentrate on liberating France, Belgium, and the Netherlands, every country the Germans had so callously invaded, push into their homeland, crossing the Rhine all the way to Berlin. It sounded like a gargantuan task, but it had to be done and Roosevelt had every confidence that the American forces, aided by their allies, could accomplish it. Once Germany was defeated, then the Allies could turn to defeating the Japanese. American forces would be fighting the War on two fronts: in Europe and the South Pacific. Kelly was right, there was no way we could sit in the middle between Japan and Germany and not get into this fight.

Twenty-One

1942 DAWNED AND WAR FEVER ENGULFED THE WHOLE OF American life. What was happening in those faraway places where our troops were pushing back the enemy permeated their very being. War rationing began: first tires and gasoline, eventually sugar and meats, and then even soap powder would be hard to come by.

"We can't complain," Americans stated repeatedly, and they didn't. "We know the war effort and the needs of our fighting men are the most important. What they need to fight the enemy, they must have, and we can make do."

They were, after all, the ones in harm's way, not the people at home, or so everyone thought.

In March of 1942, the Defense Council issued a general blackout for all coastal areas. "Them dang German U-boats have been sighted off the Eastern coast and Japanese submarines off the Western," Leon reported after listening to the radio news reports. "No American can afford to be feeling safe even in their homes anymore."

In the cities and towns across America, more and more uniformed men were seen on the streets and posters proclaimed the need to buy war bonds to support the war effort. As more and more men were called into military service and factories converted to the production of war materials, they found their employee base diminishing and the women of America stepped forward to fill the vacancies. This war challenged the whole spectrum of American life.

Elsie took a job at Burlington Mills beside her husband Fred. They had a young son, Tony, and Fred was over thirty, so there was no expectation that he would be called.

Every day, Leon went to the mailbox expecting to receive his draft notice. He knew it was coming; only the timing was uncertain. "I'm prepared to do my duty and serve; my only hope is that I will be called first and not Robert," he hoped. They were both unmarried without children of their own. Therefore, they were not exempt for that reason.

In the spring, Leon planted corn in the lower and upper fields north of the house. He helped Miss Florence plant a garden and he worked three days a week for Mr. Hoyt Senterfeit at his saw mill over near Seivern. Willie Burkett, the black man who helped him make moonshine in the old days, had agreed to help him with the planting, plowing, and harvesting of his corn. Leon knew he could depend on Willie.

* * * * *

The heat of summer arrived with a vengeance by mid-June and by the 4th of July, it was steamy outdoors with high humidity, a norm for the South. Jennie had been good enough to share some of their hog meat from last winter's butchering with Kelly's family.

The day before the fourth, Florence took a pork loin from their saltbox, washed the salt off, wrapped it in layers of heavy foil, and put it in the wood cook stove with a bed of hot embers to slow roast all night. When it was completely done early the next morning, she poured on her special barbeque sauce and sealed it back up to marinate for an hour or so. Cooking in a wood stove in July was a miserable duty, but Florence didn't complain.

I do understand why the South had separate kitchen houses in the past, not just because of the hazard of fire. With this unbearable humidity, standing over *a wood cook stove is mighty miserable,* Florence thought. Every so often, in an attempt to feel a breath of coolness, she retired to the shade of the front porch swing with her cardboard fan, her face red from the heat of the kitchen and sweat beading on her forehead. The back and forth motion of the swing also offered a little relief from the heat.

Florence was expecting company for dinner on the 4th. Miss Ella, Florence's mother, James, Eugene, and his wife Ethel were coming, and Florence looked forward to having family to share their meal. The food was all prepared by 10:00 o'clock. Florence covered the food and set it on the kitchen table, then doused the embers in the cook stove, hoping by noon it would be cooler in that part of the house; they would be eating in the dining room next door with the front and back doors open and the windows up.

It was an extra special celebration this Independence Day with the United States at war. That's what the Fourth of July is about after all, celebrating our freedom and independence. And now that they were being threatened by this war, every American felt much more patriotic this year. Kelly, with Leon's help, made it to the table at dinnertime and afterwards, while Florence, Miss Ella and Ethel washed the dishes, the menfolk, including Kelly, retired to the front porch, smoking, chewing tobacco, and of course discussing the War. It was a bit cooler on the porch; at least you were away from the heat still evident in the kitchen.

The womenfolk joined them after the kitchen was in order and the food put away in the cooling chest Kelly had made years ago. Now ice blocks had to be delivered twice a week from the ice house in Batesburg, but it was well worth the cost in the heat and humidity of this July. The womenfolk sat together on the other side of the porch, fanning with cardboard church fans to create a little breeze after the heat they endured in the kitchen. Florence told them all about her roses, holly hawks and the flowerbed Robert had helped her plant in petunias. Florence always loved her flowers and her sewing. Those were the main topics of their discussion until the menfolk started talking about the war news and who had joined or been drafted that they knew.

"I'm so afraid James will have to go," Miss Ella said in a low voice so only Ethel and Florence could hear. "He doesn't like for me to say that. He says if he is called, he'll be glad to serve, but he's thirty-four years old, not twenty like most of the young soldiers, and his health is not good. Eugene, Will, and Bunyan are older and have families depending on them; I don't have to worry about them so much."

Conversation between the womenfolk stopped as they listened intently to what the men were discussing on their end of the porch. Men, as a general rule, didn't discuss serious topics like the War in front of the women; they felt that was men's business and didn't want to upset the ladies.

Eventually, they became oblivious to the ladies on the other end of the porch in their zeal to share what they had heard. The men reported stories they had heard about the horrors of this war and some of the details were getting pretty graphic. That's when Ella decided to intervene. She felt she, Ethel, and Florence had been en-lightened quite enough through the stories of horror coming from the other end of the porch.

"It sure would be nice to have a little music while we're sitting here on the porch, James," Ella interjected.

Conversation stopped between the men and by the looks on their faces, she could tell they had completely forgotten about the presence of the women.

"That sounds like a good idea, Grandmamma," Robert answered for James. "I'll go inside and get my guitar. Uncle James, you and Uncle Eugene did bring your instruments, didn't you?"

"Why, shore we did. We don't go anywhere very often that we don't carry them along," James replied.

James fetched his guitar and Eugene's banjo from their old A Model Ford and Robert retrieved his guitar from the house. The three commenced to playing and singing, the ladies joining in when they knew the words. It turned out to be quite a celebration, sitting on the front porch, playing and singing all afternoon.

"I'm not as spry as the rest of you, but I sure do enjoy y'all's music and singing," Miss Ella exclaimed with gusto. "Almost makes me feel young again."

Shadows begin to lengthen as the sun dipped in the west over the river swamp. Florence insisted they stay for supper; there was plenty of food left from their dinner. By the time their company departed, darkness had set in completely. As they stepped onto the front porch, a whippoorwill gave its mournful cry from across the road in the woods and crickets were chirping all around.

"Now is the time we should be sitting on the front porch," commented Robert. "It's so much cooler and we would have the crickets and whippoorwills to accompany our singing."

"Well, we would love to stay and enjoy some more of that good music, but it's almost passed my bedtime, Robert," Ella answered with a laugh.

Florence hugged her mother goodbye, standing beside Eugene's Model A. "We were so glad to have all of you for the Fourth, Mamma."

"You know, child, I always like to see all my children for the Fourth. We'll be going to Fannie and Will's tomorrow and Rosalie and Lewis's the next day," Ella replied. "I want to get around and visit my children while I'm still able to go. Y'all take care now, we'll see you soon," she said as she climbed in the backseat beside James, and with a wave to Florence and a smile, they were gone.

Twenty-Two

Ella took sick the next afternoon at Will and Fannie's. They lived over behind Mt. Ebal Church near Batesburg about ten miles from Rayflin. Ella felt extremely tired and nauseous and complained of a hurting in her chest. Eugene went to Batesburg and fetched Dr. Gibson. It just wasn't like Ella to complain. Her children knew she must be feeling mighty bad. Dr. Gibson examined her. His diagnosis - acute indigestion. She passed away at about three a.m. on the sixth of July. She was seventy-four years old, a sweet, kindly little old lady, never had an enemy in the world and no worldly possessions to speak of. James and Eugene arrived at Florence's house before good daylight on the sixth to deliver the sad news to their sister.

Florence was already in the kitchen preparing breakfast on that Monday morning when she heard the automobile drive into the yard and saw the lights reflecting off the kitchen windows. She peeped out just as Eugene and James climbed the porch steps. Knowing it had to be bad news, she hesitated for a minute before opening the door, delaying the inevitable. Eugene knocked on the door and she opened it still in her nightdress. When she saw their pale faces, she knew it had to be Ella.

"It's Mamma. Florence, she died this morning around three over at Fannie and Will's house. We knew wasn't no need to wake you in the middle of night. There was nothing you could do," Eugene said.

Florence burst into to sobs as she stepped back to let her two brothers enter the room.

"Eugene went to Batesburg and fetched Dr. Gibson, but it was no use," James added softly. "He said it was just a case of acute indigestion. She started feeling pretty bad right after dinnertime yesterday and you know Mamma never complained about anything."

"You two sit down and I'll get y'all a cup of coffee," Florence said between sobs. "I'll get dressed, wake Robert up and tell Kelly about Mamma. We'll be going on back over to Will and Fannie with y'all."

The sun was coming up in the east as Robert and Florence climbed into his 1937 Ford. Florence dressed in her one good black dress, carrying a handkerchief she used every so often to dab the tears away. It was a sad thing to know her mother was gone and she didn't even get to tell her goodbye. But Florence knew Ella was saved and in a much better place; no more war or heartbreak for her, just happiness. She believed this with all her being. She was raised on the concept that after death. those who believe are transformed in the twinkling of an eye to be with Jesus in heaven. This was supposed to be a great comfort to those left behind, but the reality was quite different when the loss of someone you love is so sudden.

Eugene and James decided they best better be going to their sister Rosalie's to deliver the news, and Leon stayed with Kelly. As Robert maneuvered his automobile into the dirt road, heading towards his Uncle Will's, he and his mother talked about Ella and what her presence had meant to them both.

"Momma lived a hard life, son. It was so hard on her after Daddy died in 1913. She never had a place she could really call her own. But she made do with what she had. You remember she was born in 1868, just three years after the War Between the States. She used to tell stories about the hardships her family endured, everything her Pa and Ma had they lost after that war, and so many of her kinfolks were killed. Her daddy was a soldier in that war and had to walk all the way home from Virginia after it was over. Her Mamma told her he was barefoot, looked like an old raggedy scarecrow when they saw him coming down the road. After that war, people in the South practically starved to death." Florence began to cry softly as she remembered the hard life her mother had endured. "Well, she won't have to see any more war. This life is over for her. She loved her children and all her grandchildren; they were the most important thing in her life."

"I know Grandmamma Ella was a wonderful person and I loved her too. I don't think she would want us to be sad. She told me one time, 'Don't be sad when I'm gone, rejoice, for I'm heaven bound.'"

Florence was able to muster a little smile at Robert's remark. "That's sounds like something Mamma would say all right. She had a strong faith in the Lord. If only we could all have the kind of faith she did."

The next ten minutes passed with silence between them. Florence was trying to still herself to what lay ahead; seeing her mother's lifeless body lying peacefully in death.

They arrived at Will's and stopped the car under a huge oak in the front yard. There were no other automobiles there. Will didn't own one and they had not had time to alert family and neighbors of Miss Ella's passing. It was a small, unpainted clapboard house, shutters hanging at an angle from the front window, the porch boards sagging on one end. Pretty dilapidated looking, but Fannie kept it sparkling clean inside. She was a great believer in 'cleanliness is next to Godliness' and it was apparent to anyone crossing her threshold. She might not have the fanciest of furniture, rugs, or curtains on the windows, but they were all clean.

Ethel and Fannie met them on the front porch. They both were solemn and their faces were swollen from crying. Miss Ella was their mother-in-law, but they loved her dearly. It was impossible not to love such a kind person, and she treated them like her own daughters. They hugged Florence and Robert; tears began to flow once again as they shared their loss with Florence.

Ethel spoke first. "Miss Ella went peacefully, and Eugene was holding her hand when she passed. Fannie and I have already bathed and dressed her. We thought that would be too difficult for you, Florence. She really looks pretty and so peaceful, just like she's sleeping."

"Come on in, Florence," Fannie said as she took Florence's hand and led her inside. "Miss Ella is on mine and Will's bed. He's been just sitting there, watching over her."

Florence hesitated on the threshold of their bedroom. Will's back was to her and she couldn't see her mother's face with him between them, only her legs and her feet. She was wearing those comfort black Sunday shoes she loved with the stout two-inch heels. For a fleeting second, Florence smiled, remembering Ella would never allow someone's shoes on her good bed covers. Will turned when he heard the commotion behind him; as he turned, Florence could see Ella's face. She walked to the bedside, bent, and hugged her brother, and then stared down into her mother's face.

Ethel and Fannie were right, she thought. *My Mamma sure looks pretty. They have combed and fixed her hair and added just a hint of rouge to her cheeks. She does look like she is just sleeping.* She reached down, gently patted her mother's hand, and said aloud, "We'll be O.K. Mamma, you don't have to worry anymore." Then she turned and left the bedroom, leaving Robert to sit and talk softly with his Uncle Will.

"Eugene and James were going over to tell Rosalie and then up to Batesburg to J.L. Parrish's Funeral Parlor to buy Mamma a coffin," said Will. We talked about having Mamma's funeral service late this afternoon at 6:00 at Mt. Ebal. The weather being hot like it is, we need to get this over with."

"But how about letting all the kinfolk know?" Robert asked. "That doesn't give us a lot of time."

"Eugene and James will be going around letting some of the families know after the noon meal; maybe you can go with them. I'll just sit here beside Mamma and be here for the womenfolk if they need anything. There will be some of the family coming in later on I'm sure."

Mr. Parrish and his hearse carrying Ella's coffin arrived about 11:00, followed by Eugene and James in the Model A. Mr. Parrish and one of his helpers placed Ella in the coffin and pushed it into the front room on a wheeled cart for the viewing. Her body would not be embalmed. A white net cloth with lace edging was placed over the open coffin lid. Family, neighbors, and friends could view the deceased without the fear of flies or other insects assaulting their loved one. Those who had received the news would soon begin to arrive and all would bring food to help feed the bereaved family and guests.

Robert rode with Eugene and James over to New Holland to spread the news of Ella's death to as many of the family as possible. Ella's oldest sister, Mattie Wood, was still living and her children and their families needed to be told. They stopped at Pike Sheppard's, Tandy Kneece's, and Lee Reese's, and then went to Uncle General and Uncle Hamp Abney's, Ella's brothers, to give their family the news of her passing. By the time Eugene, James, and Robert returned at 3:00 PM, the yard at Will and Fannie's house was full of automobiles. Whenever a close family member or friend died, folks dropped whatever they were doing, put on their Sunday best, and just came to console and bring food to the bereaved family.

At six p.m., Mt. Ebal Church was half full of mourners to show respect for a gentle lady. Burial was in the church cemetery, and then the family returned to Will and Fannie's for supper.

Ella Burkett died and was buried the same day. This was necessary because without being embalmed, a body couldn't be kept out in the heat of July. Maybe it was good, too, for the family. Her passing, funeral, and burial were over so quickly; it seemed only as a bad dream. "For what is your life? It is even a vapour, that appearth for a little time, and then vanisheth away." (Holy Bible, James 4:14).

Leon stayed with Kelly the day Miss Ella died. Kelly was not physically able to attend her funeral but he mourned Miss Ella all the same. He and Leon talked about what a kind woman she was, how she made everyone she came in contact with feel at ease.

"We will all miss her gentle ways and that warm smile that she was so quick to share with everyone," Leon remarked. "She was a real Southern lady, which was evident in her words and deeds, always a very humble person; she lived by the golden rule, 'Do unto others as you would have them do unto you.' The world would be a better place if more people remembered that being greedy and putting great value on material things in the end profits you nothing. You certainly won't be taking any earthly gains with you; everyone, rich or poor, are equal in the end," Leon concluded philosophically.

"That is certainly true, son," Kelly replied. "You summed that up right nicely."

Leon walked to the mailbox that same steamy July sixth; as he took the mail from the box, he noticed the brown envelope. Turning the envelope over, he saw the stamp across the top: Official Business Department of Defense and underneath his name and address. He knew it was his draft notice; well, at least he didn't have to worry about when it would arrive anymore. He walked to the house, stepped on to the porch, and sat down in the double red oak rocker his daddy had made. Slipping the thin sheet from the envelope, he unfolded the sheet and read:

THE PRESIDENT OF THE UNITED STATES
To: Leon Odelle Gantt
Order# 247

Greetings: Having submitted yourself to a local board composed of your neighbors for the purpose of determining the place and time in which you can best serve the United States in the present emergency, you are hereby notified that you have now been selected for immediate military service.

You will therefore, report to the local board named below at Lexington Courthouse at 8:00 A.M. on the 20th day of July 1942 for military duty, dependence upon your physical and mental examination performed on that day, you will take an oath to affirm your allegiance to the United States. From and after the day and hour just named you will be a soldier in the military service of the United States.

Draft Board # 53

With Kindest Regards

Franklin D. Roosevelt

Twenty-Three

AS ROBERT OPENED HIS EYES AT DAYBREAK ON THE TWENTI-eth of July, he heard voices coming from the kitchen and could smell coffee brewing and fatback frying.

Mamma's cooking breakfast for Leon this morning before we leave for Lexington, he thought. He had requested the day off so he could take Leon to Lexington, and it had been approved.

He wearily sat up on the side of the bed and reached for his pants thrown across a nearby chair. He slept only in his boxer shorts and a sleeveless t-shirt, but with the heat of July, it was impossible to get a restful night's sleep. He had fanned with a cardboard church fan until he fell asleep, then awoke drenched in sweat and fanned some more until he fell back to sleep. That happened at intervals all night long. Even with the window up in the bedroom and nothing between him and the outdoors but a screen to keep the mosquitoes at bay, the heat was almost smothering. He stood up, stretched, and padded barefoot through the dining room into the kitchen.

Florence was standing over the cook stove, egg turner in one hand, frying flapjacks in a black iron skillet. A platter of fried fatback sat on the back-stove eye and another covered pot sat on the front. *A big pot of grits no doubt,* Robert figured. Leon was sitting at the table, fully dressed, sipping coffee and giving Miss Florence instructions about the corn crop ripening in the fields.

"Willie knows what to do with the corn, Miss Florence, he'll get a couple of fellows to help pull the ears and see about selling what y'all don't need for yourselves or the animals. I know we can trust him and y'all can pay Willie and the boys a little out of the proceeds."

Robert spoke up. "No need to worry about the corn, I'll help Willie harvest it and come fall, we'll get the fodder pulled off and the stalks cut. That is if Uncle Sam don't call me first. By the way, brother, how can you drink hot coffee in this weather? I would rather have a cool glass of water."

"Well, good morning," Leon said as he turned and looked at Robert standing in the doorway. "I thought I heard you getting up. As far as my drinking hot coffee, I guess old habits die hard. Got to have my cup of coffee in the mornings, no matter the weather. Of course, I did add a chip of ice to cool it down a bit, so it's not steaming. And I know you can take care of the harvest, Robert, but how about that job of yours in Columbia?

"It will be fine. I'm still working the graveyard shift, you know." Robert had taken a new job at Olympic Mills in Columbia in '42 working third shift, the graveyard shift it was commonly called, from 11:00 PM until 7:00 AM. It was a cotton mill that weaved material for the War effort. When Robert went to work, he rode with a few fellows from the Fairview area.

Every employee at the mill was given a nickname. The day Robert was changed to the graveyard shift, another man was hired; they became the twosome of the Lone Ranger and Tonto to their shift mates. Robert was called Tonto at work. Robert didn't mind the nicknames. Somehow it made it easier if a fellow you knew by a nickname went to war and didn't return. That way you didn't get too involved in their personal lives just to lose someone you had grown close to. He had already lost one good friend, Billy Redfern. Robert and Billy were good friends. Billy was killed in France and buried 'over there.' Robert never learned too many details about his friend's death, but he knew his family as well, so that made it hard.

"I'll come home and sleep some after my shift, then help Willie and his boys in the afternoon and on the weekends. Willie can manage without me anyway. He's better at farming than I am any day of the week. I know we can trust him. He worked a lot of years down at Rayflin in the fields down there," replied Robert. "I'll stay at Olympia as long as I can and have riders to carpool with. I couldn't afford the gas if it was just me and eventually I may have to quit; some of the guys in the carpool will probably be called into service. If that happens, then I'll get some work around here, maybe driving a logging truck for Mr. Senterfeit or Mr. Wilson. I'll cross that bridge when I come to it. I'm not worried. It will work out, I'm sure."

"It sure will be a relief to me to know you are here to handle things and we have Willie to depend on with the crops," Leon replied.

Florence spoke up. "Leon, don't you be worrying a bit about me and your daddy. Robert will be here and we'll all be fine. Now, you two sit down and have your breakfast. It's almost six and y'all have to be over at Lexington by eight a.m. I'm not familiar with the military, but I do believe they would not appreciate tardiness on any account."

While Leon and Robert sat and enjoyed their breakfast together,

Florence fixed Kelly's tray and took it to his room. She returned and sat down at the table with the two young men; they talked about the crops that needed harvesting, the family down at Rayflin, and Leon asked how all her folks were getting along without Miss Ella. She appreciated his asking, but the one thing they did not talk about was his impending departure for the Service. She knew Leon wasn't anxious for himself; he just worried about Kelly and the fact he might be away from home for a long time. Reassuring him the best she could, she said, "Your daddy has been feeling really good lately, except for his paralysis, he claims he feels just fine. I don't want your Daddy's condition weighing on your mind; no matter how long the war lasts, he'll be waiting to see you when you come home."

By seven-fifteen, Leon and Robert were ready to go to Lexington. Leon had told his daddy goodbye, saying, "I'll probably be back this afternoon, Daddy. The boys I have talked to that have been examined were sent home for a couple of weeks before they had to report for duty."

"I hope so, son. I look forward to any time we get to spend together before you are called away."

The brothers just enjoyed each other's company on the trip to Lexington. They had all the windows in Robert's old 37 Ford rolled down, and with the car zipping along, the breeze felt good. Everything by the road was a lush green in the early morning light. They passed fields of corn, stalks high as a man's head, just waiting to be harvested. When they crossed the bridge at Black Creek, there were two young boys about twelve years of age fishing from the bridge with cane poles.

"Let's just hope and pray this war is over before those young fellows are old enough to be called," Leon said. "They're at the best age of their lives and just don't realize it. I didn't either when I was their age. I'm sure they don't. No young boy worries about the future; all they're worrying about is catching a fish to take home for dinner. And that's the way it should be. When you're young like them two, you leave the worrying to the grown-ups. Speaking of worrying about the future, I talked to Uncle Roston yesterday down at Rayflin. He says he'll be glad to go with you to Lexington next week to talk with the folks at the Draft Board about changing your classification. You know Daddy and Miss Florence can't get by with both of us gone in this war."

"I know you're right about that," Robert replied. "I'm glad Uncle Roston agreed to go with me. He can explain the situation a lot better than me."

* * * * *

Fifteen minutes later, they entered the outskirts of the small town of Lexington. There were probably close to two thousand people living within the town limits and a big granite courthouse was located right smack in the middle of town. It was the county seat and all-important business for the county of Lexington was centered here: The Sheriff's office, Health Board, tax office and the Draft Board. The courthouse itself housed the Clerk of Court and the Probate Judge's offices.

As they turned into the driveway beside the granite courthouse, they saw the olive-green school bus with U.S. Army painted in gold letters on the side. A man in uniform stood beside the door with a clipboard, checking off the names of the new recruits as they stepped up into the bus. Neither Leon nor Robert could tell by the uniform what rank that soldier held; they didn't know a lot about rank or insignia when it came to the military. They could only tell that was the person in charge. Robert pulled the car into a parking space about twenty yards away from the bus and switched off the motor.

"I guess this is it and that is my ride," Leon said, gesturing towards the Army bus." He lifted the door handle and swung the door outwards.

"Do you want me to come back over here late this evening?"

"No, if they bring us back after we're examined, I'll catch a ride to Fairview and get one of the fellows from Mr. Cleve's to bring me on home. You know there's always somebody hanging around out at his store in the evenings that will give me ride. See you later."

Leon stepped out and headed towards the parked bus. Robert cranked the Ford, put it in reverse, and pulled away. He looked back but Leon never turned. He was standing before the soldier with the clipboard and then stepped on to the bus, out of sight.

* * * * *

As Leon walked towards the rear of the bus, he began to look around and observe his fellow passengers. Every seat was full of young men; some looked like raw-boned farm boys, others probably mill workers with less exposure to the sun. A few Leon could tell were from the upper class, young men from wealthy families who never did a day's hard work in their lives. He could tell by their manner of dress, the cut of their hair, and their hands: clean, manicured nails and no calluses. They pretty well represented the diversity of the county. Of course, there were no blacks among them. The other major difference Leon noticed between the others and himself was their age; they all looked to be between nineteen and twenty-five; he, being almost thirty-two, was the oldest among these new recruits. He took a seat near the rear of the bus with a big, tall young fellow and introduced himself.

"I'm Leon Gantt from near Fairview," he said as he extended his hand.

"Please to meet you, sir. My name is Tom Jeffcoat and I live near Salley. You ever heard of Salley?"

"Sure have, I used to know a couple of folks from down that way." Pretty soon, he and Tom were practically related, because of course Tom knew exactly who Leon was talking about. That is pretty much the way it is in the South; you know somebody with the same last name or from the same general location, and you find out what a small world it really is. Leon introduced himself to the others sitting around him and they got to talking about where they were from and who they knew, and within fifteen minutes, a lively conservation was going on in the back of the bus.

The soldier in charge stood up in the front of the bus and asked loudly but politely for everyone's attention.

"I am Sergeant Joseph Thomas and I will be overseeing your trip to Camp Jackson today. We will be arriving at Camp Jackson about 0930 hours; you will be transported to the reception center at the camp. There you will be examined by a group of doctors to determine if you are fit for military service. You will then be transported to the mess hall for chow. Everyone will return to the reception center, where those of you that passed their physical examinations will be administered the oath of allegiance to the United States and will be taken on a brief tour of the base to familiarize yourself with where you should report for duty. This bus will transport all of you back to Lexington Courthouse this afternoon around 1600 hours and you will be allowed to go back to your homes and families for two weeks to get your affairs in order. You will be required to report back to Camp Jackson on Monday, August 3, to begin your service in the United States Army. Orders to that effect will be issued to you before you leave the base today. Any of you that fail the physical will remain at the reception center and will be picked up by this bus when the tour is over. Any questions?"

Not a man raised his hand. The sergeant had pretty well told them what they needed to know. A few did not understand his use of military time, but they would ask one of the other fellows in private so as not to appear totally ignorant. The remaining forty-five minutes of the trip passed by in relative silence. Every guy on board was thinking of the gravity of the situation: only two weeks at home and then God knows where Uncle Sam would send him. They would no longer belong to themselves; they would basically be the property of the U.S. Army until the war is over.

Soon, they were in Columbia heading towards the northwest outskirts of the city and the military installation known as Camp Jackson, named for South Carolina native Andrew Jackson. As they went through the gate, the bus stopped at the guard shack and Sergeant Thomas opened the bus door, spoke briefly with the armed guards, and then they were allowed to proceed through the gate.

They passed row upon row of neat mustard-colored one-storied buildings with green tin roofs. Soldiers were everywhere, uniformed men marching in orderly rows, holding their rifles at their right side, barrels aimed skyward, men wearing olive green shorts and tee shirts jogging by, singing in cadence, and uniformed men lounging beside the buildings talking and smoking. The bus stopped in front of a large two-storied building with a sign over the front entrance proclaiming it as the Reception Center.

"Men, exit in an orderly fashion and line up outside the bus," Sergeant Thomas said loudly from the front of the bus. "I want to call roll, please answer present when your name is called."

After Sergeant Thomas finished a roll call of the new recruits standing apprehensively beside the bus, he led them single file inside the Reception Center and directed them to a locker room.

"Undress down to your shorts and tee shirt and deposit your clothes in one of these lockers," Thomas shouted as he banged his hand on the nearest one. "You have ten minutes, then line up in the hallway outside. I'll escort you to the examination room."

Ten minutes later, Thomas led them into a gymnasium-sized room at the back of the building. There were army medics and doctors in white standing at stations around the perimeter of the room and each man proceeded to a station. At the first station Leon visited, a medic clamped an examination form on a clipboard, filled out pertinent information as to name, address, date of birth, and recorded his height and weight. Each subsequent station he proceeded to, he handed the clipboard to the examiner, and they wrote the results of whatever test they were administering to him on the form. He had his vision and hearing checked. A doctor listened to his heartbeat with a stethoscope; a medic checked his pulse, blood pressure, and his reflexes. Even his feet were checked for fallen arches. They probed, pinched, and prodded him and his fellow recruits until they were satisfied that every inch of their bodies had been evaluated and every important question answered that would affect their physical requirements for service in the United States Army. When the results of the last test were entered on his examination form, Leon was directed to a table at the end of the room. Seated behind the table was a man in uniform.

"May I see that clipboard, young man?" he said as he extended his hand. "I'm Doctor Bradley and it is my job to review your test results." Scanning the form quickly, he glanced up at Leon. "Congratulations, Mr. Gantt, you passed your physical. Welcome to the U.S. Army," he said as he extended his hand to shake Leon's. "Now, if you will proceed through the door to your left, a medic will administer your vaccinations."

* * * * *

Leon's remaining two weeks at home passed quickly. He, Willie, and Robert harvested the corn, and every afternoon, Leon spent at least an hour sitting with Kelly and just talking. He was so afraid that once he was in service, he might not see his father again. It could be years before he came home, and he realized his father very likely could pass away during that time. And who could say, Leon himself might die on some battlefield on the other side of the world. When not in the fields with Willie and Robert or talking with his daddy, Leon spent his time visiting his kinfolks and friends. A lot could change when a body was out of touch with home for years. There would, of course, be letters back and forth. Leon knew Robert would be writing to him, but with the uncertainty of War and the chaos of the battlefront, chances were, news from home would be sparse.

Roston had accompanied Robert to Lexington on twenty-seventh of July to meet with the Draft Board. Roston was able to explain Kelly's handicap and his and Florence's dependence on Robert's presence in such a way that no doubt was left in the board members' minds that this other son had to be home for them. The draft board only took about ten minutes to confer and they agreed the classification would be changed from 1A to 3D: deferment due to extreme hardship on the family. Once the draft board agreed to Robert's reclassification, he and his Uncle Roston stood and headed for the door.

"This boy really needs to be with his parents, and we do appreciate your help and understanding of the situation," Roston told the board as they left closing the door quietly behind them.

"I wouldn't worry too much about Leon," Roston turned to Robert and said when they climbed into Robert's '37 Ford.

"Your cousin Margaret informed me yesterday that my son-in-law, Haskell, had quit his job and joined the Army. The War will probably be over in six months; Haskell Rawls won't hold no job for more than six months. I grant you, either the War will be over, or Haskell will find some way to get back. Wouldn't want to ruin his record, you know." Sure enough, Roston knew his son-in-law pretty well. Haskell was back at home in four months with some sort of medical disability.

* * * * *

On Monday, the 3rd day of August 1942, Robert and Leon once again made the trip to Lexington in Robert's '37 Ford. It was hard for Leon to say goodbye to his father and Miss Florence. Never a man given to shows of affection, he briefly hugged his father, saying, "Daddy, I'll be back when this War is over, you take care of yourself, and don't be trying to get around with that walking stick by yourself."

"Don't worry about me, son, you just watch out for yourself. Florence, Robert, and myself will be waiting here when you get home."

Sitting in the parked car at the courthouse, Leon turned to Robert. "I'm depending on you to take care of Daddy while I'm gone and to write me and let me know how things are at home." With a brief goodbye and "I'll see you when it's over," Leon climbed from the car and headed to the Army bus.

On the 8th of August, Kelly Gantt received an official postcard from the U.S. Army.... *This is to advise you that the person named below arrived this station, August 3, 1942.... Private Leon O. Gantt.* An address where to send mail to Private Gantt was also included. On the same day, Robert received a postcard from Leon.

"Hello Robert how are you and the rest, guess Dad is getting along alright this card leaves me doing very well I guess. Robert don't write me to this address for we will be leaving here in a few days and I might not get it. Wait till you hear from me again."

It was signed *From Leon.*

A letter addressed to Robert was received a week later. Leon was sent to Fort Eustis Virginia; he went through six weeks basic training there. It was a struggle for a man of his age compared to the young guys of nineteen. Fortunately, he was in good physical shape due to years of hard work saw milling, pushing a plow, and running through the swamps and woods of home ahead of the law. Marching seemed to be the main order of the day; that, and pushups. They also spent a fair amount of time climbing over walls, up ropes, and crawling on their bellies under barbed wire while live rounds were whizzing overhead. Target practice was about the only thing Leon enjoyed and he was good at it. He could shoot no doubt because Southern men, especially farm boys, learned at an early age a lot of their food depended on their hunting abilities and their proficiency with a gun. He, of course, won a marksmanship medal in Basic Training. Some evenings, his Company would march clean to the James River, stack their rifles, eat cold K rations, and prepare to bed down. Each soldier was issued a tent shelter half made of water repellant canvas, 1 center pole, tent pegs for one side and a rope. This meant you had to have a buddy with his shelter half, center pole, and pegs in order to construct a two-man pup tent.

Each man had two wool army blankets: one to lie on and one for cover. Fires were generally not needed. The men would rather eat their food cold. It was, after all, August in Virginia, and besides, seemed like the mosquitoes were worse with a fire burning. The soldiers were also issued mosquito repellent, which was more important to them lying on the ground near the James River in August than the extra blanket. Next morning at dawn, they would pack up and head back to the barracks, then hit the mess hall for chow. First order of business after chow was cleaning their rifles that had been stacked in that old heavy dew that settled in the hollows and along the banks of the James River.

Leon completed his basic training after six weeks and was issued a three-day pass, but he didn't come home. It was just too far for such a short visit. He reported to Camp Edwards, Massachusetts, in mid-October for advanced training. Leon was now a member of Battery I, 505th Anti-aircraft Artillery. He trained for six weeks at Camp Edwards, then left for Foreign Service.

Twenty-Four

LEON ARRIVED BY TRUCK CONVOY AT CAMP SHANKS, NEW York, about four o'clock in the evening of December 6, 1942. Camp Shanks, twenty miles south of New York City, was a staging area for soldiers shipping out to the European Theater of Operations. The main function of Camp Shanks and other staging areas was to ensure that every soldier was fully equipped before leaving the States for Foreign Service. The soldiers in transit at Camp Shanks were housed in 100-foot-long buildings with bunks lining the walls on both side and four potbellied wood stoves at intervals down the center. These four stoves furnished the only heat in the long building. When Leon and his fellow soldiers arrived in early December, snow covered the ground and it was bitterly cold.

"Damn, it sure is cold," a private remarked, rubbing his gloved hands together after climbing from the back of the deuce and a half ton truck. Other soldiers in Leon's platoon began to spill from the back of the trucks, jumping onto the frozen ground in front of the barracks. As they entered, faced with the sheer size of the long building and the inadequate heat source, more men began to complain about the cold and the shoddy conditions in the long drafty building. Quick thinking soldiers immediately claimed the bunks closest to the potbellied stoves and those on the outer fringes of the radiated warmth began to mutter to themselves and grumble for all to hear.

"Why aren't you complaining, Gantt?" Private Winslow from Pennsylvania asked. "Everybody else is."

"Well, I was just thinking of the time I jumped in the North Edisto River wading in water up to my neck in the dead of winter. Ice coated the trees and snow covered the ground. I've endured more unpleasant situations than this and I figure we'll have a lot worse conditions to contend with in this War. I'm saving my complaining to when I really have something to complain about. At least we have a roof over our heads. Wait till we get where we're going, we'll think this place was just like our own warm beds at home. We'll be sleeping in a lot worse places, I grant you, than this."

Platoon Leader Lieutenant Brown entered the barracks and every soldier snapped to attention.

"At ease, men, all of you need to get some chow and a good night's sleep. In the morning at 0600 hours, our company will officially be notified that we are on "alert" status. That means we will be shipping out within twelve hours from the time that status is announced. I want all of you to check your equipment; we will have final field inspection at 0900 hours. If any of you need equipment or other essentials, it will be noted at final field inspection so that any shortage can be corrected. Get a good night's sleep, boys; you're going to need it."

* * * * *

Just as the sun was setting in the west on the 7th of December, one year after Pearl Harbor, Leon's platoon fell in outside the barracks. Roll was called and instructions were given before their departure as to what lay ahead. Every man stood at attention, his duffel bag on the ground at his feet and a backpack strapped on his back. Everything they needed had to be carried with them. They were informed that they were sailing for England, but their destination beyond that would remain a mystery. Their platoon sergeant instructed them to remove their division sleeve patches for security sake; spies could be anywhere. He chalked each man's helmet with a letter and number to indicate their marching order and the rail car they would ride on.

"Atten-hut! Right face! Forward March!" Sergeant Bonner shouted, and they were off, headed east for the train depot a mile away. All was quiet in the ranks; the only sound was the crunch of hundreds of boots in the hard-packed snow. The men marched like robots, automatically moving one foot in front of the other, accustomed to the rhythm of the march, minds hundreds of miles away on home or what lay ahead. Fighting men off to War, not for glory but fulfilling an obligation to home and country. Within twenty minutes, they were at the depot. They boarded the rail cars in an orderly manner, according to their instructions, and silently began a short train ride to the New Jersey docks. From the docks, a harbor boat ferried them to their troopship, but in the case of Leon's company, to pier 90 in New York Harbor. They were sailing to England on the Queen Mary, a monster of a ship, and had to board from the pier.

After more than two hours of silent marching, loading and unloading from a rail car and a harbor boat, the men of Battery I stood at ease in orderly rows on the pier in New York Harbor. The city of New York was under a blackout; the small flashlights of the officers among them occasionally pierced the darkness. Conversation was at a minimum; the men stood quietly waiting for their officers to issue the command to board. They were instructed to line up single file according to the letter and number chalked on their helmets. Entering a huge warehouse, a short distance back from the pier, they faced semi darkness; the only light was from small blue bulbs in the ceiling above their heads and not a lot of them. They were instructed to climb stairs to the second floor; a soldier with a clipboard stood beside an open door with a gangplank extending to the Queen Mary. It was his job to make sure the men were loaded in an orderly manner. The soldier called out his number and Leon yelled, "Gantt." The number matched the name on the clipboard and he was allowed to cross the gangplank onto the ship.

And what a ship she was. The Queen Mary was a speedy luxury liner, the plum of the Cunard Line, converted to a troop ship. She was huge, 1019 feet long and 118 feet wide. With a displacement of 81,237 tons, she could travel at speeds up to 28.5 knots. Once the war began, she was painted camouflage gray and all her luxurious fittings were removed; bunk beds were installed to carry troops. She could carry up to 16,000 passengers, an entire division. Nicknamed the 'gray ghost,' she could move so fast, she frequently outran other ships in her convoy, even traveling in a zigzag pattern to avoid enemy subs.

Leon was impressed by the sheer size of the ship and the craftsmanship evident in her construction. Beautiful paintings still hung on her walls and brilliant cut glass chandeliers dangled from her ceilings. The passengers on Leon's crossing, including the crew, numbered over 11,300 souls. It was past midnight on the 8th of December before all the troops were loaded and the men were billeted to assigned quarters. Finally, the ship got underway. She slowly pulled away from Pier 90, guided out of New York harbor by four tugboats. She slipped silently past the Statue of Liberty, silhouetted against the blackness of the New York skyline, and out to the open sea. An escort and other smaller troop ships joined her.

Describing the crossing later to Robert, Leon would recall, "For six days and nights, the Queen Mary would sail in a zigzag pattern across the North Atlantic. The third day of the crossing, a strong wind from the north assaulted the ships in the convoy and the seas became violent. The ships sliced through waves reported high as seventy-five feet. Many of the troops became seasick and the stench below decks was almost unbearable. I saw men lying flat on their backs, throwing up straight into the air."

Sleeping on an upper bunk some eight feet above the floor, he was awakened during that third night at sea when the wind and waves were at their worst. The sound of voices below awakened him from his restless slumber. He peeped over the side of his swinging bunk to see two crewmembers mopping water from the floor.

"Hey down there, boys, what's with the mopping in the middle of the night?"

Looking up into Leon's face, an old man with a grisly gray beard paused in his mopping motion long enough to reply.

"Sorry to wake you, soldier, but some son of a bitch left a porthole open, and going through these rough waves, the sea splashed in. Got to get this water mopped up before you fellows fall out at daylight."

The seas calmed on the morning of the fourth day of the crossing, but the rough waves and the frigid temperatures left the decks of the Queen Mary coated with ice. No one was allowed outside on the deck unless his job required it. It was too precarious for soldiers just seeking some fresh air. By noon of the fifth day, with calmer seas and ice melting on her decks, the men were allowed outside to enjoy the fresh, crisp air above decks. It was a welcome respite from the stale air below, heavy with the stench of the vomit from seasick soldiers. They were entering the Gulf Stream that flowed northward from the equator to the British Isles, and the air and water temperatures increased. The soldiers leaned on her rails, wool scarves wrapped around their necks and heavy field jackets snapped completely closed against the crisp air, smoking and talking. There were those among the men who offered their opinions freely to anyone willing to lend an ear, especially about their final destination.

"I say this company is heading to Italy," Private Zarrillo calmly stated between puffs on his cigarette.

Zarrillo was an Italian from Brooklyn, New York, and his fellow comrades soon learned he had an opinion about everything. "And I have some kinfolks I just might look up once we get there."

"Hell, Zarrillo, that's just your opinion, none of us have a clue and that's the way Uncle Sam wants it. Your opinions don't count for nothing. You know what they say about opinions, just like an asshole, everybody has one," commented young Private Calvin Baxter from Texas. All the guys just called him 'Tex.'

The guys standing in a tight group on the deck all laughed at Baxter's remark, nodding their heads in agreement.

"Tex has sure got you pegged, Zarillo. All you have is an opinion, and you know that don't count for much in this man's army. Isn't that right, Gantt?" PFC Nelson directed at Leon.

"Gantt, what do you think?" Zarillo asked. "I know we all have an opinion, like Tex said." All the men respected Leon; he was much older than most of the soldiers, and not easily excited. He was always so calm and matter-of-fact about everything, and did his job without complaining; he was the sort of fellow you would want beside you in a foxhole under fire. They were all interested in his opinion.

"Well, boys, I don't rightly know where we might be going and I ain't about to get myself all in a quandary trying to guess. I'll go where I'm told and let the higher ups decide where that might be. I suggest you boys don't worry too much about our destination either, just follow orders and do your job."

This would be the topic of conversation many times. Soldiers going to the battlefront were always trying to figure out the next move; they wondered where they and their comrades would be tomorrow. The wondering preyed on the minds of all; in War, someone with higher rank is always the author of your destiny.

* * * * *

The morning of the seventh day, the troops on board the Queen Mary awoke to a clear, cold, sunny day off the coast of Scotland. Most ships could sail up the Clyde River to Glasgow, but not the Queen Mary; she was too big to dock. The troops disembarked onto smaller boats and were taken to shore in Glasgow. From there, Leon and his company took a train to Liverpool, England. For two months, Battery I of the 505th drilled and trained in England, just awaiting orders that would send them into the battle zone.

Leon wrote only one letter home while he was in England, just to say he was okay and to give Robert instructions as to how to address letters to him overseas. His main concern was the health of his Daddy, Kelly, but he knew his letters home would be few and far between; he would have to depend on Robert's replies to keep him informed on that score. Circumstances back home at Rayflin could change suddenly and here he was four thousand miles away. It was a worry that would keep him awake at night and remain close to the surface of his consciousness every waking hour. These thoughts of anguish were only to be cloaked by the more important business of duty and staying alive to get back home. He was careful to put 'somewhere in England' at the top of this letter. Leon was well aware of the importance of secrecy in his correspondence. He knew all letters sent home by soldiers were highly censored and the names of towns and other identifying clues as to the G.I.'s whereabouts were blacked out. Since England was the major stepping stone for all U.S. forces being deployed to the front, no mention could be made of where he actually was or the name of his company.

On the 3rd day of February he finally received a reply from Robert assuring him that all was well with the folks at home. On the 22nd of February, Leon's Company finally left England, their destination … North Africa.

Twenty-Five

AT HOME IN SOUTH CAROLINA, THAT FEBRUARY OF 1943 THE
weather was extremely cold. January and February, being the cold-
est months of the year, folks expected frigid temperatures at night-
time but even by noon most days it was still freezing outdoors. The
wind whistled around the corners of the house rattling the windowpanes and the cold air seeped through cracks around the doors and
windows. Keeping the fires fed in the fireplaces in the kitchen and
in Kelly's bedroom kept Florence busy.

True to Robert's prediction, one day in February at supper he
delivered the news to his Daddy and Mamma, "I had to quit the job
at Olympia in Columbia today, because of the gas shortage and the
shortage of men that could ride with me to share the gas expense, I
knew I couldn't afford to drive that distance by myself."

"You do what you have to son," remarked Kelly. "You'll find
something else to do, there's always the need for workers cutting
pulpwood, especially with the shortage of men at home. "That's one
job few women folks are physically able to do."

Soon Robert did find work. He was now working cutting pulpwood.

In the mornings before work Robert would build up the fires

and make sure there was plenty of wood in the boxes; in the evenings he would refill the wood boxes and make sure the fires were banked with plenty of hot coals to last through the night. During the day when Robert was working, Florence kept the fires going. At least now with Robert's job sawmilling, he was not so far from home. Some days he was able to stop by when driving a logging truck just to check on his daddy and mamma.

By the end of February, two ice storms had already hit South Carolina and the temperature hovered barely above the freezing mark the whole month. Ten-inch long icicles hung from the eaves of the house and smokehouse for nearly a week before finally melting in the winter sun. The hard freeze of that February was rough on people acclimated to mild winters and humid Southern summers.

* * * * *

Leon seemed to be faring better in England as far as the weather was concerned. The climate in England was not much difference from home due to the Gulf Stream, and from Leon's letter, Robert gathered not nearly as cold as what they were experiencing. Leon described the England in his letter: "I have seen lush green pastures and forests and the local people I have met are generous and friendly. The British people by and large seem glad to have the 'yanks,' as they called us, in their country." It did kinda rankle Leon to be referred to as a yank, being from south of the Mason Dixon line.

He wrote in his letter from England about some of the fellows he served with: "I feel like an old man living with all these young kids, and they remind me often enough about my age. But they're a bunch of good guys and we get along fine. Uncle Sam is feeding us three squares a day, but we need it with all the training we're doing. That's all we're doing day in and day out, training. I just want to get this fight over with so I can get back home."

Of course, Leon never mentioned exactly where in England he was or the nature of their training. He knew better than that. In closing, he said he was fine, not to worry about him and to write to his APO address; it should catch up to him eventually wherever he would be. He just signed his letter *Leon*.

Kelly helped dictate to Robert what to write Leon in return. "Just tell him I'm the same, feeling just fine except for this damnable infirmity. Tell him we miss him and mention to him that his Grandma Peninnah at Rayflin and all the other kinfolks are doing very well. Better tell him too that Asia had a heart attack and passed away last month. I know he will hate to hear that, Asia was always such an entertaining fool. We all have some good memories of Asia," Kelly concluded.

After adding some thoughts of his own about the hard freeze they were experiencing and how things were going with his job, Robert put the letter in the mailbox on the twenty-seventh of February with postage money and put the flag up. The mailman picked it up the next morning and it was on its way to the other side of the world. All they could do was say a prayer for Leon every night; they had no idea when or if he would receive the letter or where he might be when it finally arrived. They just had to wait for his reply.

It was like that with all families who sent their men folks off to the War. They could only sit by the radio and listen to the news reports about the progress of their troops, but had no idea where their loved one actually was unless the soldier was more of a letter writer than Leon. Robert didn't expect to hear from Leon for a while; he never had been one to ramble on about pleasantries in letters or in conversations for that matter. He said what was necessary and that was it.

Kelly spent his days in the rocker beside the fireplace, puffing on his pipe and listening to the radio. He had very few visitors during the week; gasoline was already rationed, with stamps issued giving each adult the right to purchase so many gallons a month according to their occupation. If you used up all your ration stamps at the beginning of the month, you just had to do without until the next month. Only folks whose profession was considered important to the war effort qualified for unlimited rationing stamps. Robert's employer, Grover Wilson, being in the pulpwood business was one of these. He would sometimes give Robert some extra stamps so Robert could buy more gas during the month.

Folks didn't travel frivolously; they only traveled to and from work, reserving Sundays for going to church and visiting their kinfolks. Sunday was the only day Kelly expected to see anybody besides Robert and Florence. On Sunday, they frequently had visitors for dinner, some of Florence or Kelly's kinfolks.

Florence almost always killed one of her chickens for Sunday dinner. She would say, "You just can't beat fried chicken, gravy, and rice for Sunday dinner. Add a few of my canned vegetables and some biscuits, and it's a meal."

Sundays were so special when they had company. They ate very little meat the rest of the week, only rabbits Robert caught in boxes or game he killed hunting on Saturday afternoon with Kelly's old double-barreled shotgun. Fat back and bacon was reserved for breakfast when Jennie was kind enough to share from their smoke-house. Olin, Jennie, and their boys still butchered a couple of hogs in late autumn. Peninnah and Jennie would make the sausage, mostly Jennie. Her momma was in her early 80s, but Peninnah was good at supervising. Kelly had no animals left except for the old milk cow and the mule they kept to plow and hook to the wagon.

Once in a while on a Sunday, Robert would help his daddy into the old 37 Ford and they would go to Elsie and Fred's for dinner. Kelly spent most of his time alone in his room, just sitting and puffing. No matter how alone he felt, the sounds of War were never far away.

There was constant news of the War broadcast over the radio in his room, and B25s flew over their house night and day from the Columbia Air Base; it was a training center for B25 pilots and their crews. 'Bombing Range Island' in the middle of Lake Murray was where they practiced precision bombing. At night, the island was circled with lights so that the pilots and crews in training could practice dropping the fake bombs on target. All went well with that exercise until one night a pilot mistook the lights from houses around the traffic circle above Batesburg for the island and dropped his load there, scaring the daylights out of the residents.

****

As the War progressed through the year of 1943, the United States increased the rationing stamp program. The needs of the fighting men had to come first. It took unimaginable amounts of everything to supply the millions of men fighting in the armed services of the United States. It was beginning to get tight at home; tires, meat, sugar, shoes, flour, and almost every item that could go towards the War effort was rationed. The factories producing these products began to run low on manpower, so many men were being taken away to serve. For the first time in America's history, women were called on in great numbers to leave their homes and join the work force, just like Elsie had earlier. The cotton mill produced cloth on their looms that ran around the clock. Three shifts of workers kept the looms humming twenty-four hours a day making cloth that was needed for uniforms, tents, mattress covers, and body bags.

* * * * *

"A lady working for the State is here to visit you, Kelly," Florence announced one day in January of 1943. "The State lady will help you fill out the papers necessary for you to receive state assistance due to your disabled state," Florence continued.

"Don't worry, Florence, I'm not too prideful to except help from the state; we need every penny and I don't mind having the company. Is she pretty? Not that I mind looking at you, Florence. Do send her in; I'll be glad to answer her questions."

The visit went well and Kelly did enjoy having someone new to talk to. At the conclusion of the interview, it was determined Kelly would receive $7.00 a month and he was glad he would be receiving that.

Robert's job working for Grover Wilson paid $2.00 a day. That and the welfare stipend Kelly would now receive would help them manage, but they had to be frugal.

Things were tough at home. The country was coming out of the Depression with the tremendous increase in production, but the Depression had taught some valuable lessons to Americans. Schooled by the Depression years, Florence knew how to make things last, and how to get every ounce of good out of everything, whether it was mending clothes, patching the soles of their shoes, canning the produce from her garden, or picking gooseberries and blackberries to make jelly. It was like that for all Americans; they didn't complain when the things they needed were rationed. They knew these things were going to a greater cause. They were survivors and learned to make do with what they had.

Years after the War, a book by news journalist, Tom Brokow, would call them 'The Greatest Generation.' They definitely deserved that distinction.

* * * * *

The one thing Robert told his friends, "We need a little entertainment, boys. We can't afford things that cost money, but we can get together on Saturday nights at different folks' homes and play some music, maybe have some square dancing. What do y'all think?"

So, in April 1943, the 'Crazy Band' was formed. Robert, Clyde Shumpert, Lester Gantt, Thurmond Jeffcoat, and Robert's uncles, James and Eugene Burkett, formed their own band. There weren't a whole lot of young men left in the community. Clyde was too young for the draft, Lester and Thurmond were just waiting to be called, and Eugene and James were examined but failed their physicals, Eugene because he had lost sight in his left eye in an accident. James was classified unfit for service due to an anxiety disorder. They all loved to sing and play so they decided they would use their talent for their enjoyment and that of their friends and neighbors.

After a couple of practices, the members decided they were ready to entertain in the community, and thus started the practice of having a square dance at different homes in the community every Saturday night. All their neighbors were pleased to attend and be entertained, glad to offer their homes for the get-togethers; they never had a problem finding a location to perform. With the War raging, everyone needed contact with other people, to visit with their neighbors and take their minds off the War, if only for a few hours.

The band members would arrive at the designated home after Saturday night supper, clear out all the furniture in one of the rooms, and set up in the corner to play. All that was necessary for the square dance, besides the music, was the caller. Nolan Lewis usually did the calling; he was never shy about shouting out the directions above the rhythmic strumming of guitar, banjo, and fiddle. It was his job to call out the movements while the dancers whirled and stepped around the room to the music. Four couples formed a circle, holding hands, then bowed as the music began. Still holding hands, they would step lively to the left and then to the right in time with the music.

Nolan shouted to the rhythm of the song, "Grab your partner … circle left … circle right … swing your partner … do-si-do … trade partners … promenade … grab hands and come to the middle." Then they paired off to twirl and glide across the floor. Forming a circle once again, the fellows would stand in one spot and tap their foot while the ladies weaved in and out between them, brushing each one's hands as they passed. Nolan was a master at improvising and would frequently shout his own version of the common square dance calls. But that's what made the dances so much fun and exciting. They never knew what Nolan would call; the dancers had to pay attention to follow his directions.

They soon developed a loyal following of eight couples that attended every Saturday dance and a few others that showed up depending on the location. It was never a party where food was served but always a jug of moonshine was present to be passed around among the attendees. By midnight when the party broke up some of those present were feeling mighty fine. Robert and the other band members, being more or less sober frequently had to drive their friends' home.

In mid-June, Robert and the 'Crazy Band' held a square dance at his house. Florence was not too keen on the idea. She enjoyed music and watching the dancing but she didn't approve of the inevitable jug that would be present. Heaven knew she had dealt with her share of men and their booze before; she was afraid Kelly would drink too much if it were handy. She needn't have worried; the dance was a resounding success.

Robert and the band cleared all the furniture out of the dining room. It was already warm in the evenings, so they put the windows up to let in a little breeze and opened the door onto the front porch. Whenever the room filled with people exerting themselves square dancing, it was going to get hot.

The crowd arrived promptly at 7:00 and the music and dancing began. The band warmed up with one of Robert's favorites, 'The Orange Blossom Special,' as the couples crowded to the center of the room. The music, laughter, and stomping feet seemed to shake the old house from the foundation to the rafters.

Florence smiled as she peeped in Kelly's bedroom. He sat there in his rocker, pipe in one hand and glass of moonshine on the side table; he was tapping his right foot to the rhythm of the music and grinning ear to ear. She didn't think one or two glasses would hurt so she had voiced no objection when Leon Padgett had stuck his head in saying, "How about a little drink, Mr. Kelly? It sure will increase the enjoyment of the music."

Kelly's reply: "Don't mind if I do, son."

Florence had to admit to herself, this dance was a good thing. It was wonderful to hear laughter fill the rooms again and see the pleasure on Kelly's face, something she had not witnessed in a long while.

Twenty-Six

FOR NINE DAYS, THE LITTLE SHIP, FRANCONIA, CAPTURED from the Vichy French, plowed southward from Liverpool, England, heading for Oran, North Africa. The first night out in the Irish Sea, a storm assailed the small ship and the sea was rough and choppy.

Leon was issued a hammock to attach to ceiling hooks above the tables in the galley; this was to be his bed for the trip south. The hammock swayed back and forth above the tables, making sleep impossible. It was like being permanently attached to a pendulum moving back and forth in rhythm with the ship's ups and downs in the rough sea. He slept in the hammock only one night, enduring the swinging motion above the tables. After that, he took his blanket and crawled under a table to sleep.

"I never had any use for a hammock," Leon said. "Now I know why. I lay in that contraption swinging above a table—that had to be the most miserable night's sleep I ever had. I didn't sleep; the floor had to be an improvement."

Food provisions for the company on board consisted mostly of potatoes with eggs for breakfast and goat sausage for dinner and supper. To Leon's notion, the goat sausage was impossible to eat. It looked like twists of dark brown tobacco that had been fried until all the grease was gone. It was hard, dry, and what little taste it had hinted of garlic, onion, and spoiled meat. He was not normally picky about food, but the goat sausage was too much for him to stomach.

"Not only does it look nasty," Leon expressed to the other guys, "but it also tastes the way it looks. It makes me feel queasy just smelling the leftover aroma every night from my bed under the table."

All the way to North Africa, he just ate bread and drank ginger beer, refusing to eat the goat sausage the cooks tried to feed the men.

Southward the Franconia sailed through St. George Channel and out into the open Atlantic. By the fourth day, they could see the coast of Portugal far to east. The weather and the sea were pleasant and calm enough that the men could enjoy passing the time on deck when their duties allowed. Leon spent this time smoking, talking with the other men, and thinking of home.

Some evenings as the sun set to the west, he would stand by the rail, smoking and looking out to sea, wondering what his future held and if he would ever see his home again. He knew it was like that with all the soldiers. They dreaded the coming fight, worrying if they would hold up in combat and do what they had been trained for. Most of all, they all knew death would be lurking in every skirmish with the enemy and ready to claim them or their friends. It was a dread that preyed on their minds every day and haunted their dreams at night. Home seemed so far away to these men and they feared they might never see it again.

Passing through the Strait of Gibraltar the seventh day out from

England, Leon, along with his fellow soldiers on deck, could see Spain to the north and Morocco to the south.

There it stands, Leon thought. *At the end of the Strait on the southern coast of Spain towers the great gray limestone mass known as the Rock of Gibraltar. This is considered the gateway to the Mediterranean, which I read about in my geography book at school.* Gazing upward at the great rock, Leon decided, *It surely does not disappoint. The image I have had in my head of Gibraltar doesn't compare to actually seeing it.*

Entering the Mediterranean from the Atlantic, Leon and his comrades encountered the bluest water they had ever seen. It reminded Leon of the deep blue Iris that bloomed in spring under his Grandma Peninnah's kitchen window back home at Rayflin. The water was so blue it appeared a deep navy with the sun shimmering across the surface; the small white caps that rose up with the breeze created such a stark contrast of color, the water seemed almost black on the horizon, black as the North Edisto back home.

It seems I can envision back home in everything. Even the colors of the sea remind me of home. It is the most beautiful body of water I have ever seen, and now I admit, so many things remind me of that place I sorely miss, even in a place so far away and so different. The land, the people with their foreign speech . . . how I long to hear the slow drawl of the South. I guess when you're so far away, you associate anything your senses encounter with the place you knew so well.

Once in the Mediterranean, the Franconia encountered other ships passing to the north and south, always British or American, carrying supplies and troops to and from the battle zone. But it was hard for Leon to imagine a battle zone existed so near as he stood on the deck, surveying the placid deep blue waters surrounding their ship.

The allies in North Africa had initiated Operation Torch, their plan to rid North Africa of their German and Italian enemies the previous November of '42. Leon's company was heading to North Africa to help finish the job in Algeria and Morocco. They were anti-aircraft and their mission was to destroy the enemy airplanes still menacing the area from the skies.

The first week of February 1943, General Dwight Eisenhower was made Supreme Commander of the Allied Expeditionary Force in North Africa, and by the 25th of February, the Allies had stopped the advance of Rommel's German Afrika Corps. All that was left of their mission was the complete defeat and surrender of the enemy.

By the time the Franconia sailed into the harbor of Oran on the third of March 1943, an Allied victory was almost assured. Oran was a Mediterranean seaport in Algeria, North Africa, originally built by the Moors centuries before, and had been taken and retaken by the Spanish, destroyed by an earthquake in 1791, and abandoned by its invaders. The French took over the city in 1831 and rebuilt the place; Leon had been enlightened to all this history by one of the younger guys in his company, a college boy called Grimsky who had been a history major in some northern college. Grimsky was just full of interesting information and Leon didn't mind his sharing. Some of the others thought him a nerd and were not at all interested in the knowledge he had to impart. Not Leon. He figured the more you know about a place, the better off you are. He had always heard, 'If you don't know history, you are doomed to repeat it.'

The Allied Armies now occupied Oran. It was an interesting old city; some of the original Moorish buildings of pink sandstone still stood, lining dusty streets in the oldest sections of the city. It was so foreign to Leon, raised in the slow-paced Deep South with only two races, black and white, and one shared language. This land's history was ancient, stretching centuries into the past, and though there were many dark-skinned people in Oran, their dress and speech was more than he could comprehend. So totally opposite from what he had experienced up until this time of his life, it may as well have been another planet he had landed on. The sand he could cope with—he had been raised in the sand hills of Carolina, where wheels were often mired in the deep sand beds of the back roads—but the trees were what he missed about home. Pines, cypress, and oaks were abundant back home; here, most were of the palm variety. He wondered how people existed in a land like this, but he figured it was all in what you were used to.

The first few days, Leon and his comrades of Battery I remained in Oran, awaiting orders and the arrival of their equipment they had loaded in Boston before leaving the States.

On the fourth day, their Company CO, Lieutenant Lewis, passed on to the men, "The ship carrying all our equipment was sunk by a German U Boat in the Atlantic. A new shipment of equipment, 90-millimeter guns, 40 millimeters, P68 radars, searchlights, and their transportation is being dispatched as soon as possible. Until then, we have been given an assignment, MP duty guarding prisoners at a POW camp in the northern highlands of the Atlas Mountains visible just to the south of the city."

Arriving by convoy at the POW camp the following day, Leon was amazed at the size of the stockade. It was as big as the town of Batesburg back home; laid out in blocks, it was a city surrounded by barbed wire. Each block had a thirty-foot wooden corner guard tower with a searchlight manned by an MP equipped with a 30-caliber machine gun. Between these corner towers stood another tower manned by an MP with a rifle. Leon was assigned to stand guard in one of the corner towers overlooking the compound where the prisoners were housed in pup tents. Prisoners arrived at the camp daily by truck convoy from the battlefront. Most had no pants or shoes, just ragged uniform shirts. After they were run through the showers, their heads were shaved to keep down the threat of head lice; all were issued blue fatigues with big white letters, PW, on the back.

One morning while Leon stood guard in his corner tower, an enterprising German prisoner slipped out clinging underneath the water truck. He didn't get very far, unfortunately for him; a French policeman riding a big white horse captured him just outside the gates. Every morning after that while Leon stood guard duty, a circle was drawn near his tower and the escaping prisoner was told to stay in the circle.

Leon's orders: "If he steps outside the circle, drop him."

The prisoners were kept in the tent city until arrangements could be made for their transfer from North Africa to other permanent prison camps in England or the United States. Then they were loaded onto a train, sent to the port of Oran and by ship to their final destination. Early one morning at sunup, Leon helped guard a trainload of the prisoners on their trip by train over the mountains to Oran harbor. The MPs were all over the train, carrying M1 Grandes and 45 caliber side arms. Riding on top of the train, whenever it stopped, Leon and the other guards hit the ground. Another engine was coupled to the rear of the train to help push it over the mountains. They left at sunup one morning, crossed the mountains, supervised the loading of the prisoners on a British ship in Oran harbor, and returned to the camp two days later at dark. His company guarded the camp for almost six weeks, then was sent back to Oran to unload their equipment from the ship that had finally arrived. They set up their gun emplacements near an allied airstrip south of the city, ready to do what they had been trained for: shooting enemy planes from the sky.

It wasn't long before the men were thrust into action. His baptism under fire came one night soon after the company was entrenched near Oran airfield. Air raid sirens began to blast after good dark; a formation of German 88 Bombers was approaching from the South. Leon and two others manned a searchlight to help direct the fire of their 90-millimeter guns as the German 88 Bombers came in low over the city, dropping bombs near the airfield. The sky was lit up like the fourth of July as the searchlights weaved back and forth, directing the fire from their 90 millimeters. There were eighteen German Bombers in the formation that night and the guns of Leon's Battery shot down eight. After the raid was finally over, Leon and his searchlight squad were relieved to get some rest. All the guys in Leon's tent that night was bone-tired but still on an adrenaline high from their first experience in combat.

He remarked to his tent mates right before the weariness finally overtook him, "Well that ain't exactly like shooting doves, is it, fellows?"

> *Somewhere in North Africa*
> *May 23rd 1943*
> *Robert,*
> *I received your letter and was glad to hear that everyone back home is doing very well. I was sure sorry to hear about Asia's dying. He was a good old soul and will be missed. That's*

something we'll all have to face one of these days. I am now in North Africa and doing O.K. This country is really something to see. In the daytime, it gets up to 120 degrees, and at night, I sleep under two wool army blankets and almost freeze. You would think the whole place was a desert, but I have seen grape orchards with grapes so big a bunch wouldn't fit in a ten-gallon bucket. I've made some good friends among the men. One guy, Talmedge Pressly, is from north Georgia and we get along really good. He was raised in the country just like I was and even had some moonshiners in his family. There are several Italian guys here from New York City, different upbringing, but good guys all the same. I hope Dad and Miss Florence are well and everything is going good with you and that job working for Wilson. I'm going to write a letter to Elsie and Fred too. Write me soon with all the news from home. I'll answer when I can; we got bogged up in this damn thing right once we got to North Africa.

Leon

The 505th Antiaircraft and Leon's Battery I stayed in position before Oran, ready to protect the city from enemy aircraft. The 13th of May 1943, the Germans in North Africa surrendered, along with 250,000 Axis troops. The Antiaircraft Unit had no mission without the threat of enemy aircraft attacking the city. They would be reassigned where they were needed. The Germans were effectively kicked out of North Africa and it was time for a second major Allied offensive.... Italy.

Twenty-Seven

STANDING IN FORMATION IN FRONT OF THEIR COMPANY AREA
on the outskirts of Oran, Leon could feel the sweat running down
between his shoulder blades. It was mid-July and the temperature
soared. It reminded Leon of July and August back home, except for
the humidity. At home, it was steamy hot in mid-summer; here it
was just hot. The merciless sun beat down on the soldiers, the only
shade offered by tall palms beside the company headquarters tent
fifty feet to their left. A rustling sound reached his ears as the hot
breeze stirred the leaves; conversation was not allowed in formation.
For fifteen minutes they had stood in the ranks, the only sounds
the stir of the palm fronds and the near-inaudible conversation of
a group of officers standing in front of headquarters. It was midday
and his Antiaircraft Company was awaiting the arrival of a very important person, General Dwight Eisenhower himself, the Supreme
Commander of all Allied Forces in North Africa. General Eisenhower, along with other military brass, was inspecting the troops
still entrenched around Oran in anticipation of the next big push
against the enemy.

A convoy appeared in the distance, approaching from the direction of the airstrip. Leon could see the vehicles heading towards

them, but because of the intense heat from the ground, the vehicles appeared wavy and their numbers were unclear. It almost seemed they were crossing water—a mirage, Leon realized. When the convoy got within three hundred yards, Leon could make out a deuce and a half in front and back with three jeeps between. He could tell there were two men in the seat behind the driver of the middle jeep, one in uniform. A small American flag was fluttering from the right front bumper of the middle jeep and a small Union Jack fluttered from the left. The three jeeps came to a halt amid a cloud of dust some fifty feet in front of Leon's formation. The occupants climbed from the jeep and approached the Company. The silver-haired gentleman hung back a bit, letting the General observe his men. Just as he approached, the order of 'atten-hut' was shouted and the men all snapped to attention. General Eisenhower walked over to within twelve feet of the front line, stood at attention himself, and returned the salute to the soldiers in formation. He then announced, "At ease, men, good job against those German 88s, keep up the good work." Short and sweet words of praise from Eisenhower but any notice received from him was important. It was a morale builder to Leon and all of Company I. He then turned back to the gentleman accompanying him and they proceeded to join the group of officers in front of the OD (olive drab) green headquarters tent. After greetings with handshakes and big smiles, Leon's company officers listened intently to the two visitors' questions, responding when necessary. The small gathering assembled in the meager shade available closest to the tent. They were soon absorbed in deep conversation, including the silver haired gentleman, a mystery to all the soldiers standing at ease in the blistering sun.

All Leon and his comrades could think about was being dismissed to seek someplace even a little cooler and some water. The breeze did continue to stir the palm fronds thankfully. *Without the breeze,* Leon thought, *if they continue to leave us standing here, we'll be dropping like flies.* The thought had barely crossed his mind when the order was given to be dismissed.

The Company would not learn until after their visitors had departed that the gentleman was George VI, King of England. It also surprised the men that the General would mention their assault against the 88 bombers.

"I suppose General Eisenhower knows pretty much what his whole Army is doing, probably received a report about our Company's activities before he arrived," Leon commented to his tentmates before lights-out that night. It was an honor, the bit of praise from General Eisenhower, they all agreed with Leon on that.

* * * * *

It was mid-September 1943, and the evenings were just beginning to cool enough to tolerate sitting on the porch after the sun had set. The regular Saturday night dances had continued throughout the summer. Robert looked forward to seeing his friends and playing his music; there was nothing he enjoyed more. They had held one other weekly dance at Robert's since June.

"The two dances y'all had here," Florence told Robert, "were such rousing successes, as far as I'm concerned, I don't mind volunteering our house for another weekend shindig. Kelly was so pleased. It was good to hear him laugh and tell some of his stories again. Now that the weather is cooler, why don't y'all have another dance here next weekend?"

Kelly seemed to enjoy the music and the crowd so much, not to mention the spirits. Florence knew he had so little pleasure to look forward to in his handicapped condition. The 'Crazy Band' was welcome to play for another square dance.

Saturday arrived. A crowd of neighbors would begin to arrive about seven p.m. so Florence knew she had to have their supper over and done with by that time. Their suppertime was always five p.m. Supper was over and Florence had finished clearing away their dishes before six, when the first automobile pulled into the yard. It was Clyde, Lester, and Thurmond. They arrived early to help Robert clear out the furniture in the dining room and get things set up for the dance. Florence lit kerosene lamps to place on the mantle and on small tables near where the band would be set up.

"I'll go check on your daddy while you boys get things ready," she said to Robert as she disappeared towards Kelly's room.

They joked and laughed while emptying the room, then went back to the automobile to retrieve their instruments. Robert noticed that Thurmond and Lester were not as talkative right away, and when Lester returned carrying a jug and plunked it down on the kitchen table, he knew something was up. Lester didn't as a usual thing bring a jug to their get-togethers; he occasionally took a drink, but rarely when he was playing.

"What's with the jug, Lester? You usually leave the liquid refreshments at home when we're playing," Robert asked, a wide grin on his face.

"Well, Robert, Thurmond and I just feel like a little celebrating tonight. We both received our draft notices the other day and there won't be too many more opportunities to play with our buddies before we'll be going into service. This might be our last. We have to report for our physicals next week."

"Lester's right about that," Thurmond chimed in. "I don't know if celebrating is the right word. We're sure going to miss the playing and singing with you boys. I guess both of us just feel like getting a little drunk tonight, but don't worry, we'll behave ourselves and it won't affect our playing none."

The yard and road in front of the house were soon crowded with automobiles, and the music and dancing commenced right on schedule. Leon Padgett brought a jug along and those not square dancing in the middle of the floor sat around the kitchen table or in chairs along the wall, the menfolk sipping and the womenfolk laughing and talking.

Kelly sat in his usual place before the fireplace in his bedroom, puffing his pipe, listening to the laughter and music from the other room. He was not able to join them, but eventually, as the evening wore on those menfolk not occupied with the dancing gravitated to his bedroom to join him in a drink. He seemed to end up 'holding court' in front of the fireplace from his rocker. The windows were up; crickets, frogs, and the occasional whippoorwill or owl competed with the music in the dining room, adding their night chorus to the band's music.

Kelly was a wonderful storyteller and all the menfolk present enjoyed sitting with him while he spun one of his tales about his moonshining days and the trouble it brought him. With the music and singing in the background and an audience before him, Kelly was in his element. A drink on his little semi-circle table to his right and his pipe sending spirals of smoke upward resting in an ashtray, he told his stories with relish. He might have been a cripple, but there was nothing wrong with his memory. He could describe in detail the principle participants in his stories, the weather conditions, and time of day each event took place, which was quite amazing considering he was drunk at the time. Secretly, some members of his audience thought he made up what he didn't remember, but his stories were so vivid and entertaining that no one would dare suggest such a thing. That fantastic memory for details would be inherited by his two sons, Leon and Robert.

At 9:30, the band members took a break for some refreshment, a smoke, and a breath of cool air on the front porch. Thurmond and Lester, true to their earlier announcement, poured themselves a drink from Lester's jug. They'd already had at least two, Robert noticed while playing. Their glasses were filled when the playing started, placed on the small table against the wall near them and refilled when emptied, compliments of one of the menfolk present. Whenever they paused between songs, they would reach for their glass. Robert never took a drink himself; he had been around Kelly and Leon too many times when they were drunk to be attracted to the fiery liquid. He knew that he and his mamma would have to get Kelly undressed and in bed when the party broke up. Someone would have to drive the rest of the drunks home tonight. He would probably have to help with that chore and replace the furniture later on.

The band members and a few of the partygoers relaxed on the darkened porch without the wonder of electric lights, not yet extended this far into the sparsely settled countryside. There was no need to bring a kerosene lamp to the porch; the bright yellow orb of a moon provided enough light to see the outline of the automobiles parked in the yard once the eyes adjusted to the dim light. The outline of the men sitting in the chairs on the shadowy front porch was easily visible. There were also the bright coals on the ends of their cigarettes to pinpoint exactly where the others sat.

"There's a bit of a breeze blowing from the south," Robert commented. "Cool compared to inside and quite pleasant with the full moon shining above and the sky full of stars. The combination of the breeze, the darkness and the smoke seems to keep the mosquitoes away too."

Sitting on the porch in the darkness, the men and a few ladies enjoyed a leisurely conversation. No one wished to dominate; only one spoke at the time and the others listened. It was a calming atmosphere; the liquid spirits had begun to mellow out Lester, Thurmond, and the others present. There were no loud drunks here to contend with. They were all content to enjoy the breeze, the drink, and the company of friends. There were long pauses in the conversation when they all just seemed to meditate on what had been said by one of the others, listen to the crickets and a pair of whippoorwills calling to each other in the distant woods. They talked mostly about the War and friends that were in the service. All were interested in what news Robert had from Leon.

"We received a letter from Leon two months back. You all know Leon was never one to talk a lot, except maybe in his drinking days. He's still in North Africa, I guess. In his last letter, he said he had seen and saluted some really important people when they were in North Africa inspecting the troops. Of course, he didn't mention any names, censorship of course, to prevent the enemy from knowing where these important people were. I guess that will be one of his stories to tell when he finally gets home. He seemed right proud of that. His letters are always short, and we all know he has always been direct and to the point. It's about time for him to write again."

There was a brief pause while they all thought about Leon and all their other friends so far away. Robert broke the silence. "We better get back to our playing. We've been sitting on this porch a good forty-five minutes—time for the dancing to continue."

Twenty-Eight

"THE PLAN FOR AVALANCHE WAS TO LAND AT SALER-no, seize nearby Naples and establish airfields further north. A major amphibious expedition needed three to five months to plan. Allied planners gave Clark only forty-five days. It was hastily devised and poorly executed; due to the belated discovery that Salerno Bay was protected by minefields. Operation Avalanche was to commence at dawn on September 9th, 1943." (Atkinson 224)

Participating vessels would have to drop anchors nine to twelve miles from the beach; the men would climb down the heavy rope netting to the landing craft and head to the beaches from that distance.

"At midnight the night before ship captains of all participating vessels ordered engines stopped and anchors dropped at the hundred-fathom line." (Atkinson 244)

Eisenhower said of Clark, *"He is the best organizer, planner and trainer of troops I have ever met."* (Atkinson 222)

Clark would definitely be put to the test with Avalanche.

"Some 55,000 assault troops were set to invade at Salerno with a comparable number of reinforcements to follow." (Atkinson 241)

It was hard fighting on the beaches for the thousands of American and the allied forces involved.

"The 5th Army's beachhead stretched for forty miles, at an average depth of six miles Dday+3. The fighting was fierce but there were now roughly twenty-eight thousand Americans ashore with roughly twice that many British troops to the north at Taranto on the other side of the Italian Boot." (Atkinson 265)

The arrival of more ships and troops seemed to seal the fate of the Germans. The message that the Germans intended to abandon the fight at Salerno and move northward proved true. Pressing on, the Eighth Army on September 27th captured the Foggia Airfields, northeast of Naples, almost across the Italian peninsula and near the Adriatic Sea. The Americans entered Naples on the west coast four days later on October 1, 1943.

* * * * *

Leon's unit, Anti-Aircraft Artillery Company, Battery I of the 505th, left Oran in Africa the last week in September aboard the USS James O'Hara. Crossing the Mediterranean, their ship sailed north-westward around the island of Sicily and nearly half way up the distance of the Italian peninsula to arrive in Salerno Bay. Leon was not in the initial invasion that landed on Salerno in early September, but some of his outfit was.

Leon and the remainder of his AAA unit landed on the beaches at Salerno, south of Naples, Italy, on October 3, 1943. By then the beaches had been wrestled from the Germans.

'Of course, at the time," Leon remembered, "we didn't know that the beaches at Salerno had already been secured by the Allies. Me and my fellow soldiers rode in a landing craft from our ship, The USS James O'Hara, to within a hundred yards of the shoreline. The front ramp of the craft was dropped and all of us just spilled out into the gray waters, carrying a full pack and an M1 Grande; we waded ashore unmolested by enemy fire."

When he and those with him came ashore, they had no opposition from the enemy, only a photojournalist taking pictures to document their landing. The soldiers assembled on the beach, loaded their gear and themselves in deuce and a half trucks, and headed for Naples.

The allies entered the Naples, Italy, on October 1stjust two days before Leon and the remainder of Battery I arrived on the outskirts of the city. The Germans had retreated to the north abandoning Naples, leaving behind a bombed-out city. Basically, there were few complete buildings standing.

Leon would relate the still painful memories of what he saw and witnessed forty years later. "The Allies would soon learn the Germans had left in some buildings explosive devices set as booby traps to main and kill Americans soldiers. There were also snipers left behind in some of the buildings and in any high vantage points around the city to kill soldiers unlucky enough to end up in their crosshairs."

First order of business when the Americans and their Allies entered the city was to seek and destroy any German snipers left behind. Then they begin to help the civilian population.

The refugees had no homes left and were so dirty one soldier said, "They didn't look human." The Germans had mined at least fifty buildings, Italian bodies lay in the streets of the city.

"Three-quarters of the city's bridges were demolished, along with electrical generators and substations. Industrial plants were gutted; others had been wired for demolition though they had not been fired." (Atkinson 289)

Weeping and plucking at the uniforms of the liberators, Italian citizens flung themselves at their feet. Pandemonium soon spread throughout the city.

"The people left in Naples were pitiful to look upon," Leon remembered. "They had no food, no electricity, no water, and the children's faces, I'll never forget, they were totally devoid of any hope. It was as if there was no feeling at all. They just stared into the distance, would barely respond if asked questions. It was as if they did not exist at all. The blank stares of the young ones reminded me of the lifeless eyes I witnessed on so many dead soldiers, Dirty children best describe what a defeated, hopeless people look like."

The once beautiful city had been bombed by the Allies when the Germans held the city, but the Allied liberators found the Germans had mutilated what remained before they departed.

"One half the city's population of one million remained through the German occupation. None now had running water, dynamite dropped down at least 40 manholes by the Germans wrecked at least that many sewer lines. Robert Capa, a photographer, photographed a schoolhouse converted into a morgue with twenty boys arrayed in crude coffins. Crying women held up pictures of their dead children hoping to find their bodies for burial. One hundred fifty dead civilians on stretchers and window shutters with their names and addresses tucked in their closed

hands lay outside a hospital; no trucks were available to transport these dead to graveyards. "(Atkinson 288).

The Harbor so important to rebuilding the city and supplying food and armaments to the allies was completely impassable.

"Not a single vessel was afloat in the port. It was a drowned forest of ship masts, funnels and cranes. Thirty major wrecks could be seen, and ten times that amount had been sunk. Vessels had been scuttled, often one atop another. A German ship with seven thousand tons of ammunition had been blown up, wrecking four adjacent city blocks. Only rats still inhabited the waterfront. "(Atkinson 291)

All this devastation lay in shadow of the great volcanic mountain called Vesuvius.

When Battery I of the 505th Anti-Aircraft Artillery (AAA) entered Naples, it had been less than a week since the Allies gained control of the city. The dead had to be buried first, the living fed and given medical attention, the rubble removed and cleared from any usable buildings, and most importantly, the harbor cleared so ships could supply the city. Although the Army engineers reported the sabotage of the port was done "by a man who knew his business," after closer examination, it was discovered and confirmed that the "demolitions of the port were planned more for revenge and to wreck the economy of Naples, rather than just to prevent the Allies from its use." (Atkinson 291) The success of the Fifth Army's survival and triumph in Italy depended on Naples. It would be done with manpower and determination. No soldier of Fifth Army doubted their success.

Leon, now a Private First Class (PFC), remained at Naples for two months with his Unit. There was plenty of work for everyone, and the anti-aircraft equipment had to be set up around the city—

generators, searchlights, and 90 millimeter guns—in the event that the Germans would attempt more destruction from the air, which from Fifth Army's point of view, was practically impossible in Naples. But they had to be prepared.

Germany was already dangerously low when it came to planes and pilots, so that was not a major concern. The men of Battery I guarded the city from the air at night using their searchlights to keep any ambitious German fighter planes at bay. If they were on duty, the crews had to get some rest during the day, but even the crews that worked at night protecting the city from air attacks spent their afternoons working alongside civilians and other units. They helped their fellow soldiers and civilians with clearing rubble from buildings and removing the wrecked ships from the harbor. The feeding of civilians and the Army already entrenched at Naples required the unloading of supplies brought up from the beaches by trucks; the port was not yet sufficiently ready to accept the docking of Allied vessels to deliver the needed supplies.

Leon had not written a letter home since his outfit landed in Italy, but his two months remaining in Naples gave him the opportunity. He had time in the evenings to think about home and to write his family. The searchlight crews of the AAA rotated so that they had some time for rest and reflection; staying in one place for a while did have its advantages. He knew that his dad, Miss Florence and Robert were anxious about him and whether he was alive. He wrote to Robert first from Naples, Italy.

* * * * *

Somewhere in Italy

October 27, 1943

Dear Robert,

I'm alive and well and wanted to let you and all the family know. I pray that Daddy, Miss Florence and you are all OK. Read this letter to them please, I know they are concerned but in this War, I'm on the move so much, I am not able to keep in touch with you too often. The powers that be dictate what and when I have some spare time. Of course, I can't tell you where I am exactly or what my job is here for security reasons. I can tell you I am now in Italy, a beautiful country until the ravages of war took its toll. This is a very mountainous country; the weather at present is cold and I am told by others a harsh winter will soon be upon us. It has already begun and I fear not only our troops but the people here, so dependent on us, will face an even worse winter without the food and supplies we give to them.

I have seen so much death and destruction. It haunts me even in my dreams at night. I can't describe in words what the people of this country have suffered, or the deprivation of all our men. Even the bodies of our dead suffer degrading treatment at the hands of our own. Just yesterday I stood and watched a deuce and a half pass through our camp with our own dead stacked like cord wood. Sitting in the back on top of our dead were two soldiers, not from my outfit, but Americans. They were smoking cigarettes and laughing about some joke while underneath them our dead lay lifeless. Where has our decency gone, the reverence for those that gave the ultimate sacrifice? It's as if in war, civilized people no longer exist. It makes me sick to my stomach that our soldiers have come to this. That's war, I guess and a sorry state of affairs I believe. Don't read this part to Daddy and Miss Florence. They may think my mental state is slipping away too. I don't want them to hear what I have just written. They probably hear far too much of the harsh realities on the radio already. I wouldn't want my words to add to their distress.

Tell them I am well and that the Allies have conquered another big city and have the Germans in retreat. Thank Dad and Miss Florence for the little pocket Bible with the steel cover that they sent. I keep it in the breast pocket of my shirt over my heart and read some from it almost every night. It does give me a small measure of comfort in these dreadful unavoidable circumstances; I and thousands of other American G.I.s find ourselves embroiled in a chaotic state that we have no control over. The little Bible is one of my most treasured belongings at the moment. Please let them know that I ask only for their prayers and I am proud to do my part for freedom. If God wills it, I will make it through and come home. I so miss all of you and the place that is home.

Give my love to Grandmamma and all my kin at Rayflin. I will write a letter to Elsie and Fred too and let them know I am well.

Leon

* * * * *

"There's something you fellows should see," Leon said to some of his buddies. "At night, we have the most beautiful fireworks display from Mt. Vesuvius. You all do realize Vesuvius is only nine miles from Naples. It appears like a giant bowl of fire from the air, I've been told by some of our pilots. Volcanic rocks and flames are frequently flung from the mountain and can be seen from the city."

During the two months he spent in Naples, many evenings, he would enjoy the sight of the giant sparkler of Vesuvius. It was still the only active volcano on the European continent.

There is still some beauty in this place even with all the death and destruction. It is almost bearable in Naples with the evening fireworks, the prettiest I have ever witnessed, Leon thought to himself. *The calm at present, no bomb blasts and sniper fire filling the air day and night, is only a brief respite from what is sure to come.*

Twenty-Nine

WHILE THE GERMANS WERE RETREATING FROM NAPLES TO the north, half a world away, so it seemed, life went on at its own slow pace. At Rayflin, Leon's kinfolks felt the pinch of the war effort through the allocation of certain items that were more necessary to the War than to the people safe at home. Stamps were issued for such things as sugar, rubber tires, and shoes and, from the beginning, gas.

Florence and Kelly didn't dwell on the lack of these items. Both had lived through the Great Depression and knew how to conserve and reuse things they already had. When clothing was worn out and there was no money to buy new ones or if stamps were required, as with shoes, they just made do. Florence could patch clothing, and rubber soles on their shoes could be replaced. Old bald tires could be cut and used to re-sole shoes. Kelly had a shoemaker's iron form in the old smokehouse and a tact hammer, and he knew how they could be fixed. Of course, in Kelly's crippled condition, he could not patch the bottoms of the shoes himself, but he taught Robert. Florence often took old quilts that were worn and used them inside of a new quilt top she had patched from the best parts of old clothing. Cotton was too important to the war effort to be used for batting to put inside a quilt. Heavy canvas tents, duffle bags, and uniforms for the soldiers all required cotton. All resource materials that were deemed necessary were set aside for the war effort, which was of utmost importance. Supplying the materials for the War had to come first. Civilians understood how important the need was 'over there' and didn't complain.

* * * * *

On Sundays, Florence, Kelly, and Robert could count on having relatives or friends for dinner; sometimes invited but more often, they just turned up around dinner time, bringing their own meager food contributions to add to the noon meal. Sundays were visiting days for people in the South. The women folk did the cooking and clean up afterwards; the men folks would sit on the front porch if the weather was nice. They smoked their pipes or cigarettes, or chewed tobacco, and speculated about what was going on with the War. Most everybody had a family member in service, so they all shared what news they had recently received from their soldier, even though letters were few and far between. Kelly enjoyed the visiting with kinfolks, neighbors and friends. He could get about with his cane and Robert's steady hand as support.

Elsie and her husband Fred and son Tony always came to visit on Sundays. Elsie looked forward to visiting her daddy. She and Fred had been married in 1935 and Tony was their only son. Elsie sometimes would bring a letter from Leon and share its contents with Robert, her daddy, and Miss Florence, and she always brought food to help with the meal. After all, she and Fred had jobs at the cotton mill and steady paychecks.

Entertainment was at a minimum. The War in Europe and the Pacific was so important, people back home dedicated their whole being to it. Robert did get together with his uncles Eugene and James to play music some Saturday nights. Most of the guys Robert played music with were now in Foreign Service. Robert, Eugene, and James still played if they had an invitation and a place to play.

The only other social activities centered on the church. Most everyone attended to sing and socialize with friends. Unfortunately, Kelly, due to his physical condition, could not attend. The pews were just too hard for him to sit on for any length of time. Negotiating the steps at the church was too difficult. He and Florence stayed home but Robert always attended.

"There's always a sermon being preached on the radio," Kelly remarked. "Florence and I are content to receive our divine instruction from Pastor Charles Fuller of the 'Old Fashioned Revival Hour' or some inspirational Christian music. There's always some good gospel music to listen to on Sunday mornings. While Florence is busy preparing dinner, I always turn the music up, so she can enjoy it too. Sometimes Florence and I have our own little prayer service. She'll read a chapter to me and we'll discuss what the Word of the Lord means to us. It's usually a book in Psalms; that's the easiest to understand. It's not like attending church, but we still feel we are worshipping, even if we aren't sitting in the pew, and I'm sure the good Lord understands."

This was the life of Kelly, Florence, and Robert while Leon was away at War. The timing of it seldom changed, and receiving a letter from Leon or a visit from kinfolk were the two things that kept them going. Everything else they did was just the necessary comings and goings to survive. Robert sometimes felt he wasn't accomplishing anything. To him, it was like standing still in one spot, marching in place, not going forward or backward. Life was the same each day, only a different day. During the week, with no gas to waste visiting with friends, the only way to stay connected was through the mail. They all looked forward to the mailman stopping by with letters or postcards from family. Florence's siblings and cousins didn't live nearby like Kelly's. Some of her family, aunts and cousins mainly, she had not seen since before the War; letters were the only way to keep in touch. Getting letters and postcards from her kin was a special treat for Florence.

Thirty

THE GERMANS RETREATED NORTHWARD IN ITALY, CROSSING the Volturno River and the Liri Valley. The Germans always occupied the high ground. The American and British Forces were left to dog their enemies from lower altitudes. The Allies were stopped by the combination of German firepower, the Italian Winter, and the mountainous terrain.

"The Germans had prepared a series of fortifications in mountainous country just south of Rome called the Gustav Line. It was studded with pill boxes on high ground that hinged on the town of Cassino above the Liri Valley." (Atkinson 305)

* * * * *

While Naples was literally coming back to life, Corporal Leon Gantt of I Battery 505th Anti-Aircraft Artillery (AAA) was leaving Naples to protect Foggia Airfields near the Adriatic Sea. It was late December, three days before Christmas, and all Allied troops were on the march. Leon now held the rank of Corporal and was a member of one of the searchlight crews needed at Foggia.

The Eighth Army had captured the airfields at Foggia on the 27th of September. Control of Foggia would provide bases for the bombing of Austria, southern Germany, and the Danube basin. Getting the men and necessary equipment to Foggia was not an easy task. They had to face floods, mud, mountains, and winter cold on a slow convoy of deuce and a half trucks. The roads were slippery with snow and ice. The trip across the peninsula on highway number 6 was treacherous; there were still pockets of German resistance, and caution against snipers had to be considered. The convoy arrived after four slow days of agonizing cold and began to set up of their tents and equipment

* * * * *

"In the meanwhile, Clark's Allied legions faced a formidable obstacle twenty miles north of Naples. Here, at the wide Volturno River, Fifth Army would make its first crossing in Europe of a contested river against the German Tenth Army." (Atkinson 298)

The fight for the river crossing was only the beginning of a great battle. The prize was the town of Cassino at the head of the Liri Valley.

"Beyond the town of Cassino, set in the Apennine Mountains, there were higher mountains and then 130 miles beyond those lay Rome." (Atkinson 302)

The real objective at Cassino was a Benedictine Abbey setting on what is called Monte Cassino. The Abbey controlled by the Germans was believed to be the optimal vantage point from which to rain destruction and death on the Allies below. The first attacks towards Cassino, Italy, begin on January 17, 1944. The Battle for Casssino was destined to be a long one. The Allies bombed the monastery at Monte Cassino for three days in February '44 and perpetrated an Allied final attack on the mountain beginning on March 15th. All the Allied planes that bombed Monte Cassino took off and returned to Foggia Airfield, where Leon was stationed.

* * * * *

The airfields at Foggia were nothing short of an engineering marvel. The landing strip alone was 7000 feet long made of steel mats, which went together like a hinge and locked kind of like a puzzle. The matting was anchored at one end, a large section was rolled up and buried in the ground in a deep ditch, constructed as an anchor so it would stay put when planes took off and landed. According to some of the soldiers Leon and his buddies encountered upon arriving at Foggia, there were thirty-six hundred four-motored bombers there and the airfield was twenty-five miles across.

"That's according to what Captain Walker said," Leon told the others quartered in his tent. "I never counted them myself, nor did I measure the landing strip or the distance across. I guess I'll just have to take Captain Walker at his word. Being a Captain, he should know what he's talking about. It is an awfully big place."

Leon did, however, know something about the airplanes that

landed and took off from Foggia. "There are Snelling planes, Wellingtons, B17s, Halifaxes, Manchesters, P38s, P51s, P47s, and Spitfires. That's just the ones I'm familiar with," Leon commented.

After their arrival, tents were assembled at one end of the runway. There had to be a mess tent, sleeping quarters for the crews and officers, a Headquarters tent where all administrative business concerning the Anti-Aircraft Artillery (AAA) personnel stationed there would take place. No serviceman would be granted a leave, transfer, or furlough from Foggia without a formal set of orders. After these tents were assembled, all the (AAA) equipment—searchlights, generators and 90 millimeter guns—were placed for best advantage of protecting the airfield and guiding our planes in night combat against the enemy. German planes attempting an attack over the airfield would be pinpointed by our searchlight beams, enabling our 90 millimeters to destroy them. Allied planes landing at night would have to be guided by the searchlight beans to a safe landing.

As a searchlight crewmember, Leon's job was as follows: He worked with the crew setting up, operating, and maintaining the portable power generator. He also operated and maintained searchlights, did maintenance on equipment, and connected light to power. He was responsible for checking dials for proper amperage. He had to hook up station to radar and to the searchlights and maintain synchronization between them. He had operated this equipment in North Africa and now in Italy under numerous air raids. He served in this capacity at Foggia until March, when he was promoted to Sergeant and listed as Searchlight NCO.

Foggia Airfield was the largest airfield in the world at this time. There was a gas pipeline that pumped gas to the airfield from tankers at Beri, Italy, a seaport town on the Adriatic Sea. There was also a railroad built from Beri to Foggia in order to ship equipment for maintaining the airfield and airplane parts. The railroad brought replacement motors for planes in boxes on flat cars, boxes made out of 2x8 lumber painted blue. If a plane came in from a bombing mission damaged, a motor could be readily shipped by rail from Beri, and airplane mechanics could have the plane repaired and ready to fly again on short notice.

The runway mats ran southeast to northwest with the railroad on a rail bed about waist high at the southeastern end of the strip. One morning, Leon witnessed a B17 taking off about 500 yards away, heading towards the south east. "The B17 was carrying seven tons of bombs, a fourteen-man crew and ammunition for the guns mounted on the plane," Leon noted. "The pilot could not get his landing gear up before reaching the rail embankment, and the wheels got caught on the rails and flipped the plane over on its back. Fortunately, no one got hurt and no bombs exploded. What could have been a major disaster was prevented by luck and the grace of God."

* * * * *

In February, a major bombing mission was mounted against Monte Cassino. At dinner time on the 15th, Leon and a fellow soldier, Talmadge Pressley from north Georgia, were driving down the field towards the mess tent when Leon noticed a pilot walking in their direction.

"There are a bunch of fellows coming back from a mission flying

B17s," Leon commented. "Evidently, that guy has just landed his plane. Stop, Pressley, and offer that fellow a ride," Leon said. Pressley stopped and Leon asked, "Need a ride, sir?" The pilot was a 1st Lieutenant.

"Sure, appreciate the offer," the pilot said as Leon opened the passenger door and slid over to make room.

"Have you boys heard of a place called Cassino?" the pilot inquired.

"They tell me it's pretty rough up there," replied Leon.

"There ain't any Cassino there," was the Lieutenant's answer.

"Where is it then?" asked Leon.

"Our boys blew the damn thing away this morning."

"What, it's completely gone?"

"Three hundred of us dropped 7 tons apiece on it, nothing left but rubble."

They reached the mess tent and the pilot hopped out. "Thanks for the ride, boys, and good luck."

"Same to you, Lieutenant," replied Leon.

Turning to Pressley, Leon said, "I guess now we know what all that thunder was to the northwest this morning. I thought old Vesuvius might have blown her top. It was just our boys giving the Germans a wakeup call."

When Leon's promotion to Sergeant came through, he became NCO of a searchlight crew. That job entailed a lot more responsibility. He directed and supervised the crew operating the searchlights, specialized in pin-point directing of lights necessary to expose by light hostile bombers and yet not expose friendly fighter planes engaging bombers in combat. He headed a twelve-man crew in this capacity until May 1944.

Thirty-One

"BEFORE MEMBERS OF THE ANTI-AIRCRAFT ARTILLERY HAD been in Italy a year," Leon said, "we would all be assigned to other units: infantry, military police, trucking companies, field artillery and combat engineers. We had done our primary job of destroying the German Luftwaffe so well, the AAA units were no longer needed in the fight the Allies waged to claim all of Italy. We had literally done our job so well we had made our job as Anti-Aircraft Artillery almost obsolete.

In May of 1944, Sergeant Gantt was transferred from the Anti-Aircraft Artillery at Foggia Airfield to the 85th Combat Engineer Unit attached to the II Corp of the Fifth Army with the title of Construction Foreman.

The combat engineers were as important as any unit in the 5th Army.

"They cleared minefields and tank obstacles, destroyed enemy bunkers, cleared roadways, built many bridges to replace those destroyed by the retreating enemy, removed barbwire obstacles, built enemy prisoner of war compounds and fought as Infantry when the need arose." (169th Engineer Battalion Unit History)

Leon would end up at war's end transferred to the 169th. Basically, if the Army needed something cleared, detonated, built, or torn down, they called on the combat engineers.

Allied troops landed at Anzio Beach south of Rome Jan 22, 1944 while Leon was still at Foggia Airfield. In February, the Germans counterattacked against the Anzio Beachhead. Finally, at the end of May, the Germans retreated completely from Anzio. In May, the 85th Combat Unit, with Sergeant Leon Gantt, was supporting the Allies in the area of Anzio. Sergeant Gantt dealt with mines. He cleared mines during the rainy, cold weather near the town of Anzio.

"I lay flat on my belly, searching for land mines, scratched the dirt from around them, and then very carefully screwed the detonator out to disarm each mine. I got my 'bunkum' wet as hell," Leon proclaimed to fellow soldiers.

"When clearing mines beside roads to park repair machinery and dozers, minesweeping crews were used. They advanced in couples; the sweeper first swinging side to side his iron pancake on a long instrument set handle; followed behind was his partner carrying a rifle, binoculars dangling from his neck and long tasseled sticks to mark suspicious spots. The second man's job was protecting the sweeper from snipers." (Burke-White 42).

Anzio was only thirty miles from Rome and was especially important to the German Army. Now, as of early May, they had been forced to retreat. Unfortunately, the Germans had left behind booby traps, mines, and snipers to harass and maim the Allies. The mines had to be cleared and any suspicious places booby traps could be placed—road culverts, innocent looking deserted buildings, even a rock outcropping beside the road—needed to be investigated.

"Not only were all roads mined by the Germans; but so were alleys,

goat trails and streams. Germans even booby-trapped doorknobs, desk drawers in empty buildings and grapevines and haystacks in the fields." (Atkinson 303-304)

Chasing the Germans was dangerous business, especially for the Combat Engineer Companies. Soldiers would soon learn mines could be waiting anywhere for some unlucky soldier to discover.

The weather was miserably cold and wet during the early phrase of the Anzio invasion. The roads were now muddy bogs and the mountains treacherous; trails were steep, slippery, and overgrown. It was almost impossible to supply any of the Allied soldiers fortunate enough to gain any high ground.

"The engineers sometimes built bridges across deep ravines sunlight could not even penetrate. But German binoculars could probe into most of them and enemy spotters could choose which half-track, jeep or road gang to target." (Bourke-White 40)

Sergeant Gantt said, "At night, sometimes we were out in front of the infantry and had to move trucks. I, along with other soldiers, sometimes guided the way with flashlights. No headlights could be turned on; that would make it too easy for snipers to find a clear target, even though the noise of moving machinery could only be silenced by slow travel and then only minimally. We also didn't dare light a cigarette, too dangerous." Sometimes bridges had to be built at night. Leon recalled, "We built a ninety-foot bridge completely in the dark. We put it across a gap in about an hour, never had any light, and couldn't even smoke. Every man knew his job and did it, very little talk allowed either. You knew what to do so you were not putting yourself or your buddy next to you in avoidable danger."

* * * * *

On May 11, 1944 the Allies attacked the Gustav line, the name of the German fortifications just to the south of Rome. The Allied Forces, British, Canadian, and Polish troops were able to breach this German line on the 24th of May. The Germans were in retreat towards northern Italy. The next day, the Germans retreated from the Anzio area, leaving all the Boot of southern Italy in Allied hands.

Thirty-Two

"TWO NIGHTS BEFORE THE ALLIED TROOPS WERE planning to enter Rome, the eternal city, leaflets were dropped by the American forces, written in Italian, encouraging the Roman citizens to safeguard their city's public services, telephone and telegraph plants, and railways. They were asked to remove obstacles that blocked the streets, leaving them free so that the Allied troops could pass through unencumbered. It was evident to the citizenry that the Germans were deserting the city. Suddenly, senior German officials' luggage was sent to the north from the Via Veneto Hotel." (Clark 363-364)

The evening of June 2nd, the Pope's message was broadcast to the world. "Whoever raises a hand against Rome will be guilty of matricide to the whole civilized world and the eternal judgment of God."

Even Hitler was decent enough to send a coded message to General Kesselring, the commander of the German 10th. "Rome," Hitler said, "was a place of culture and must not be a scene of combat." Hitler gave permission to Kesselring for all German troops to vacate the city.

The Roman citizens hated the enemy, the German Army; now the Germans were demoralized and beaten, retreating to the north.

Their hope was to cross the Arno River near Florence and fall back to the well-fortified Gothic line before the Po River Valley. According to the scuttlebutt that circulated among the Allies, This was the Germans' greatest defense between the Apennine Mountains and the Alps of Switzerland and Austria. They intended to make the Gothic Line their final stand to keep the Allies from winning the prize of Italy.

* * * * *

Mark Clark was determined that his Fifth Army would beat the British Eighth to be the first liberators to enter Rome.

In the early morning hours of June 4, 1944, our Allied troops entered the outskirts of the city. Officially, the liberators with General Mark Clark, among the first, entered the city on June 5, 1944. Sergeant Leon Gantt was attached to the 2nd Corp that entered Rome the first day, following General Mark Clark.

"The Fifth Army, with General Clark in one of the lead jeeps, entered the city of Rome at 8:00 A.M. that morning, June fifth, followed by his entourage of staff officers. Following behind their leaders was a long column of vehicles: tanks, jeeps, guns and large trucks. The snake-like column stretched as far as the eyes could see. Clark drove first in his jeep to St. Peters, and there posed for a photograph with a priest. The priest said, "Welcome to Rome, is there anything we can do for you?" (Clark 366). Bells were ringing all over the city. General Clark had the right to be proud; he was considered the conqueror of Rome. The Roman citizens welcomed the

Americans and were happy to be their hosts. The Italians danced in the streets, pretty Italian girls kissed Allied soldiers as they marched by and there was all manner of celebration, including champagne corks popping.

Sergeant Leon Gantt remembered the excitement and pride he felt entering the 'eternal city.' "An enthusiastic soldier removed the road sign at the edge of the city boundary and presented it to General Clark as a souvenir," Leon recalled years later.

* * * * *

After their unit, the 85th, found quarters on the northern outskirts of the city, the members received official orders from their superior officer for a three-day leave. General Mark Clark decided the liberators of Rome deserved a brief leave to enjoy the hospitality of the grateful Romans before moving northward in pursuit of the Germans.

"Before that order took effect, the 85th Combat Engineers had to construct a bridge over the Tiber River in Rome and a foot bridge attached for pedestrians. Bridge construction was delayed several times by enemy artillery but was completed by Sergeant Gantt's unit on June 6." (85th Combat Battalion Website).

Sergeant Gantt and two of his buddies, Corporal Juhlin Golden and Corporal George Shimmel decided to see some of the beauty of ancient city. The 85th had two days before their unit would move out, heading north up highway 9 toward the cities of Florence and Bologna. The German Gothic line of defense was just to the north of Bologna in the Apennine Mountains. Leon was no longer a drinking man, since he quit back in 1937; neither were Golden and Schimmel. Most of their fellow soldiers were more interested in frequenting the cities' bars and bordellos with their free time. Leon was just thankful to have a real bed for a couple of nights and a roof over his head for a change. Being a farm boy from the backwoods of South Carolina, the very idea of being in the city of Rome, Italy, was almost beyond his comprehension, especially after the carnage and destruction he had witnessed so far in this Great War.

Sergeant Gantt and his companions, Golden and Schimmel, visited the Coliseum, the Spanish steps, St. Peters Basilica, and the Cemetery of the Capuchin Fathers. The Cemetery was to the right of the Church of the Immaculate Conception. There was an underground passage with a long corridor and six arched compartments. The walls, archways, and candelabras were constructed from the bones of some four thousand religious people who died between 1528 and 1870. The underground passageway was lit only by small lights and appeared quite eerily and somewhat grotesque, considering the decorative use of human bones. Leon was fascinated especially when he took a flashlight from his coat, peered into the mouth of a mummified woman, and saw a few snags of teeth remaining. Supposedly the woman had died some five hundred years earlier. Here, her remains were displayed in a glass coffin. His two companions, Cpl. Golden and Cpl. Shimmel, were not as fascinated as the Sergeant. Every place they visited, Leon purchased a postcard as a souvenir, hoping to show the folks at home, if he was lucky enough to survive and make it home.

Two days later, the Fifth Army and all units were on the move, chasing the Germans northward. On June 17th, Fifth Army Headquarters was relocated at Tuscani, some seventy miles north of Rome.

* * * * *

Somewhere in Italy

June 1944

Dear Robert,

I am writing to let you know I am alive and well. We're in the low lands (I guess it's OK to write that) of Italy. Seeing how most of the country is mountainous you might be able to approximate my location. I don't relish the weather at present. It has been raining continuously, but I am thankful, the road has not been too boggy as of yet. It is no fun however sleeping in a tent. At present, I have a lantern sitting on a wooden crate and am writing by lantern light. It kind of reminded me of home, knowing you still have no electricity there. I try not to think too much of home because I realize I may never see the old house Daddy and his brothers built so long ago. If I do make it home, I plan to spend the rest of my days there. I think of the times we sat on that porch with kin and friends; just sitting, rocking in those chairs daddy built, or swinging in the porch swing, talking about everything and nothing, listening to the whip-poorwills, crickets, and watching lightening bugs flit back and forth in the front yard. Sometimes I would catch a whiff of Miss Florence's roses on that big bush under the window if the season, the breeze and sitting in the right spot. We always had Will, James, Bunyan or Eugene to talk with. It seems funny when I think of it now. What I miss the most are the little things; the sun sitting over the river swamp, the darkness on the porch with only kerosene lamps shining from the windows, and if there is a full moon, it illuminates the whole yard. I do believe the moon shines brighter from that front porch than it does in this foreign place. That's what I'm hoping for if I make it home; peace. Tell Daddy and Miss Florence I miss them and remember me to Grandmamma Peninnah and the rest of the family at Rayflin.

Leon

Thirty-Three

THE LIBERATION OF ROME ON THE FIFTH OF JUNE 1944 WAS overshadowed by the landings at Normandy a day later. Operation Overlord, commanded by Supreme Commander Dwight Eisenhower, took precedence over the liberation of Rome the day before. But there was very little bitterness that Normandy pushed the liberation of Rome from the headlines. The troops called themselves the 'D-Day Dodgers.' The veteran troops in Italy began to take a perverse satisfaction in being overlooked. Between June and August, the troop strength of the Fifth Army fell significantly due to troops being reassigned to France, code name – Anvil.

Two months after the liberation of Rome, in August the Allies captured Florence, made a turn to the west toward the Italian coast, liberating Leghorn, then crossed the Arno River and entered Pisa to the north. They had now conquered what the Germans called their Arno line of defenses. The Allied troops broke their way through line after line of German defenses, crossed mountain after mountain and river after river to find north of Florence the same German Army.

"The Germans took up position in the Apennine Mountains behind

their last line of defense the indestructible Gothic Line." (Atkinson 672)

The Allies comrades in arms, the Eighth British Army, and all their units reached the Gothic line first and attacked the fortifications there on all fronts.

Their first strategy was to take the coastal plain around the mountains on the eastern side of the peninsula. General Alexander was the supreme commander in Italy at this time. Under Alexander, General Mark Clark commanded the Fifth Army and General Sir Oliver Leese commanded the Eighth British Army. Both the Fifth and the Eighth Armies were in position before the Gothic Line. Alexander ordered all bridges over the Po River destroyed from the air; this would limit the Germans' escape route and the possibility of their being reinforced. The Gothic Line was a tough nut to crack, but the Allied armies kept pounding away.

Mark Clark faced north from Florence towards Bologna, a distance of only fifty miles, but over some of the most rugged country God could have created for a military to conquer. The roads through the mountains were narrow, with substandard construction and hairpin turns. The roads were not built for large trucks, tanks, or trucks carrying the portable Bailey bridge components necessary for crossing the Po River when reached.

Before any of the vehicles could get through the mountains, the enemy dug in up and down the mountains' sides, with many fortified cement machine gun nests that had to be cleared. The enemy was hidden in caves and camouflaged by every imaginable and ingenious trick possible. The Germans were determined to kill or main as many Allied soldiers as they possibly could. The German commanders, however, had underestimated the American soldiers' ability to transform what was the most difficult country into a viable ground for attack.

The Second Corp pushed through the center, flanked by the left and right wings of the Fifth Army. By the last half of October 1944, Clark and the Americans were within eight miles of Bologna and were determined to break into the Po Valley before winter clamped down on the Apennines. Winter was fast closing in on the Fifth, but they pushed on toward their objective. On November 24, 1944, Clark was placed in command of the Fifteenth Army group, British Eighth, and the Fifth Army. He had taken Alexander's place and was directing all ground forces in Italy. Clark went to the front every day and was very popular with all his troops. There was always one more ridge to cross, it seemed. The joke was the Germans had left and took the last ridge with them.

Leon, historian though he was not, could see some parallels with their position in the freezing snow-covered Apennines before Bologna and the Po valley and General Washington at Valley Forge. They did have better accommodations, warm uniforms, and supplies, whereas the Continental troops had none of these. It was just a fleeting thought, but lent some credence to the American soldiers' spirit of determination and hardship no matter the cost.

In one of Leon's letters, he shared his grim perspective of War and the degradation it caused in the moral fiber of civilized people; this letter Robert did not share with Florence and Kelly. He knew it would only make their lives more depressing, but he figured Leon told him because he needed to share it with someone.

Leon penned the letter when he was serving 'somewhere in Italy' in the freezing cold of the Apennine Mountains in the winter of 1944-45. The letter was not dated and he had addressed it to Robert, knowing after he had read it, he would keep its contents secret from their daddy and Miss Florence. No need to burden them with the horrors of the War he had personally witnessed.

Leon wrote, "I try not to become too close to the new guys in our unit. They always seemed to make some stupid mistake on the front lines and became casualties of the enemy. It took a while to become battle hardened veterans and you don't reach that point in a few days, weeks, or months.

"Let me tell you something, and I think it affects every soldier this way. You get over here in this kind of damn mess and you get to wondering, when you see all them fellows killed and lying dead, run over by tanks and all that blood, gore, and disregard of human life and stuff that no human should have to see; you get to saying, "Well, I wonder if I'll get to go back home or not, bogged up in this kinda damn mess." You'll go that way for a few months and then you get to where you don't give a damn if you go home or not and that's when you raise plenty of hell. When you reach that mindset, I would consider you a battle-hardened veteran."

* * * * *

Sergeant Gantt was billeted in an eight-man tent. It now seemed like he might get a little rest at night; at least they had broken through the mountains at the edge of the Po Valley. He had just fallen asleep when 1st Lieutenant Russell came into the tent with a light.

"Sergeant Gantt?"

"Yes sir, Lieutenant, what you want?"

"Be ready to leave here at 0300 hours. Me, you and five others have got to go to Rome."

"What are we going back there for, sir?" Leon asked. "We've done been there."

"That's true, Sergeant, but we've got to go back there to engineering school to learn how to construct Bailey Bridges. Just Sergeants and officers have to go. Our company leader feels we, being fairly new to a Combat Engineer unit, need some more training on bridge construction."

"How are we going, Lieutenant?"

"We're going to the airstrip to catch a plane."

The next morning, a truck was waiting there to take those chosen to the airstrip. They got out to the strip and there was just one little tent beside the strip. They waited and waited. Finally, an officer went to the tent and asked the personnel inside about a plane that was supposed to take them to Rome.

"Sorry, sir," the man in charge told the Lieutenant. "I haven't received any communication about an airplane designated to transport you and your men to Rome." Finally, late in the morning a phone message was received for Lieutenant Russell.

"We'll have to go by truck, I'm afraid. No plane has been reserved for us," Lieutenant Russell informed the group.

One can only surmise how downtrodden the men felt. But they had their orders, and no one complained; they all climbed in the back of the deuce and a half and started for Rome. They rode all day long until, late in the evening, they reached Florence, Italy, spending the night there. Rising again at 0300 in the morning, they rode all day and entered the south side of Rome at almost sundown. The school was going on when they arrived. The days' instruction and demonstration were almost over. They were dismissed and were assigned a barracks for the night.

Sergeant Gantt and the others showered. "Boy, am I whipped and give out, but I don't think I am the only one," Leon noted. They ate and showered. "This almost feels like home, sleeping in a house with electric lights, not in a tent or outside looking at the stars," Leon commented.

They next day, they worked all day on Bailey Bridges, being trained on how to assemble and disassemble the lightweight sections that could be locked together quickly with enough know-how and co-operation. Team work was the key, Leon soon realized, and of course knowledge of the construction. He was beginning to feel confident about his training and so were the others. They all took a bath that evening. It was already dark outside and Leon was writing home when a fellow entered their barracks with a message.

"How many of you fellows in here are from the 85th Engineers?"

Several spoke up in the affirmative.

"You're going to leave in the morning," said the fellow.

"What's this all about?" Lieutenant Russell inquired.

"Your outfit has been alerted that you are being reassigned and all that are in the 85th need to get back to your outfit as soon as you can. Your orders should be ready at 0500."

No soldier went anywhere without orders to that effect.

Two days later, four members of the 85th reached their bivouac on the outskirts of Bologna in the Apennines at the edge of the Po Valley. There was only one member of the 85th left, Sergeant Gilbert. Engineering Companies were in great demand for the operation in France. General Clark allowed the Seventh Army Commander, General Alexander Patch, to choose which of the Fifth

Army Engineer Units he wanted, and he chose the 85th. General Clark released them to the Seventh Army; their next stop would the beaches of Nice, France.

Gilbert had not gone with the others because he had 85 points, enough to go home to the states. Leon only had 83 and therefore would be reassigned somewhere else.

"Where in the hell am I supposed to be?" Leon asked at headquarters. Everyone who returned with him from Engineering School in Rome was being assigned to different units.

"Tomorrow, Sergeant, you are going to the 169th Combat Engineers," replied the clerk. "I have your orders right here," he said.

At first, Leon did not have a good feeling about being in the 169th. They had been formed in 1943 at Camp Beale, California, and arrived in Italy in September 1944. *In my outfit, the 85th, if you didn't know your stuff, you didn't get no strips. The 169th was not a real outfit; those guys in there got their strips from shining officers' shoes, buckles, and stuff. Now I am in a real mess,* he thought to himself. He was an old guy, thirty-four, compared to the others in that new unit, the 169th Engineers, and was a veteran who had seen the horrors and destruction of war in Italy and also North Africa. Most of these guys were just shave tails to Leon.

After being in the 169th a few months, he realized that these younger guys looked up to him because he had more experience, and he became an asset to the unit. *At least these boys know how to construct bridges and clear mines.* There grew a mutual respect between Sergeant Gantt and his new unit.

The Fifth Army really had the Germans on the run. They had to conquer the heights at Bologna to get into the Po Valley proper. The men had shivered and endured another bleak winter of snow, rain, fog, cold, and general misery before Bologna. At Bologna, located at the northern edge of the Apennines and at the edge of the Po Valley, winter had set in with a vengeance. The letter home Leon was writing back in Rome was never sent. The 169th was too busy battling the freezing landscape, the slippery roads, and the enemy advancing ahead of them towards the Po River. Mark Clark was determined to reach the Po River and trap the Germans there. The Fifth, in pursuit, dealt with sniper fire, mines and booby traps the Germans left behind to slow their progress.

* * * * *

With the arrival of spring 1945, the Allies made a push forward to trap the Germans before they could cross the Po River. On April 21, 1945, Bologna finally fell completely to the Allied forces.

The Allied Armies were crossing the Po valley, pushing to trap the Germans before they could escape further north. The Germans, realizing the Allies were nipping at their heels, had reconstructed the pontoon bridge across the Po that had been destroyed earlier by Allied planes before the siege at the Gothic line began. The German engineers hurriedly rebuilt their bridge when it was evident that they would be trapped there. Some of the German Tenth Army had escaped before the Allied planes destroyed their escape route once again. Many were trapped and surrendered to the Fifth Army. Those that escaped were fleeing across the Po Valley for the Swiss and Austrian borders and the Alps.

Thirty-Four

NOW THAT THE FIFTH ARMY HAD FINALLY REACHED THE PO River, it seemed that all of Italy was theirs. The German units that had not surrendered to the Allies were fleeing to the north in hopes of making a stand with their comrades in Austria or the Fatherland, Germany. Many had been indoctrinated by their Fuhrer Hitler's words, and his elite SS troops made sure Hitler's orders were followed to the letter. Most of Hitler's troops believed they were obligated to the Fatherland to fight to the death for their cause.

There were those in the German Army that were beginning to realize their comrades were dying for a lost cause. There was even an attempt to assassinate Hitler in July of '44 by some of his own men. This attempt was perpetrated by some officers in his high command. The attempt was a failure and those involved were executed.

The German people were not total barbarians as portrayed; a great many were just following orders. Leon realized this but kept his opinion to himself. He knew evil when he saw it and had seen a lot perpetrated by the Germans who followed Hitler and his Generals. But he had also seen frozen corpses of American soldiers disrespected, piled together, arms and legs frozen in grotesque positions, ignored by other American soldiers as if they were just a part of the landscape. All he could think of when he saw this kind of treatment was, *Those boys are loved by their families, they have mothers, fathers, sweethearts, and wives back home that would be totally mortified that their remains were treated this way.* He tried to push these thoughts from his mind, knowing that if he dwelled on all this death and destruction around him, he would very likely go insane. There had been a few guys in his unit who had gone completely mad. He was determined to do whatever it took: kill German soldiers, destroy innocent people and towns. Like he had told Robert in his last letter, *You get to thinking you won't ever see home again and that's when you do raise hell. That's what it takes to survive.*

* * * * *

Standing on the bank of the Po River, the 169th Combat Engineers knew they had a job to do, and a dauntless task at that. There were no mines to remove now, just a bridge to be constructed in record time across fifteen hundred feet of swift flowing water, the Po River. Leon told the other engineers, "It is at least that distance to the far bank, but we will know for sure once it has been completed."

"The Bridge would be constructed for the first 200 feet with Bailey bridge components. The Bailey bridge was a marvel for bridge construction and the portable design made it the most remarkable bridge in the history of military operations. It can cross two hundred forty feet without pontoons; bridge parts were interchangeable and light weight, the heaviest part requiring only six men to lift. It was prefabricated in ten-foot sections, and only one steel pin is needed for each joint. The

Bailey, after being built on rollers on the edge of the river, can be pushed over by the building crew without mechanical aid. Because of the Bailey's simple design and light-weight construction it can be put together in record time and used for tanks and artillery pieces. It was constructed for bridge approaches and exits. The triple-single Bailey bridge went down two hundred feet on the near bank. The rest of the bridge was set on steel pontoons across the water." (Bourke-White 55-56)

The Engineers had to stretch a steel cable across the river to within two hundred feet of the far bank, where the portable Bailey bridge was again constructed. The bridge over the Po River was constructed in twenty-four hours with the combat engineers working eight hours shifts until completion.

Once reached, the far bank had to be cleared first by the engineers. "We have to be sure there are no mines the Germans may have left before fleeing," Leon assured those in his platoon. After this task was completed, the bridge was operational for vehicles and infantry. Soldiers had to stand guard on both banks of the river to watch for floating objects large enough to break the bridge cables.

Shortly after the bridge was completed, Leon saw a jeep floating down the river. "Help me get that jeep between the pontoons!" he shouted to a group of fellows above the noise of the swift running river. "We have to push it between the steel pontoons—can't afford to have it hung up, liable to break the cable, and then we would have a mess on our hands. The whole damn thing could unravel and down the river our bridge would go." They had to stay alert when it came to large floating objects, or the result could be disastrous if the steel cable was broken.

Thirty-Five

BENITO MUSSOLINI, HIS MISTRESS CLARA PETACCI, AND FIVE of his fascist followers were captured in Milan, Italy, by Italian Partisans and executed on April 28, 1945. The next day, their bodies were hung upside down with piano wire at an Esso station in the center of Milan, Italy. The crowds desecrated the bodies hanging there, striking them with all manner of objects, spitting on them, and taking out their hatred on the remains until they were pushed back by law enforcing authorities. The bodies were finally cut down and put on public displace in wooden coffins, propped up so that photographs could be taken to record what was their final deserved justice. The story had been told to Sergeant Gantt by some of the British Eighth soldiers who had witnessed the execution.

Leon was in the vicinity of Milan at that time and was told of the exhibition of Mussolini and his mistress's dead bodies at the center of Milan. Two British soldiers told him of the macabre spectacle they had seen and asked if he wanted to go see them, since it wasn't very far to Milan.

Leon refused. "I have seen enough death and mutilated bodies already in this war and have no desire to purposely see anymore, no matter who they are."

* * * * *

Sergeant Gantt and his unit were in northern Italy now, the brilliance of the Alps rising to the north, the Apennines to the south.

"Our unit got up there one afternoon near the town of Verona," Leon recalled. "Verona is a pretty big place. They were fighting in the town; I could hear snipers shooting at our boys. We turned right at the edge of town and went out into a big barley field. It was May and I could see the Alps in the distance. They looked like fields of cotton with the snow on the tops. About night, our platoon officer came to me.

"'Gantt, I want you and your squad at the edge of town tomorrow; be up there a little after daybreak, there will be trucks arriving about 0900. The trucks are coming in advance of the Fifth Army's Headquarters and you will be needed to help unload the trucks.'

"We took out our little old tents, set them up for the night, and got some chow. When the moon came up, we could hear sniper fire and artillery rounds exploding in Verona. There was a tent set up with radio equipment, so our unit could stay in touch with what was going on in our area. One of the fellows came out of the radio tent; I could tell he was excited about something," Leon remembered

* * * * *

"Sergeant, do you know the War is over?"

"You're damn right I do."

"How did you find out?" he asked Leon.

"Hell, I've been knowing it all the time."

"How did you find out?" the radio guy asked Leon again.

"You didn't know it was over?" he asked the radio guy.

"Not until just a minute ago," the radio guy replied. By this time, he was beginning to get a little unnerved by the Sergeant he was addressing.

"Hell, it's all over this place here and all over the mountains," Leon replied with a wave of his hand towards the mountains.

"I'm not joking, the Germans are surrendering by the thousands, and there are some pockets that haven't gotten the word yet. Some right here close to us."

"How well I know that too," Leon answered.

By this time, the radio guy was ready to give up. His exciting news seemed to fall on deaf ears when it came to Sergeant Gantt.

That was just Leon's personality. He was like a modern day 'Columbo' of 1960s television fame. He played dumb, just like asking the Lieutenant at Foggia where Cassino had gone; actually, he was really a very astute and intelligent fellow. He had just learned early in life that you find out more if you just keep people thinking you know nothing. Like the radio guy, they give up explaining and leave you the hell alone.

* * * * *

Leon's squad was waiting at the edge of town near daylight and waited till late in the day, just like they were told by the platoon officer. The trucks still had not arrived; their platoon officer told them to go back and get some rest and he would send another squad to help unload when the trucks arrived.

The next morning, May 3, 1945, the trucks arrived loaded with prefabricated buildings, bolts, and all the needed tools to assemble the buildings. Sergeant Gantt and his squad went into town and unloaded the trucks. They immediately began to assemble the first building that would be part of Fifth Army headquarters in Verona. An officer walked up and addressed Leon.

"Sergeant, what are y'all doing in here working?'

"We were told to do it," Leon replied.

"Well, y'all are the only ones working, the whole Fifth Army is sitting down today."

It wasn't long before their Commanding Officer came up and told them to quit. "Germany has surrendered; your mission in Italy has been accomplished. Disassemble this building and reload it on the trucks. We'll decide where we want them later. Thanks, Sergeant, you and your men did a great job here."

Leon and his squad returned to their bivouac, tore down their tents, pulled back three miles from Verona, and set them up again. "Maybe we can get a little sleep tonight, boys. I'm sure headquarters will soon let us know what our new destination will be and will give us a new set of orders."

* * * * *

Our Soviet allies captured Berlin at the end of May. Adolph Hitler and his wife Eva Braun had committed suicide in the bunker that Hitler had ordered built under his headquarters in the city. Hitler shot himself and Eva took cyanide. He had requested that his elite SS troops burn their remains in the garden in front of the building where his bunker was located. Hitler didn't want Eva and himself to have their bodies treated like his comrade Mussolini and his mistress had been treated in Milan, Italy.

The unconditional surrender of all German troops to the Allies was made formal and was signed on May 7, 1945 in Rehims, France. Officially, the next day, May 8th, was celebrated as VE day, Victory in Europe. The Germans had been defeated and were no longer a threat in Europe.

Thirty-Six

THE 169TH COMBAT ENGINEERS, LEON'S UNIT, WAS, FOR THE time being, ordered to stay in northern Italy. They had gone all the way up to the Austrian border and the Alps. They were awaiting formal orders from Fifth Army headquarters. In the meantime, they did what they were trained to do; their commanding officer approved the engineers to help the Italian citizens.

They built bridges, restructured roadways, clearing burnt out vehicles blocking the roads, and basically helped the Italians in rebuilding their infrastructure. Of course, the Italians were very grateful to have the American and British help in making their home country livable once again. But the Italian population realized that this was just an interim job for the Allies. They were still fighting in the Pacific against the Japanese. It was only a matter of time until the Allied soldiers in Italy would be ordered elsewhere.

"Almost two months later, at the beginning of August 1945," Leon recalled, "the 169th Combat Engineers finally received official orders from Fifth Army Headquarters. We were to report to Leghorn, Italy, to be transported by the USS General M.B. Stuart from the Italian theater to the island of Okinawa in the Pacific in preparation for the invasion of Japan."

* * * * *

As the soldiers ascended the gangplank of the General Stuart with their backpacks, carrying their duffle bags, their faces and countenance were that of depressed and downtrodden men. Their ship, the General M.B. Stuart, with some three thousand servicemen on board, was to proceed from Leghorn, Italy, across the Mediterranean, stopping only to refuel at Gibraltar, then across the Atlantic through the Panama Canal into the Pacific Ocean and to the island of Okinawa.

As the General Stuart pulled away from the Italian shore, many felt a twinge of nostalgia for the friends they left behind, for the places they'd lived in and for the sights they had become accustomed to. Hardiest of all for Leon was he knew he was leaving behind buddies that had died defending North Africa and Italy.

I have seen so many friends dismembered and mutilated by bullets and bombs; a few were right beside me in foxholes or behind cover of a rock outcropping. They died and I was spared. Spared for what and how; by the grace of God for a purpose only He knew or by just plain dumb luck. How long will I survive, going into battle again? Leon wondered.

He determined he would survive no matter how many enemies he had to kill, how many innocent people were destroyed, or how many innocent people lost their homes and livelihoods. He had become a hardened veteran. As he told Robert, "When you reach this point, that's when you really raise hell."

* * * * *

The men aboard the General Stuart learned of Truman's authorizing the dropping of an atomic bomb on Hiroshima, Japan on August 6, 1945. Leon recalled, "The news made our spirits lift. Perhaps, we thought, this is the end. Some of us thought we would endure this long journey and then end up spending a year over in the Pacific area even if the Japs did surrender." Their planned voyage on the General was a direct route, with no stops in the States.

"Our spirits continued to rise with Russia's declaring war on the Japanese on August 8. On August 9, Truman dropped another atomic bomb on Nagasaki, Japan. Surely the end must be near, but the General Stuart neared the 'Rock' on the tenth. It loomed ahead through a veil of mist. Everyone ascended from the bow of the ship to give Gibraltar the once over at close range. Here, we made a scheduled stop to refuel on the eleventh. Rumors abound that the Japs have offered to surrender; the rumors were confirmed. The Allies wasted no time in replying to the Japanese; nothing but unconditional surrender was acceptable. Emperor Hiro Hito had to take orders from the Supreme Allied Commander. On Monday the thirteenth, still no word from the Japanese. Every man on board strained to hear any announcement over the loud speaker on the starboard side. On Tuesday, sailing weather was fine. We were now out in the Atlantic, heading straight across till mid-ocean, then southwest towards the Panama Canal."

What is taking so long? The suspense is so thick you could cut it with a knife. Why haven't the Japs replied?

"Lights out was called at 2130 hours, turn in to your bunks –

silence about the deck; the War was still on and we were still rolling towards the Pacific; another day of disappointment. By 2200 hours, most soldiers were in their bunks. Only a few remained on deck, still praying, hanging on the rails, watching the North Star and straining to hear. Yes, we were in the middle of the Atlantic, now heading southwest towards Panama."

Then from the speaker came the long-awaited announcement. "President Truman has just announced the surrender of Japan. The War is over." The time was 2235 hours and all hell broke loose on the quiet deck. The cheers of the men on deck yelling, "It's over! The War's over!" brought three thousand wild-eyed, jumping GIs on deck, most in their shorts. It was the wildest, happiest three thousand men ever to ride the waves of the Atlantic. They jumped, they yelled, they screamed, some with tears streaming down their faces. They slapped each other on the back, officers hugged privates; rank did not matter to the three thousand ecstatic men that night. They were all equal in that time and place. Then someone started singing 'The Star-Spangled Banner' and every man on deck joined in. Then came 'God Bless America'; it was all spontaneous, the songs just burst out like fireworks on the 4th of July. Cold chills ran up and down the men's spines. It was a grand and glorious night. For the first time in years, the world was at peace.

One black soldier yelled, "Now is the time to turn on them lights again, all over the world."

In answer to his exclamation came, "Navy, fire the guns...turn on the lights… … .let's go home!"

It had been a dark night, a rough sea, but suddenly if you were watching, you could see the moon come out from behind the clouds. The sea was calm as glass. To the soldiers and sailors on the

General M.B. Stuart, it was a wonderful, glorious night that they would never forget.

Yes, the 14th had been a big night for the fellows onboard the General Stewart, but the morning of 15th would be even better. The first question that morning was, "Are we still headed south?" Arguments, rumors, and reports floated in air that morning. "Can't we just change course and dock somewhere on the east coast?" But the ship just kept rolling along to the south and Panama.

Then at 1020 hours that morning, Wednesday morning, August 15th, 1945, a loud whistle blast came over the loudspeaker. The announcement came in a dull, quite tone … "The ship's destination has been changed to New York."

Wow! Talk about celebration!

"We are going home, can you believe it? I'm going home after three and a half years of not seeing my family or home. I'll be there in a few days!" Normally calm, Leon laughed, jumped, cried, and slapped his buddies on the back, just like all the fellows did that wonderful morning. There was a rumor that the Captain's brother worked for the Pentagon and had arranged for the change of destination.

All day long, the men hugged the rail, just waiting, standing there, watching the water. Even late at night, men still lined the rails. No one wanted to go to bed; their minds were in turmoil over what had actually happened in the last three days. They went from highs to lows and back again, like the pendulum on a clock. But the last three days had been mostly highs. The dropping of the atomic bombs, the Japs' surrender, the War declared over. And now they had changed course for New York City. It was almost too much for their minds to comprehend.

Early Sunday morning, August 19th, the General Stuart was in sight of New York City. The tall skyscrapers could be seen before they actually entered the harbor. The soldiers, most whom had been hanging on the rails long before daylight, finally saw home. When Liberty Island came into view, the Statue of Liberty with her torch held high, many of the men just stood quietly as the ship slipped passed her. Tears ran down their faces; the emotion of actually being in this place at this time was too much happiness at once. It was really overwhelming. All their senses were heightened at once. Some still believed it was all a dream. Home at last to some; they were only hours away from those loved ones they had left behind. To others like Leon, there would be a long trip before they actually got home, but at least they had reached the USA. Some among their shipmates would be traveling across the entire country; it would be days before they made it home.

"On Sunday August 19th, around 1200 hours, the USS General M.B. Stuart docked at Pier 83 on 42nd Street in New York City. The General Stuart was the first troop ship to land in New York after the War ended." (The Trooper Souvenir Edition, printed aboard the Gen. M.B. Stuart and distributed to the 3000 troops aboard).

Thirty-Seven

THE LOUDSPEAKER HAD BEEN GIVING INSTRUCTIONS FOR days as to the procedure for disembarking the ship once she had docked in New York City. The men would leave the ship in groups every thirty minutes; their company commanders had been busy dictating orders to clerks, so every soldier would have his orders in hand and could travel for free. All men were to receive a thirty-day furlough at home, and then would report to their original training center to be mustered out of the service or to receive new orders if they had not served their time. Leon had done his time and would report to Fort Belvoir, Virginia, to be discharged after his furlough and to receive his discharge papers.

The men left the ship on trucks every thirty minutes and were dismissed by companies. They already knew their departure time before the ship docked. They would be initially taken to Camp Shanks outside of New York City and would make arrangements from there to head home.

Some guys were in no hurry and wanted to see the city. Some lived in one of the boroughs around the city, the Bronx, Brooklyn, Queens, Staten Island, or Harlem, even Long Island and Manhattan Island itself. It was such a huge city, lots of guys lived in neighborhoods dominated by their ethnic groups; Irish, Italian, Greek, African, they all lived in New York. And everyone considered New York City their home town, no matter what section of the city was home. When the General Stuart docked, they were home.

Leon cared nothing of seeing the city; he wanted to catch the first conveyance heading south to where he belonged, the sparsely settled country of South Carolina. They still didn't have electricity in the world he considered home, but that's where he longed to be, and the sooner he got there, the better.

Finally, at 2:30 PM, Leon disembarked from the General Stuart. Heading down the gangplank, he never looked back. He was wearing his backpack and carrying his duffle bag. Throwing his duffle bag into the back of the truck and excepting a hand up from another soldier, he was seated and ready to go. None of his family had a clue he was on his way home so soon after the War had ended. They thought it would probably be months, at least weeks, before he arrived.

"Boy, are my kinfolks going to be surprised when I show up!" Leon commented.

Leon got to the train station not far from Camp Shanks and requested a ticket on the quickest train heading south. He showed the agent his orders and was promptly booked a seat on the Atlantic Coast train.

"The train will be pulling out in about thirty minutes," the agent said. "We will be pleased to have you aboard, Sergeant Gantt and wish you well. Thanks for your service."

"Can I get some supper on the train?"

"You certainly can, sir, just make your way to the dining car."

Leon put his backpack overhead and dropped his duffle bag in the empty seat facing him, thinking, *I'll move it if the seat is needed.* In two minutes, he was hard and fast asleep with his feet propped on his duffle bag. He didn't even think of food. He was just tired and emotionally drained. Now that he knew he was on the way, his body began to relax. With no unforeseen delays, the train would be in South Carolina in about seven hours. It could travel fast, faster than a car for sure, just a straight track and very few stops.

Leon woke up just as the train crossed into South Carolina. When it stopped in Sumter, he grabbed his gear and got off. He didn't want to end up in Miami; changing trains would be necessary. He ate fried chicken in Sumter at the station. Man, he had missed fried chicken. He took another train across Lake Marion to Fort Gordon, Georgia.

His appearance crossed his mind. *Boy, I am a mess. I haven't shaved and need a bath. I look like I've been making liquor and have been on a week-long drunk.*

When he reached Fort Gordon, he was able to have that bath and shave.

He got in the chow line, but the line cut off so he didn't get any food. From Gordon, he took an Army bus to Augusta, and then caught a Greyhound to Batesburg. It was in the early morning, about 4:00 AM, when the bus pulled into the station in Batesburg. Leon got off with his gear and started walking, figuring he could make it to Mr. Ed Ridgell's house. Ed was Fred's daddy. It was still dark so he sat down on the front porch. Mr. Ed heard someone on the porch and told his wife, Miss Sallie, to get up and turn on the porch light. They were sure surprised to see Leon. He went in and Mr. Ed called Fred at home. Elsie was working at the mill on 3rd shift. Fred came right over and picked him up."

"I'm taking you to the mill to surprise Elsie."

Elsie had her back to them, running a loom.

Fred said, "Elsie, there's somebody here that wants to see you."

She turned around and saw Leon. She froze for a minute, couldn't believe he was actually there. Then she rushed over to her big brother and threw her arms around his neck in a tight embrace, almost a bear hug.

Leon blurted out between tears, "It feels so good to have my little sister in my arms after two and a half years." They were both in tears by the time Elsie released her grip.

Elsie got off work and she and Fred took Leon down home to see their daddy, Kelly, Miss Florence, and Robert. The eastern sky was just beginning to turn light pink as the sun started to come up.

"Considering Daddy's health, having a stroke and all, I think Fred and I should go in first and break the news of your return to Daddy. I'm afraid the shock might cause him to have another stroke."

"Well, do try to break it to him gently," Leon replied as Fred pulled the car into the driveway.

After they exited the car, Leon sat ever so still, taking in the vision he had carried in his mind every waking hour, and even in his dreams: home. A tear slipped down his cheek as he gazed upon the old house and yard, still in disbelief that he was actually here.

Of course, it was odd for Elsie and Fred to arrive so early in the morning, and in the middle of the week. Miss Florence was already up cooking breakfast. She let them in and welcomed them, noticing the conspiratorial gleam in Elsie's eyes.

"Is everything OK, Elsie?" Miss Florence asked, concerned.

"Of course, it's absolutely great; do you think Daddy is awake yet? If not, we'll just have to wake him up." In a low voice, she whispered, "Leon's home and is waiting in the car."

"Imagine that, is all Miss Florence could think to say. "Kelly will be so excited. Let's go see if he is awake."

When they entered Kelly and Florence's bedroom, a faint hint of daylight was beginning to peep through the windows; Kelly was sitting on the side of the bed holding the walking stick Robert had made for him.

"Well, I heard a car drive up and could see through the window that it was Elsie and Fred. What in the blazes are they doing here this early and in the middle of the week? I figured something bad or good had occurred." He could now see that Elsie and Fred were standing behind Florence. "Well, get in here and tell me what's going on right now. Florence, go ahead and light the lamp by my chair please."

"Oh Daddy, it's the greatest news. We just didn't want you to get overly excited, so we left him in the car."

"For God's sake, Elsie, who did you leave in the car? Damnation, woman, you know I don't like surprises!"

"It's Leon daddy, he's home from the War!"

"My boy's home and you left him in the car! Go tell him to get in here, his daddy has been waiting for this day for too long. Florence, you better wake Robert. He'll be just as excited to see Leon and it's about time for him to be up anyway."

Fred hurried out to car to get Leon while Elsie slid Kelly's rocker to the bedside and helped him get into it.

Florence woke Robert and told him, "Leon's here, get your pants on. I'm sure you'll want a little time with him before you go to work."

Kelly looked up from his seat near the fireplace and in the doorway stood his eldest son dressed in his uniform. "My son, you are a sight for these old eyes. I was afraid I might not get to see you again."

Leon crossed the room, shook his daddy's hand, bent over, and gave him a long hug. "It's wonderful to see you too, Daddy." Raw emotion sounded in his voice. He had a hard time controlling his feelings but didn't want to get all blubbery in front of Kelly. It wasn't the manly thing to do.

From the doorway, Robert said, "Good to see you, big brother, and welcome home. It sure has felt empty without you in this old house." Robert rushed over and hugged Leon and gave him a pat on the back, something unusual for both of them. They normally didn't show affection, but this was a special occasion and they both felt the need just to touch, to make sure the other was real flesh and bone, not an apparition.

Robert continued, "Let's help Daddy to the kitchen so we can sit around the table, have a cup of coffee and maybe some breakfast. I think we have a lot of catching up to do, don't you?"

They did sit around the kitchen table that morning. Leon looked from one face to the other. He had thought of his family so much in the last two and a half years, he would have been content to just sit and gaze on the faces of these loved ones he had longed to see.

Elsie and Fred soon left. Elsie gave Leon a final hug. "I'll see you for Sunday dinner. Maybe y'all can come to our house for a change, if Daddy feels like getting out."

Robert got ready for work and Mr. Wilson picked him up in the logging truck. He purposely waited until they reached the highway before he told Mr. Wilson the good news, knowing his boss would want to at least take the time to welcome Leon home. Robert didn't want to delay the work day by even thirty minutes. He knew the sooner he got to work, the sooner he would be done for the day and would be back home to sit and hear all Leon's experiences, both good and bad. Robert was really looking forward to the end of his work day. He could have probably told Mr. Wilson and requested the day off, but he had a job to do. They really needed the money, and if he missed the day, he wouldn't be paid.

Leon helped his daddy back to his room. "We'll talk some more later, Daddy. I just have to lie down for a spell. I might go down to Rayflin this afternoon and see Grandmamma Peninnah. Is she doing OK?"

"I would say tolerable for a woman her age. At least she can move around, that's a hell of a sight more than I can say for myself. She'll be so happy to see you, son. Now go and get you some rest. I'm mighty glad you made it home."

For thirty days, Leon just enjoyed basking in the glow of his family's affection, walking the fields and sandy roads of home. It was so quiet and calming without the clang of medal, the sound of gunfire, or the sight of destruction and bloodshed. At first, he had some bad dreams that he was back in the thick of the fight and would wake up in a cold sweat when the dreams were too vivid. Eventually, the bad dreams would fade away for Sergeant Leon Gantt and the quiet of the countryside, the crickets chirping, and the breeze stirring the magnolia leaves outside his open window would lull him from fretful to calm sleep. Many soldiers would never overcome the bad dreams and flashbacks. They would be diagnosed with 'shell shock' and suffer the remainder of their lives, never recovering from the horrors that the War had inflicted on their minds.

* * * * *

After thirty days furlough, Elsie and Fred took Leon to Fort Belvoir, Virginia, to be mustered out of the US Army. He had fulfilled his obligation but was required to stay at Fort Belvoir until all his paperwork could be sorted out.

There were so many men in uniform, Sergeant Gantt was given a patch to sew on his uniform. The soldiers called this patch 'a ruptured duck.' It was khaki in color and had a duck in flight on it. The purpose was to distinguish the soldiers who were no longer on active duty from those that were. Sergeant Leon O. Gantt was presented with an Honorable Discharge, a Good Conduct Medal, and four battle stars for combat in Italy and North Africa, along with orders to the effect that his debt to the United States Army was paid in full.

Fred and Elsie drove back to Fort Belvoir and brought Leon home for good. He would never set foot on foreign soil again.

Thirty-Eight

THE REMAINDER OF THE DECADE OF THE 1940S, LEON worked mostly for Hoyt Senterfeit and Tracey Gunter cutting timber. He also helped survey what was left of Kel and Peninnah's original acreage. There had been 504 acres in their place, but long before Kel's death in 1930, Woodard had asked his father to give him title for his part. Kel had cut off 40 acres down near the North Edisto River for Woodard.

Jennie and Olin had moved into the house with Peninnah and raised their family there Leon had been made aware of this arrangement when Kelly had been, but what occurred while he was overseas, he did not know

Kelly's sister, Aunt Corrie, told Leon, "I was down there visiting Mamma; Jennie had to go to the hospital for an operation. Olin had sugarcoated Mamma into signing the place over to Jennie, but when Jennie went to the hospital, Olin accused me and Mamma of trying to find the dowry papers to tear them up. Olin came in, cussed me out, cussed Mamma out, and told us to get out of there, *damn it and stay out, don't come back!* I went up to Steadman to stay with Woodard's family and Mamma went to stay with her niece, Pauline Matthews."

"This all happened while I was in service?" Leon asked his Aunt Corrie.

"Yes, Leon, you were in service, or you would have been the first person I would have told, to think Olin run our mamma out of her own house."

"If I had been home, Olin Rish wouldn't have dared to cuss Grandmamma and you out, Aunt Corrie, much less run you off. He is a sneaky, mean man. He will cuss out little children and old people who are defenseless; he wouldn't have messed with me. I wish I had been here to take care of his sorry hide."

Olin's brother, Arthur Rish, was a good man. Arthur said, "Olin will beat me, beat me bad too if he can. You know, if he'll beat *me*, what will he do to other people? I'm his brother!"

When Jennie got home from the hospital, she straightened things out; Peninnah moved back into the home place and lived there with Jennie and Olin until she died on November 17, 1949. She was eighty-nine years old. Leon frequently would walk down to Rayflin to visit her and his Aunt Jennie before her passing, but he never had any use for Olin Rish.

Shortly after Grandmamma Peninnah died, the land was going to be sold for back taxes, auctioned off at the court house in Lexington. Aunt Jennie came to see Leon.

"Leon, you helped survey all these lands. If anybody asks you where the lines are, don't tell them. I'll have my lawyer, Milo Smith, at the auction, and if we're able to buy it, can you pay the 5% down on the sale price? If you will, I'll cut you off whatever part of the place you want."

"Yes, Aunt Jennie, I will. I would hate for a stranger to own this land." Truth be told, there wasn't much land that Jennie didn't already own, once the back taxes were taken care of, that is. With Peninnah's dowry and her 1/9th of the property, she had control of over half of the land, about 258 acres. When the actual auction took place, not too many people bid; they didn't know where the property lines were. There was a couple of timber companies that were interested, but without knowing the property lines, they couldn't figure the value of the timber.

Milo Smith, Jennie's lawyer, won the auction and the land was hers, as soon as Leon paid the 5% down on the sale price. True to her word, she let Leon have the acreage he requested put in his name. At the time, he said, "I didn't foresee the need for more than thirty acres and the house where Daddy, Miss Florence, and Robert live."

* * * * *

The other eight children got fair market value from Jennie for the acreage she did not own. Binnie, as Buck's widow, received his share. To pay them, Jennie had Uriah Collum cut a stand of timber off her part.

"Rion, Sammy, Corrie, and all of Peninnah and Kel's children got the same amount that my daddy did," Leon said. "About $200.00. None of them even had a rabbit box on the place, much less a house. If I hadn't paid that 5%, my daddy Kelly would have lost the house he lived in. I just don't believe Aunt Jennie would have kept her word to him, not being married to Olin Rish."

Kelly was happy that Leon was able to make an arrangement

with Jennie so that the house he and his brothers built was still their home. Leon did not discuss the situation with Kelly; he thought it best not to share his personal opinion of the whole affair with his daddy. It would probably just upset him and he didn't need the irritation due to his health. But Kelly knew Olin Rish too well and knew he was probably behind the whole land affair. He just pretended to Leon everything was fine with him. And it was, as long as they still had the house and some land, of course, after all the years and work he had personally put into the place; it never really belonged to him, never was legally put in his name, but now it belonged to Leon and Kelly was satisfied. He knew his son was an honest and fair man and would always watch over Robert and Florence.

Thirty-Nine

CHRISTMAS 1950, ELSIE, FRED, AND THEIR SON TONY WENT to Miami, Florida, with Ryan, his wife, and Aunt Peggy Shealy. They went to visit Elsie's cousin, Willie Mae, her Aunt Peggy's daughter and Ryan's sister. While they were gone, Kelly had another stroke and lingered, ill, but conscious of his surroundings for several days. The stroke itself may not have terminated his life, but then the cough and low-grade fever started; they had the doctor from Batesburg, Dr. Brodie, who had taken over Dr. Gibson's patients, come and examine Kelly.

"I'll be honest with you fellows," he told Robert and Leon on the porch before he left, "it doesn't look good for your daddy. I'm afraid he will develop pneumonia and in his disabled condition, with another stroke, he can't get around. He's in the bed all day; I don't think he'll last long. It's not pneumonia quite yet, but that's probably what he'll develop within the next twelve to twenty-four hours. I know tomorrow is Christmas, but I'll still drop by late in the evening to check on him."

"Thanks for being absolutely honest with us," Leon said. "Our sister is in Florida visiting a cousin for Christmas. I guess we better try to get in touch with her."

"I think that would be a good idea if she wants to see her daddy before he's gone," replied Dr. Brodie.

They now had electricity in the old house. It was installed in 1948, but they had no phone. Robert was determined to contact Elsie and let her know the seriousness of their daddy's condition. He made a trip to Batesburg and stopped off at Fred's sister Nezzie's house. He was sure Nezzie would know how to contact them.

She had a phone and knew the number to call. She did this for Robert and he talked to Elsie.

"I'm sorry to have to call you, Elsie," Robert said, "but you should know Daddy is bad off. He had another stroke three days ago, but the doctor thinks he is developing pneumonia, and if that happens, he won't survive long. I didn't know if you, Fred, and the rest wanted to drive home or not. Y'all are so far away."

Elsie didn't even hesitate. "We'll leave as soon as we can get our things packed. If Daddy can understand you still, please tell him I love him and we're coming home." Those with them all agreed. There was no hesitation from the rest of the family; they realized how important it was to get Elsie home. Fred, Elsie, Tony, Ryan, his wife, and Aunt Peggy hurriedly said their goodbyes to Willie Mae and her husband Crawford, loaded their suitcases in the trunk, and piled in Ryan's car with him behind the wheel. It was late afternoon on Christmas Day, and they had a long trip ahead.

Tony sat between Ryan and his daddy, Fred, in the front seat. The three ladies were in the back. Elsie was in such a state of anxiety, almost unable to function due to the stress. Knowing her daddy could not survive long, she had an almost fanatical need to speak to him before he was lost to her forever. Her mind was in such turmoil, with memories of her daddy and all their shared experiences flooding her consciousness. She did finally sleep a little, crying herself to sleep while leaning against the window, head on a rolled-up cardigan as insulation against the cold glass. Aunt Peggy, sitting by Elsie in the back seat of Ryan's 1949 two-toned green Chevrolet Bel Air, patted her hand softly as she whimpered in fitful sleep. She could only think of things that needed to be said; these things filled her dreams. Why do people wait too late to tell those people they love how important they are in their lives and what they mean to them? It's just human nature. No one seems to realize that the here and now is what is important; no one is guaranteed tomorrow.

Highway 301, the main artery north to south on the east coast at that time, was a good road, but because of holiday travel, it would be busy. Highway 301 was officially named a Federal Highway in 1932. Over the ensuring years, it was extended northward and southward, eventually passing through seven states, from Delaware to Florida, and became a favorite of travelers up and down the east coast because it did not pass through any major cities and the travel time was faster. It eventually acquired the name 'The Tobacco Trail.'

Thinking that would be the quickest way home, Ryan and Fred decided on that route. When they finally reached Allendale in South Carolina, they then proceeded cross- country through Barnwell, Williston, Wagener, and Fairview Crossroads. Two miles past Fairview, they turned on a dirt road to Pine Grove Baptist Church, towards Elsie's home. Just one more turn to the right, and they were on the dirt road that led to Kelly's.

They drove all night through the cold dark countryside, from Miami to the Fairview crossroads in South Carolina. Exhaustion had set in and both Fred and Ryan were blurry-eyed from watching the constant ribbons of white lines passing on the highway. The menfolk thought it best if the women didn't drive, especially Elsie; she was too anxious to get home. Tony sat between them in the front seat, nodding off when his lids got too heavy to stay open. Most of the time, he kept up a conversation to help his daddy, Fred and Elsie's cousin Ryan, stay awake.

They didn't get to Kelly's until early in the morning on December 26th. They didn't even head to Batesburg to unload the car, since coming from the south, they could easily go to Kelly's first, and Elsie just wanted to get to her daddy to say good-by.

Fred, Elsie, Tony, Ryan, his wife, and Aunt Peggy arrived about 7:00 AM on that day. The sun was barely up, shadows still flooded the yard, and smoke was pumping from the kitchen fireplace. As soon as Fred stopped the car out front, Elsie jumped out. There were lights on in the kitchen, dining room, and her Daddy's bedroom, but none outside. No one was sitting on the shadowy porch; they had no way of knowing when Elsie would actually arrive, and it was too cold outside to watch for her from the front porch.

Elsie didn't even bother entering the kitchen. She ran to the end of the porch and entered the hall; her daddy's room was on the right. With faltering steps, she approached the doorway. His body lay on his bed, eyes closed as if he were sleeping; Elsie could tell he was already gone. Tears streamed down her face.

Leon sat in a chair beside the bed watching over their daddy. Seeing Elsie enter, he jumped up, ran around the end of the bed, and embraced her.

"I'm so sorry, Elsie, but we couldn't contact you, knowing you were on the road." She untangled herself from Leon's embrace and stared down at Kelly's peaceful face.

"Daddy died peacefully about five this morning, just as the eastern sky began to lighten a wee bit over the dense woods across the road. At the end, he was totally unresponsive," Leon recalled. "But around suppertime yesterday, he told me, 'Tell Elsie not to be sad for me when I'm gone. She was a wonderful daughter and I love her very much.' I had to lean over to hear him whisper those words, he was so weak. Those were the last words he uttered, a goodbye to you. After that, he was barely breathing, as if suspended in a gossamer web between life and death, his body not knowing how to break free. He lay resting until the end, no suffering or pain, not anymore."

Robert was sitting with him when he finally crossed over. He just stopped breathing suddenly. "It was a peaceful passing, but I'm sorry I was not beside him. He wouldn't have known, he didn't know if any of us were present in the end. I had gone to get some fresh air, put on my denim flannel-lined jacket, and stepped out on the front porch for a cigarette. The air was so cold, my breath hung in the air as thick as the cigarette smoke."

Robert had come to the hall door, cracked the door and screen, and whispered, "He's gone, I need to tell Mamma."

"I snuffed out the cigarette and rushed inside. Daddy lay there so still, but his face had this look of peace about his features. I knew he was knocking on the pearly gates. He's with our Mamma now; he's not a cripple any longer, and I know we will see them again."

Elsie placed her hand on the metal curved rail at the end of the bed and, touching the cool metal, walked around to the side where her daddy lay. She bent over and kissed the top of his head. "I love you too, Daddy, and I hope you know that." Elsie realized, with all her feverish longing to see her Daddy before he was gone, it was not to be. She slumped down into the chair where Leon had been sitting. Bending over, she held her head in her open hands and sobbed, loud agonizing sobs. Leon had never heard such sounds of torment as those that now came from his sister. He knew there was no comforting her at this point. It was best to let her dispel her anguish alone.

He quietly addressed her, hoping she would comprehend what he was saying. "Elsie, Daddy took a turn for the worst on Christmas Day. Dr. Brodie stopped by and told us there was nothing to be done. He could not survive."

"I can hear the rattle in his lungs, its pneumonia, I'm sorry," Dr. Brodie had said.

"All we could do was make him comfortable and wait for the end. Robert and I took turns sitting with him. Miss Florence wanted to, but she is just too distraught, so we thought it best for her to try and get some rest. We haven't contacted Mr. Attaway at the funeral parlor yet. We knew you would want to see Daddy before he was taken away, and with the weather turning so cold, it would be okay to just let him rest here until y'all arrived."

Elsie accepted the handkerchief Leon extended and dried her eyes. Blowing her nose loudly, she attempted to compose herself and stopped sobbing. Looking around her daddy's bedroom, she kept wiping moisture from her eyes with the corner of Leon's handkerchief. Kelly's rocker sat to the right of the fireplace. He spent so much time sitting there smoking his pipe. The pipe now lay in the ashtray on the semi-circle table to the right of the rocker next to the wall. It was in easy reach whenever Kelly wanted to smoke his pipe, something he enjoyed so much while listening to the radio placed under the front window. Elsie noticed the much lighter mark on the wall beside the fireplace. Kelly always struck his matches there, had been doing so for eleven years, so there was a definite worn area on the wall, testament to the many times he had enjoyed lighting his pipe. She took it all in one last time; her father's world was this room almost exclusively; now that would change. She wanted to remember the way it looked; closing her eyes, she could almost see the smoke from his pipe rising towards the ceiling and smell the wonderful cherry smell of his favorite tobacco. She was making a memory in her mind that she would revisit whenever she would enter this room or think of her father.

Fred, Tony, Aunt Peggy, and the others were in the kitchen with Miss Florence and some neighbors. They knew Kelly was gone and thought it best to let Elsie have some time alone. Fred knew he would be no help when he heard the sobs coming from Kelly's room. Leon was with Elsie, and sometimes mourning requires solitude, not someone just saying it's going to be okay, because it won't be, at least for a time. Healing comes with time, after all.

Forty

THE WEATHER, ALREADY BELOW FREEZING, TURNED EX-
tremely cold before mid-morning on the 26th. Fred, Elsie, Tony,
and their companions went on home after talking with the family.
They were totally exhausted from the trip home.

Miss Fannie and Mr. Reedy Gunter were there. So were Jennie,
Olin, Roston, and Sam. They were all sitting in the kitchen having
coffee, trying to console Florence. Robert and Leon were grown
men and felt they had to keep their emotions in check.

"We'll go to Batesburg after dinner and make arrangements for
Daddy," they had told Elsie. "Y'all go home and get some sleep."

Robert and Leon went to Attaway Funeral Parlor in Leesville
about ten miles away after dinnertime on the 26th to make arrangements for their daddy's body. They picked out a nice casket, gray
metal with a tucked, white satin interior. There was embroidery of
praying hands in blue yarn inside the lid.

"We'll be down there shortly with the hearse to pick your daddy
up, boys, get him fixed for viewing and have him back home by
6:00 this afternoon. Don't worry about the cost, we'll settle that later," Mr. Attaway said. "I knew your daddy for nigh on thirty years
and he was a friend and a good man."

Forty-One

IN ORDER TO GIVE ELSIE, FRED, AND TONY TIME TO GET SOME rest, the funeral was set for the afternoon of December 28th at Pine Grove Church. There was a crowd; Kelly had made a lot of friends during his life that wanted to show respect to the family. Even though it was bitterly cold and the ground was covered with snow, they came.

The service was scheduled for two in the afternoon and was conducted by the Reverend Jacob Felder, pastor of Pine Grove at the time. Almon Gunter had been a good friend of Kelly's all their lives and had asked Leon if he could say a few words about the character and life of his good friend. Almon wanted it to be a tribute to the kind of person Kelly had been, a true depiction of who he was and the progression of what he became to all that knew him.

Pastor Felder made some brief comments and the congregation sang 'Amazing Grace,' a favorite of Kelly's. Then the pastor turned the podium over to Almon, not having a clue what he would say about the deceased.

Almon began and told exactly what he knew about the man. "Kelly Gantt was quite a character," Almon began. "He led an interesting life, made his share of moonshine, drank his share, and could hold his own with any man spoiling for a fight, in his younger years, at least. The stroke he had in January 1940 slowed him down, but it didn't get him down. He lived eleven more years. He loved his family and was proud of his children. At his death, he held no grudge against any man. Kelly is gone but his legacy will live on in his two sons, Robert and Leon, and his daughter, Elsie, and all those he called friend. He also leaves behind a wife, Florence, who he dearly loved. Florence took care of Kelly; she was his nurse the last eleven years, doing everything she could to make him comfortable. The highlights of his life will be repeated many times. His children will tell many stories about their father; he will be remembered as long as his descendants are alive to pass on his stories. He did some things in his early life that some members may consider sinful, like his drinking and making moonshine, but we all must remember those were desperate times and we all did things, desperate things, to feed our families, things that we did to survive. In the end, I believe, Kelly Gantt was an honest, true Christian, and that today he is singing with the Saints in Heaven. No one leads a perfect life, but he was a believer and I thank to God that's what counts in the end."

Those in the congregation knew Kelly for who he was and agreed that Almon's tribute was right on all accounts. Those present knew he had done a lot of good for the community and almost every person there could have shared a personal story of Kelly's generosity and fortitude. He was a good carpenter and had voluntarily, before the stroke disabled him, built whatever he could to help his neighbors. He helped build some of their homes, barns, and fences. There was hardly a family present that had not called on Kelly Gantt to construct a coffin for one of their family members. He never said no, and they would always carry good memories of the man, Kelly Gantt, helper and friend.

Forty-Two

MEMORIES OF RAYFLIN LIVE IN THAT PLACE. THE LAND IS still there, along with the smokehouse and Kel's corn crib, both having survived more than a century. All the other buildings are no more. The fields are overgrown, strangers live on the land that Kel and his children cherished and nurtured throughout their lifetimes. But the memories are always there.

As for the house Kelly and his brothers built in 1912, it still stands as strong as a lighthouse in the storm. Kelly's grandson and his family live there, and its appearance has changed overwhelmingly, and for the better. It was a house that was built to last, and it still survives, having seen four generations of Gantts grow to adulthood within its walls. This house too holds lots of memories for us all.

Memories are powerful things. The smell of yellow jasmine on the spring breeze, the flash of color from a red bird on the wing or the deep blue of a blooming iris can elicit a memory. The pinpoints of light flashing in the dark woods, as lightening bugs flit to and fro, the sound of ice-coated limbs cracking in the stinging cold of winter wind or the warmth of wooden steps under bare feet. For some, it may be the sun beating down on their bare limbs while working in the field, or the taste of fried chicken at Sunday dinner. And how can anyone living in the country, away from city lights, noise and people, not remember the lonesome cry of a whippoorwill floating on the night air and a moment in time associated with that sound?

Sight, sound, smell, touch, and taste all serve to remind folks of memories that have been tucked away deep in our unconscious minds; that is, until something, perhaps a small thing, brings them to mind. The sight of quart jar filled with water and spring flowers sitting in the center of a kitchen table, or the smell of roses blooming on a bush fanned by a warm breeze towards the porch rocker we sit in under a cloudless, starry black canopy. The brilliant color of some article of clothing that reminds us of a frock that was Grandma's favorite or patches in a quilt from our childhood clothing. Small, almost insignificant things can elicit a moment in time, a memory of a person or place we cherished from our past. Life's experiences are remembered and recalled through our senses. A smile or frown may cross our face depending on what memory is brought forth. At the end of our lives, all that will be left are the memories we leave in the minds of others left behind. All we can hope is that the good memories outnumber the bad.

"It's surprising how much memory is built around things unnoticed at the time." ~Barbara Kingsolver, *Animal Dreams*

Photographs

Willie Mae Vann (woman with the scarf) with Virginia Rish, Elsie, Louise, and Leon (in overalls), Mildred Rish & Ramon Gantt, and two infants. Picture taken at Rayflin 1920-23, one-room house in background was home of farmhand Arthur Moore.

Buck Gantt & brother Woodard Gantt

Robert and mother, Florence

Robert, Nathan, and mother Florence

Jacob Kelly 'Kel' Gantt

Jim Barfield, Florence, and brother Will

Leon & Robert

Reedy Gunter & Olin Rish

Kelly Gantt with his shotgun

Kelly Gantt behind the old house, pipe in hand

Greco Gunter, Mildred Rish, Leon Gantt, Virginia Rish and J Hugh Gunter
sitting on the ground Buck Gantt

Daddy Robert and the boys in his FFA (Future Farmers of America) at Fairview School: Everett Padgett, Lewie Hallman, Luther Waters, Robert, Billy Redfern, Kenneth Miller, Lloyd Taylor, Harold Shealy, Leon Padgett, JW Lorick, Cyril Gantt, Hubert Watkins, Drayton Gunter, Chalmus Gantt, and William H. Howell (teacher)

Elsie Gantt at 15 in 1930

Sis, Uncle Jule Smith, Aunt Corrie, and Nina Lee

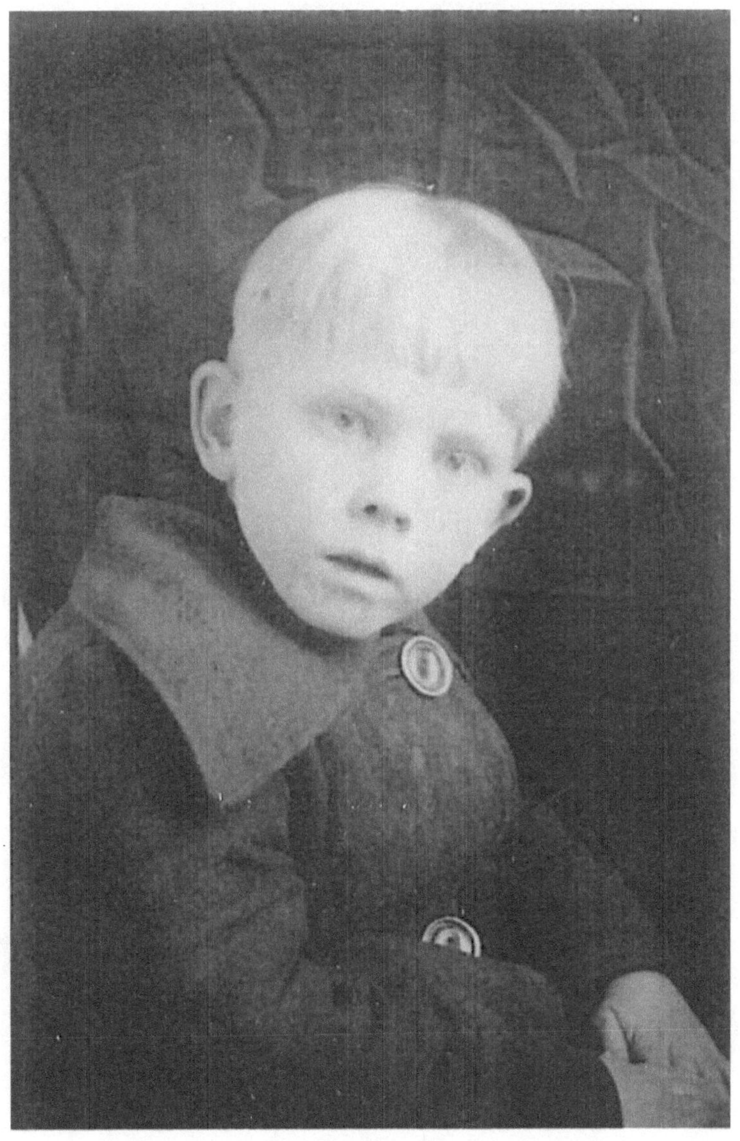

Robert, 1930, wearing the coat his mother cut down to fit him

Elsie Gantt

Leon Gantt

Ramon Gantt, son of Roston and Leon. Uncle Leon said he was high as a Georgia pine in this photo

The smokehouse Leon wrote his name on in red paint, late 20s or early 30s. The smokehouse still stands today in 2018

Aunt Jennie Rish

Daddy and his guitar, purchased for $12.00 at a pawn shop in Columbia

Daddy and his fiddle

Granddaddy Kelly Gantt, picture taken at Rayflin

Grandma Florence

Greco Gunter, Buck Gantt, Kelly Gantt, and J Hugh Gunter. Young man in front is Crum, Buck's son

Rion Gantt

Greco and his knee-high laced boots

Tony, Uncle Fred, and Aunt Elsie

Daddy, Robert, in his graduation robe

Granddaddy Kelly & Grandma Florence

Grandma Ella Abney, mother of Florence & one of her grandsons

Daddy Robert Gantt, Hilton Gantt, distanct cousin, and Linbergh Gantt, son of
Roston

The Crazy Band – Clyde Shumpert, James Burkett, Eugene Burkett &Robert Gantt

Florence and Granddaddy Kelly

Grandma Peninnah at the homeplace, Rayflin

Granddaddy Kelly

Daddy, Robert, with his guitar

Daddy Robert

Leon Gantt in his uniform, member of the AAA anti-aircraft artillery, 5th Army

Leon Gantt stationed at Camp Edwards, MA, before being shipped to the European Theater

Sgt Leon Gantt

Leon somewhere in Europe

Leon and good friend Talmage Pressley

After being transferred to the Combat Engineers, Leon was a construction foreman

Marvin Chalmus Gantt, son of Uncle Woodard. Chalmus served in Patton's

Army

Ramon Alton Gantt, son of Uncle Roston, Raymond was at Schofield Barracks at Pearl Harbor when the Japanese attacked.

Selected Sources

Books

Atkinson, Rick, The Day of Battle. The War In Sicily and Italy 1943-1944, Volume Two Of The Liberation Trilogy, Henry Holt and Co., New York

Bourke-White, Margaret. They Called It Purple Heart Valley. NewYork: Simon & Schuster, 1944.

Clark, Mark W. Calculated Risk. New York: Harper & Brothers, 1950.

World Book Encyclopedia. World War 11. Volumne 21 pg 365-379. World Book, Inc. 1983

Pamphlets

Prepared by the Antiaircraft Artillery 5th Army Headquarters. Salerno to Florence. 5th Army Antiaircraft Artillery Unit History. First year of fighting in Italy.

Prepared by U.S. 5th Army Headquarters. Road to Rome. 1945

Narratives

Recorded & Written Stories From Two Major Characters. Leon O. Gantt & Robert K. Gantt. All Stories Based on True Events.

Newspaper

The Trooper. Published Aboard the USS James B. Stuart & distributed as a souvenir copy to all 3000 troopers, passengers on that vessel, arriving in New York, August 19, 1945.

Websites

169th Combat Engineers Website
85th Combat Engineers Website

About the Author

KATHY GANTT WIDENER WAS BORN IN LEXINGTON COUNTY, SC in the small town of Batesburg. One month after graduating from high school, she married the love of her life and spent the next seventeen years raising their three children. At age nineteen she developed an obsession for genealogy and spent endless hours in cemeteries, archives, courthouses, and interviewing older family members. After eighteen years she decided to attend college part time. In 1990 she received an Associates Degree with high honors, her major was history. Kathy and her siblings grew up in the same old house built by her granddaddy, Kelly Gantt, and his brother in 1912. Kathy and her siblings grew up listening to their Uncle Leon's stories about his youth, making moonshine and his service in WWII. Uncle Leon had a phenomenal memory and loved to share his stories. He kept Kathy and her siblings mesmerized for hours with his tales. After his death in 2002 at age 91, Kathy decided these stories deserved to be shared and began to weave them into a narrative based on true events and real characters.